THE POISONED SPY

The Poisoned Spy

In Flight from Iron-Curtain Romania

Muriel Bol

FAIRMILE PRESS

First published in 1994 by Fairmile Press
P.O. Box 494, Norwich, NR2 2SX, England

© M. E. Bol 1994

Typeset in Scotland by Black Ace Editorial
Ellemford, Duns, TD11 3SG

Printed in England by Antony Rowe Ltd
Bumpers Farm, Chippenham, SN14 6QA

A CIP catalogue record for this book
is available from the British Library

ISBN   1–899594–00–0

ACKNOWLEDGEMENTS

I wish to acknowledge my gratitude to Mr David Nutt
for his help and encouragement, and especially
for having designed the jacket for this book.

I am indebted to Miss Bita Hariri
for producing the final manuscript on computer.
Also to Miss Parissa Etessami
for her help in this connection.

HISTORICAL NOTES

1. Russian Intelligence:
   N.K.V.D., up to 1946
   M.G.B., from June 1946 until March 1954
   K.G.B., from March 1954

2. During 1949 Trieste was a Free Territory under an Allied (British and American) Government. There was a strong Italian influence.

3. In 1949 the Transport International Routier (TIR) agreement came into force, allowing lorries to cross mainland Europe's borders without Customs hindrance.

4. Marshal Tito, President of Yugoslavia, broke away from Russian control in 1948, and Yugoslavia became independent.

This book is dedicated to Mila and Emile.

We were strangers and you took us in.

1

Ron Fenton was dead. It was poison that had first paralysed and then killed him. British Intelligence were worried; he was their man in Trieste with special responsibilities for agents in Austria and the Balkan countries.

He had been good, as had all the others, but over the past few years they had been picked off one by one. Morale was low and to make matters worse the Americans were beginning to withhold information. There were whispers of a mole, but all attempts at finding one had so far failed.

In the decaying splendour of the Athénée Palace Hotel in Bucharest, James Wilson was enjoying a drink in a quiet corner with Radka Antonov.

Someone was playing the grand piano and strains of a sonata floated past them as they sat on delicate French-style gilt chairs looking out on to a small courtyard where a fountain sparkled in the sunlight, surrounded by a blaze of red canna lilies.

It was summer 1949. The elections held two years ago had been a farce. The king had been driven out at gunpoint and Stalin had imposed a puppet communist government headed by Petru Groza with Anna Pauker in charge of foreign affairs. The Ceausescus had already begun their meteoric rise on the political ladder and had started to lead a lavish lifestyle while the country starved. The Iron Curtain was firmly down.

James had joined MI6 some years ago and, having done his stint at the Foreign Office in London, had been sent to join the staff of the British Embassy in Bucharest a year ago. Although he kept the Ambassador briefed, the person he reported to was Ron Fenton. The fact that he had been murdered had not yet penetrated the Iron Curtain and, so far, James was blissfully unaware.

He was mature at thirty and his fair hair and dark blue eyes had the Romanian women falling over each other trying to get his attention. He was of average height, slim and fit with a distinctive bump in the middle of his nose where it had been broken when he was boxing at school. He was endearingly natural and straightforward with a quick, intelligent grasp of the situation. He was not married but was feeling it was time to settle down and have a family. There were plenty of beautiful, marriageable girls in Romania but James always had a nagging doubt as to whether he was loved for himself, or as a means of getting a British passport.

He rang for a waiter and ordered tuica for himself and Radka. She was wearing a lime-green linen dress which showed off her slight, athletic body to advantage. She had been born in Sofia twenty-two years ago and was now the wife of the Press Attaché to the Bulgarian Embassy in Bucharest.

Radka was good company. She did not chase men, there was no need. She was always radiant and the moment she entered a room there was brightness and laughter. Sex was not foremost in her mind; she just wanted fun. It was never safe to tell her a secret. She simply did not understand secrets.

Her green eyes looked laughingly at James as they sipped their drinks. Her chatter came bubbling out quite effortlessly as she tossed her flowing, chestnut hair about. 'Come to the theatre with us tonight,' she was saying. 'We 'ave four tickets, my 'usband cannot come but my brother and 'is girlfriend will be coming. We will 'ave dinner together afterwards,' she continued, taking it for granted he would come; that was Radka's way. 'Come at seven, then we can 'ave a drink before we go.'

'Thank you, I shall look forward to that,' James replied.

As they left the coolness of the hotel's white marble floors and stepped outside, the torrid heat hit them and the sun scorched their skin.

'Let me give you a lift,' he said. He looked forward to an evening at the theatre and wondered how much longer they would be able to enjoy these light-hearted entertainments. Romania was rapidly being transformed into a fully-fledged Soviet satellite with purges of all political opponents. The church was under state control and the death penalty had been imposed for even minor offences against the state. Night clubs had been closed.

The British Embassy was a large, old building of classical design in a good part of Bucharest. To the rear of the building were some garages, screened by trees and shrubs, while to the front and sides there were well kept lawns and flower-beds. An underground passage went from the Embassy and came up in the house where the Military Attaché lived, which was in a street a short distance away.

James made sure he was seen entering the Embassy. Once inside, he slipped into the secret passage, came up into the Military Attaché's house and through a door into a garage where a shabby and old-looking Skoda was kept.

The windows were seldom cleaned and this made the identification of the occupants difficult. The grey exterior was still stained by mud, where it had been through the slush of last winter. In winter the roads were appalling; snow, mud and pot-holes. In summer the mud turned into dust which covered everything.

James got into the car and drove out of the garage, remembering to close the garage doors behind him, and out on to the streets of Bucharest, he hoped unnoticed. He took the first turning right, then left, then left again and kept a watch in his rear mirror. All was well, no one was tailing him. He drove to Strada Popovic, parked the car and got out.

He had received a message from an agent in Vienna, who used to work for him in Bucharest. A fellow agent, codename Charlie, had fled from Vienna and was in hiding in a safe house in Bucharest. It was urgent that he should visit Charlie but no one must know about it. He had carefully never memorised the address; he just knew how to find it.

He walked hurriedly down two more streets, then turned a sharp corner where four roads met. On each corner was an identical high block of cheap-looking concrete flats. He glanced quickly around and walked past the first block. He crossed the road and passed the next block where some children were playing on the narrow pavement. A lorry went by. He crossed over the next road, glanced around and slipped into the third block of flats and sniffed.

Cats!

Yes, that was right, the entrance always smelt of cats. Up the steps he went; steep, stone steps, dirty, chipped and with rubbish lying about everywhere. On and up he went until he could go no further. He had not counted the number of floors, or the number of doors. He didn't want to know. He was now at the very top, right under the roof.

He stood still, listened, straightened his tie and knocked gently five times, then again a little more loudly. Nothing happened. He tried the door but it was firmly locked. He knocked once again. A bolt was pulled back and the door was opened just a crack. 'I am James Wilson,' he said quietly.

The door was opened wider.

'Charlie,' came the response.

James went inside, locking and bolting the door behind him. 'Welcome to Bucharest,' he said, smiling and holding out his hand. 'I have a few things for you.' And he took from the various pockets of his jacket, bread, cheese and apples. He searched again and found milk powder and coffee.

'Thank you,' Charlie said quietly, as she took them from him. She did everything quietly; in fact she was the epitome of quietness and composure. Her fair hair, brushed straight back from her forehead, fell to her shoulders and curled slightly. Her eyes were large and grey, set far apart in a pale, oval face. Her features were regular and small. She had a well bred air about her and a whimsical charm that captivated both men and women; her smile began in her eyes and then spread to the rest of her face. She sat upright on the sofa listening as James explained the procedure for her stay in the safe house.

Baroness Elisabeth Maria Christine von Althof (Lisl to her friends), codename Charlie, was Austrian and twenty-four years old. She had been working successfully as a British agent in Vienna, moving in international circles, making use of her linguistic ability, particularly fluent Russian. She was always in demand at diplomatic social functions where her humour and wit were appreciated.

She was working on the case of a young British agent called Josef who was seen in Vienna being bundled into a large, black car. The last communication Fenton had received from him indicated that he had finally penetrated Russian intelligence in Austria. It was feared that he had been kidnapped by the Russians.

Through contacts, Lisl made the acquaintance of Colonel Aleksandr Petrovich Ivanov, born in Leningrad in 1915, head of the MGB in Austria. He had previously been working at MGB headquarters in Moscow, where Stalin had kept him fully occupied on detailed investigations of people's private lives so that purges could continue. He had been sickened by this work and in Vienna he had come into contact with the West and with western ideas for the first time.

Aleksandr, called Sascha by those who knew him well, was drawn irresistibly to Lisl. Their meetings had to be clandestine because the Russian forces were forbidden to fraternize with foreigners; the punishment was severe.

Their friendship blossomed, they became lovers, and Lisl fell deeply in love for the first time in her life. She had enjoyed many friendships with men, but this was different; this was the real thing. This was what she had been waiting for. She knew it was dangerous for him and crazy on her part, but she couldn't help herself, she was powerless. Her love was passionate; he returned it and they were both starry-eyed and helpless. His young, dark-eyed wife and two small children back in Moscow were forgotten; the lovers just lived for today and for each other.

They thought their meetings had been undetected, but one day Sascha was instructed to return to Moscow immediately. He knew this meant disgrace and punishment, perhaps hard labour, or even death – if he was accused of passing on information to the West. But uppermost in his mind was the certainty that he wanted to spend the rest of his life with Lisl.

He immediately left his office and went straight to Lisl's flat. He knew there would be a search for him the moment he was found missing. He poured out his feelings to her and between them they planned that he would defect and claim asylum in England in exchange for highly classified information. He outlined to her the information he intended to give to British intelligence. He was going to bargain for his freedom with it. She listened with concentration and stored every detail in her trained memory.

He then told her something so important that he had kept

it apart. He took her hands, looked straight into her eyes and said, 'you must swear by your love for me and by all you hold most sacred, that you will never, under any circumstances, tell anyone what I have told you, because this is all I have in exchange for living in England with you. If I'm killed, you should get to England and then disclose everything.'

He looked at her pleadingly, 'Do you promise me?'

She forced herself to speak, 'Yes, I promise,' she whispered. 'I'll keep your secret. I'ts safe with me.' Tears were running down her face.

Sascha took her in his arms and gently kissed the tears away.

'Surely there is someone amongst the British here we can trust? Then we could go together and it would be so simple,' Lisl insisted.

'No, my love, I know and have evidence that they are infiltrated. We can't trust our lives to them. Remember what happened to Vladimir Romanovich? Someone came from London and the next thing that happened he found himself on an Ilyushin on his way back to Moscow and the firing squad. I would rather risk my luck and go to your friend Fenton in Trieste, and that you go directly to England.'

They embraced and clung together, knowing that he must leave at once.

When Sascha had first gone away, Lisl had been quietly content to while away the hours thinking of their love which had begun tenderly and romantically and had then become so passionate and consuming. It was difficult for her to think of anything else; she was absorbed in their relationship and relived over and over again the times they had spent together. Hers was the love that knew when her lover was thinking of her, if he was well, happy or in trouble. She lived

15

with him mentally, whether he was near or far away. There was this intangible bond that could span time and space.

Lisl was waiting for news from Ron Fenton that Sascha had arrived in Trieste before making her own plans to go to England. Time passed and there was still no news. She knew she must be patient because Ron would want to investigate Sascha thoroughly before contacting her, which he only did whenever necessary.

About three weeks after Sascha had left Vienna, Lisl felt desperately depressed. She was conscious of this feeling the moment she opened her eyes. She could think of no reason for it; she had a quiet, happy nature and depression had no place in her life. But now she felt sad even when playing golf, one of her favourite pastimes. Her play was deplorable and became worse as they went round. Her friend Ilsa suggested they go back to the club house and give up playing for the day. Seeing the depressed state of her friend, Ilsa invited Lisl to come to the theatre with herself and her husband in the evening.

Lisl gladly accepted.

It was a serious play dealing with political and religious ideology, and accompanied by appropriate music. Towards the end of the play the music became solemn and sacred then rose to a crescendo as peasants, dressed in national costume and rags, struggled up a hill and embraced a rugged, wooden cross.

At that moment Lisl was aware of a sudden pain, so intense that it took her breath away. It felt like a knife cutting through her body diagonally from her left shoulder to the top of her right leg. She could see it. Straight, with no curve. It was flat but sharp at the edges and bright like a blade of steel. She tried to breathe, just enough to keep alive, just a very little breath, then she knew nothing. When she regained consciousness, she found herself lying on a narrow bunk in a small, untidy room with clothes hanging about everywhere. She looked up and leaning over her was a tall, thin, young actor, smiling down at her. He held a little visiting card and one red carnation. This was his dressing room. With his free hand he raised her hand and kissed it.

'Here's my card,' he said. 'Please get in touch with me – you are lovely.' He pressed the card and carnation into her hands. Lisl gradually regained her senses and to her relief Ilsa came into the room and immediately took control. She swept the young actor out of the dressing room, sat Lisl on a chair and found two strong men to carry her – on the chair – to the car. Lisl now realised she had no pain but she felt ill and utterly exhausted.

Ilsa took her back to her flat, helped her get to bed and promised to ring in the morning to find out how she was.

Lisl knew that she had gone through a great emotional experience; she had been torn in two. It was then she knew without doubt that something terrible had happened to Sascha. She felt desperate.

'Oh my darling, my dearest!' she cried into the night. 'What is it? Where are you? Oh Sascha, I love you so much.' She sank to her knees weeping and cried herself to sleep on the floor. She knew that he was dead.

Next morning she bathed her face in cold water, tied a scarf over her head to help hide her face and put on sun glasses. She could wait no longer; she must find out what had happened.

She left her flat and hurried down the Westbahn Strasse, past the St Laurenz Church and on until she could turn into Neubau Gasse and then the Maria Hilfer Strasse. As she passed the Maria Hilfer Church she realised people were looking at her because she was almost running. She slowed down and walked more sedately past the Kunst Historis

Museum, turning right into the Opern Ring. At the Opera House she turned left into Kärtner Strasse and, as casually as possible, turned the corner into the Philomoniker Strasse and walked through the doors of Sacher's Hotel.

Coming in from the bright sunlight Lisl had to remove her dark glasses. The heavy curtains and the dark Biedemeier furniture cast a sombre gloom throughout the hotel. She made her way to what used to be the separate little rooms, and sank on to a wooden pew-like seat with the back rising high up like a wall. There were red velvet cushions on the seats and beautiful old paintings on the walls.

She was desperately in need of coffee, a lot of it and black. She looked at the paintings and noted that they were badly in need of cleaning – the sky would never have been brown originally; all those cigars, she thought. The waiter came over and she ordered black coffee. Then Johann appeared. He was always there in the mornings, overseeing that all ran smoothly. He had done so for over twenty years; he could remember the day he first began working at Sacher's Hotel because it was the day Hitler arrived in Vienna, a day he would never forget.

It was soon after the British army arrived and took over Sacher's Hotel that he met the young, slight army officer from London. Eventually he agreed to work for British Intelligence and he became Lisl's contact.

'Johann,' she said, looking around to make sure they were not overheard, 'I need some information urgently. I must know what has become of Aleksandr Petrovich Ivanov. He is a Russian friend of mine who has defected and gone to Trieste to give himself up to Ron. I must know if he has reached Trieste.'

'Why did he not give himself up here?' Johann asked. 'There is the British Embassy and the British Army with their Intelligence units, it could have been done so easily.'

'Aleksandr Petrovich told me that he could not trust the Intelligence in Austria because last year a friend of his gave himself up to the British and a few days later he was at the airport, as he thought on his way to England, but instead he was handed over to the Russian military, frog-marched on to a Russian plane and flown to Moscow, where he was shot.'

'I heard rumour of that,' replied Johann. 'As you know my contact is with Trieste direct. I will do what I can to find out what you have asked. Please return in four days time, in the morning.' The waiter was approaching; Johann bowed slightly and walked around the room greeting known customers.

Lisl poured out the coffee and, picking up the large cup in both hands, admired the design and the high quality of the china. She sipped the steaming coffee and sat back knowing she had done all she could. She must now wait four days. She idly ran her hands over the silk tablecloth and decided she would spend the day walking in the shops and perhaps visit a gallery, where the beauty of the paintings would soothe her troubled spirit. That evening, footsore and weary, she let herself into her flat. She stood there shocked. 'My God!' she whispered, and put a hand to her mouth to stifle a cry. She felt sick and frightened.

Tables were overturned, cushions torn apart, papers scattered everywhere, soles ripped off her shoes, floorboards taken up, the furniture moved and the pictures flung on the floor.

The bedroom was even worse. The mattress was slashed from top to bottom, the floorboards were up and split into jagged pieces with long nails sticking out. Her clothes were strewn about the room and the drawers of the dressing table had been turned upside down on to the bed.

She did not attempt to go into the kitchen. Bread had been broken into pieces and flour, sugar, tea, coffee, jam and the contents of all her jars and tins had been emptied on the floor and the whole mess was swimming in milk. The flat had been thoroughly ransacked.

As she stood amidst the chaos the telephone rang. She jumped, then stood undecided what to do and listened to it ring; it went on ringing. She walked over to the table and picked up the receiver as if it were something that would bite her, and put it to her ear.

'Hello,' she whispered.

'Go! Go immediately. You are in great danger.' It was a male English voice. He rang off without waiting for a reply.

Her mind raced. Where to go? What to take? How to get away? She must remain calm. Lisl walked quickly from room to room stuffing essentials into a small brown leather suitcase. She gathered up all her jewellery, all the money she could find, her passport and her address book, then went out of the flat locking the door behind her.

She stood on the doorstep uncertain where to go. She knew that people just disappeared, were spirited away and never heard of again. She was beginning to feel afraid and half ran, half walked to the house where her cousin Freiheer Rudolph Tiergau und Tammin lived.

She ran up the steps to the front door and rang the bell. The door was opened by the butler, who bowed and took her suitcase.

'His excellency is in the drawing room.' He went before her, opened the drawing-room door and announced her arrival.

'Lisl my dear, what a lovely surprise,' said her cousin as he rose to greet her.

'Oh Rudi, I'm in great trouble. I came to you for advice. I don't know what to do.' Lisl fought to hold back the tears.

'Tell me about it, perhaps I can help,' he replied soothingly.

She sank on to the sofa; the down-filled cushions felt
comforting. Her cousin was twenty years her senior and
was leaving Vienna in two days time to take up his new
appointment as Austrian Ambassador to Romania. Lisl was
the youngest child of his youngest sister; both her parents
were dead and he felt protective towards her. His wife came
into the room.

'Thérèse, see who is here,' he said.

'Lisl my dear, how good to see you, but you look
unhappy, what is the matter?' she asked as they embraced.

'Tell us your troubles,' he said with a tolerant smile.
'Thérèse and I are good listeners.'

'Everything was so wonderful and I was so happy, but
now my world has fallen apart and I'm in real trouble,'
explained Lisl. 'I had never told anyone, but I'm working
for British Intelligence. I became involved with a Russian
MGB Colonel and am hopelessly in love for the first time
in my life. The Russians found out and ordered him back to
Moscow, so he had to flee to the West and we planned to
meet in London and to spend the rest of our lives together.
But tonight when I returned home I found my flat ransacked
and someone rang and told me to leave immediately because
I'm in great danger.'

'Oh, how awful!' exclaimed Thérèse, 'You must stay
here.'

'Why should you be in danger? Have you any idea who
warned you?' asked her cousin.

'My Russian friend had some important information he
will disclose when he reaches London.'

'And do you know what that important information is?'

'Yes,' she replied, 'But I'm sworn to secrecy. I'll never
disclose it.'

'Rudi, we must help her. Where can she go? What can she do?'

Rudolph frowned. He had steered a careful diplomatic path, avoiding controversy and keeping his character and his political dealings above suspicion.

'I do not like the sound of this at all, Lisl,' he said. 'I have always avoided getting mixed up in these clandestine affairs. You should never have taken on this sort of work and I really would prefer to keep out of it.'

'But Rudi, you must help her! She has no one else to turn to, and she has always looked upon you as upon her father. Surely you know someone who can help,' pleaded his wife.

'I know someone in the British Embassy. I will talk to him tomorrow morning. Now not a word of this to anyone and be careful what we say in front of the servants. Lisl you must stay in your room. We will say you are not well. Thérèse will bring you some food.'

'Oh, Rudi, I'm so grateful,' said Lisl. 'I'm so sorry to be such a nuisance – but I'm so worried and so desperate.'

'You need rest,' said Thérèse, 'I will show you your room and you can borrow anything from me that you need.'

Lisl kissed her cousin good-night, Therése put her arm around her and they went upstairs together.

The next day, just before lunch, Rudolph visited Lisl in her room.

'The news is not good,' he told her. 'Your life is in great danger and the British cannot find a safe way of getting you out of the country immediately except by suggesting that I should take you with me when we leave for Bucharest tomorrow. They have given me a safe address where you can stay and you must remain there until an Englishman called James visits you. You must be prepared to travel

22

in the boot of the car when we cross the frontiers. As you know, because I have a diplomatic passport and number-plates, my car will not be searched.'

'I don't know how to thank you,' Lisl said. 'I know how you hate doing this sort of thing. If you would rather not take me, I will stay and take what comes.'

'No, no. You come with us, but once you are in Bucharest you are on your own. Promise me you will never come near me or the Austrian Embassy. Never tell anyone how you got there – it could cost me my job. I have never before abused my diplomatic status and I shall never do so again.' He walked out of the room.

The next day they began their journey to Bucharest and, as planned, Lisl was packed into the boot of the Mercedes in a quiet place just before the Hungarian frontier. Because of their diplomatic numberplates, they were waved through. At the first convenient place she was released and made comfortable on the back seat.

She got into the boot again just before the Romanian frontier. It was most uncomfortable and claustrophobic locked in there. She felt the car stop. She heard footsteps; she heard voices; she heard her heart beating. It seemed a lifetime before the car moved on. Then she breathed normally again.

During the remainder of the journey she travelled in the back of the car and her cousin drove to the address of the safe house. He stopped a little way from it and told Lisl it would be wiser for her to walk the rest of the way alone. They embraced and she promised to let her cousin know when she reached London. She watched them drive away.

Lisl looked around; the street was empty and very quiet. She carefully followed the directions she had been given, entered the shabby block of flats, climbed the stairs and stopped on the top floor in front of the only door. She had been told that the door would be open and she would find the key behind the lavatory. Once inside she should lock and bolt the door and open it only to James Wilson.

'I had to see you urgently,' James was saying as he and Lisl sat on the only two chairs in the dim, low-ceilinged attic room. 'Be prepared for bad news. Ron Fenton has been killed. We've only just heard and know no details.'

Lisl said nothing. She just looked at him silently with large, round, unblinking eyes. She rubbed her hands together and a shudder went down her spine. She had gone a shade paler and the shadows under her eyes were a shade darker. She was thinking of Sascha. Had he reached Trieste? Had he and Ron met?

Aloud she said, 'I'm so sorry about Ron. He enjoyed life so much, I can't imagine that I shall never see him again. Has anyone taken his place?'

'No one as yet, so you'll have to make do with me for the time being. Is there anything you need?'

'There is just one thing I am desperate to know. Colonel Aleksandr Ivanov has defected and was making his way to Trieste – to Ron. Can you find out if he had met up with Ron and what is happening? He's a particular friend and I am so certain that something awful has happened to him. I must know, do you understand?' She looked at him imploringly. She was feeling so helpless.

'Tell me why you have to go to England and about your friend Colonel Ivanov.'

Lisl sighed deeply, then told him briefly what had happened and about the secret she had promised to keep.

'It might be better if you shared your secret with me,' James suggested. 'Then should something happen to you – which God forbid – I could go to England and disclose this vital information.'

'No. I can't tell you, I can tell no one. I promised.'

'All right,' James conceded, seeing how determined she was, 'I'll do all I can to find out and let you know. Remember, answer the door only to me or to a Romanian called Radu Negulescu. You can trust him absolutely.' James handed her some Romanian money. 'Take this,' he said. 'Go out as little as possible and try to be patient. We'll get you to England just as soon as we can.'

He stood up. 'I must be going,' he said. 'You'll find some books and magazines on the table.'

Lisl locked and bolted the door behind him. Then she looked around the flat and thought: *So this is to be my home: almost a prison.* She noticed the Romanian hand woven rugs on the floor; their bright colours made the room feel warm. Besides the two chairs there was a sofa covered in red and gold. There were two tables, one square and one low and round. She saw the books and magazines lying on the smaller table. In a corner stood a wicker basket.

In the bedroom was a small double bed with an attractive white, wooden headboard. This was hand-painted with bright coloured flowers and leaves. There was a small table and a chair, and more handmade rugs on the floor. A small kitchen and bathroom completed the flat. Adequate, she thought, so long as I don't have to stay too long.

She went back into the sitting room and looked out of the window. All she could see was the neighbouring block of flats. She sat on the sofa and wished she could dispel her fears about the man she loved; they nagged at her incessantly. She selected one of the books and attempted to concentrate on the story.

Back in the Embassy, James sent a message to London telling them that Charlie had arrived in Bucharest. He also asked for news of Colonel Ivanov.

2

Meanwhile in London there had been the usual soul-searching when an agent was murdered. All the doubts surfaced again and were chewed over. There were veiled innuendos. As people passed each other in the corridors there was the muted word, the clipped sentence. Nothing would come of it, the matter would die and a new man would take over.

The head of section 'B', responsible for Trieste, Austria and the Balkans, was sitting in his office deciding who to send to Trieste to replace Fenton. Hugh Compton was well groomed, in his late forties with blue twinkling eyes and thinning hair which had once been sandy in colour but was now going grey faster than he cared for. The lines on his face were from thought and laughter; there was nothing unkind in his expression. He was tall and slight and his clothes, although good, hung loosely on his thin frame. He had been in the Intelligence set-up from before the war.

He picked up the telephone. 'John, can you come and see me?' He replaced the receiver and sat studying his nails.

A quick knock, the door opened and in walked John Harcourt, exuding the vigour and verve of a fit, happy twenty-eight-year-old. He had been a brilliant wartime officer, serving with the Chindits in Burma, where he won two D.S.O. decorations and the M.C. He had a keen sense of humour and a sense of responsibility beyond his years. His light-brown hair had touches of auburn and his blue eyes were flecked with brown. He was well-built and athletic. His mother was Irish and his father English and he had inherited charm from one and reliability from the other.

'Sit down. What are your views on Fenton's death?' asked Hugh.

John paused before replying. 'In the land of the Borgias one must always expect poison. The Italians didn't want Ron dead but they could have done it for someone else, sir. Do we have details on his last movements?'

'The only information we have is that his last meal was fish. He had been seen with a girl aged about twenty-two with dark hair and olive skin. Probably Slav or Greek. We know that five days before he was killed he sent a Top Secret message to us.'

Hugh handed John the signal. It read:

Interrogating MGB Colonel Aleksandr Petrovich Ivanov defected from Austria. Claiming asylum in England. Will disclose information of great importance only when in London. Charlie connection.

'What reply did we send?' asked John.

'We told Fenton we would make arrangements to get Ivanov out and would let him know by the end of the week. Then a final message from Fenton: *Ivanov dead. Investigating.*'

'There must be a connection, sir.'

'Yes,' agreed Hugh. 'Now I want you to go to Trieste immediately and carry on where Ron left off. Find out the reason for these two murders and who did them. He must have been close to something important. We have all the interrogation reports on Ivanov so read these straight away and leave tomorrow if possible. Be discreet, and be careful.' He stood up. 'Good luck,' he said, smiling.

'Are you sure I'm the right person for the job, sir?' John asked, thinking of the disruption to his private life.

'Yes,' replied Hugh. 'You have the imagination, patience

27

and tenacity required for a job like this. You speak Italian, Serbo-Croat and some Russian. You are the best person we have for the job.'

John signed for the Ivanov interrogation papers and did not leave the office until he had assimilated them. He would be up most of the night, cancelling engagements and sorting out his private life before leaving for Trieste the next day. What a strange life, he thought, as he stuffed some clothes into a bag. We are all expendable and only one thing really matters: the Intelligence game must go on. One must for ever be looking beneath the surface and never talk about one's work. Thank God he was blessed with a cheerful disposition and a sense of destiny which enabled him to cope with and to enjoy the uncertainty and the danger.

He was looking forward to revisiting this beautiful, turbulent city wedged between the lovely Adriatic Sea and the mysterious Guilian Alps. The population was composed mostly of Italians, Croats and Slovenes. Since the end of the war the Yugoslavs and the Italians had fought over who should possess it. A few years previously the Yugoslavs held Trieste for forty days; during this short time they arrested and marched off about two hundred people, killed them and threw their bodies into a pit.

A military Government of British and American forces was then set-up and the area declared Free Territories with Zone *A* Italian and Zone *B* Yugoslav. The town was in Zone *A* which became Italian in character and Italian was generally spoken. The Italians continued to stir up unrest, with demonstrations and riots, while there was occasionally sabre-rattling on the Yugoslav border.

John had no intention of getting involved with the Allied Intelligence organisation. He intended to give them a wide berth; he preferred to work alone; he felt safer that way.

3

To begin with it was bearable, but as time passed Lisl felt lonely. The days were long and the nights even longer. When she could bear the solitude and silence no longer, she would leave her room silently, creep down the stairs and walk out into the bright sunlight, down the Strada Popovic and on to a group of small shops to buy an item she needed. Other days she would walk to the Parkul Juano and wander about among the trees enjoying the refreshing scent of the magnificent lime trees.

These walks made her tired and helped her to sleep. The nights were the worst; that was when she missed Sascha almost unbearably. He was never really out of her thoughts, that was the trouble with the intense way she loved; it was all or nothing. When Sascha had decided to defect it was like a dream come true; she would follow him to England and they would live happily together. He had taken her advice and set off to contact Ron in Trieste – and now Ron was dead.

What had happened to Sascha?

Time and time again her thoughts returned to this question, to which there was no answer. She prayed that her forebodings were wrong, but in her heart she know that something terrible had befallen him.

This morning she could wait no longer. She *had* to have news of some kind. She would go to the British Embassy and find James Wilson or the Romanian, Radu Negulescu.

She knew where the Embassy was; she had walked past it on several of her outings. Today she walked with a purpose; she must find out if Sascha had arrived in Trieste and where he was. Would they tell her?

She had been walking quickly and was hot and a little

out of breath when she reached the Embassy. She crossed the road, ran up the wide, stone steps and rang the door bell, ignoring the policeman in his sky-blue uniform and white summer cap, standing on duty at the bottom of the steps. He made no attempt to stop her, but gave her an appreciative glance and a smile, which was what she had become accustomed to from men of all walks of life. The heavy door opened slowly and a uniformed porter asked what she wanted.

'I have come to see Domnul Negulescu.'

'Have you an appointment?'

'Yes. He's expecting me,' she lied.

'If you would wait here, I will telephone him,' he replied and gestured towards a chair in the entrance hall.

Lisl walked to the chair and sat down gladly. 'What name shall I say?' he asked her.

'Rodica Popescu,' she replied without hesitation. She had no wish to advertise her whereabouts by using her own name.

She had only a few minutes to wait before a short man with a swarthy complexion and black, thinning hair came down the stairs and across the hall towards her. He was squarely built, middle-aged and on the heavy side. He had a most distinguished air, bowed stiffly to Lisl and asked, 'What can I do for you, madame? I do not remember making an appointment to see you.'

Lisl smiled, 'How could you have ever forgotten so soon?' she said. Then she looked at the porter and added, 'but we can't talk here. Is there anywhere more private?'

Radu Negulescu opened a door nearby and showed her into a small sparsely furnished room. There was only a heavy square mahogany table and four mahogany chairs with green leather seats.

Lisl sat down, took off her sunglasses and headscarf and

shook her head so that her hair fell loosely round her face and on to her shoulders.

'My name is really Elizabeth von Althof. I need to know what has happened to Colonel Ivanov.'

Radu Negulescu drew in a quick breath. 'Madame la Baroness,' he said sternly, rising to his feet, 'you should not have come here. It is dangerous for you and not good for the British Embassy. It is not allowed. You must forgive me, but it is important you abide by the rules. If you will please wait for a moment, I must consult.' He stood up rather stiffly and, with a bow to Lisl, left the room without actually turning his back to her, an art acquired from service in the Royal Romanian Court.

Now that Lisl had taken this decisive step she felt much calmer. The atmosphere in the Embassy, with its solid furniture and Radu Negulescu's old-fashioned courtesy, put her at ease; it was the world she knew. She did not mind how dangerous her visit was, so long as it brought her nearer to finding out what had happened to Sascha.

Suddenly the door was flung open and James Wilson strode into the room. 'What are you doing here?' he demanded angrily. 'You know how important it is that there is no connection between you and this Embassy. You could compromise us all and there would be an unpleasant diplomatic incident. This Embassy is under constant surveillance and by coming here you endanger your own safety. This is unacceptable behaviour.' He was blazing.

Lisl stood up, 'I know, I know I shouldn't have come here, but I couldn't wait one minute longer.' She grabbed his arm. 'Please listen to me!' she implored. 'I must go to Trieste myself and find out what has happened to Aleksandr Ivanov, I think he's dead,' and she sank back on to the chair sobbing.

She took out a white handkerchief and dabbed at her tears. 'Colonel Ivanov and I planned to make a new life together in England. I love him and would die for him, but I can't help feeling he's dead. What can I do to find out?'

James was at a loss when dealing with weeping women. He stood looking out of the window and was relieved when Lisl regained her composure.

'Your fears may be groundless,' he said gently. 'Someone should have arrived to replace Ron by now. I'll find out all I can and will come and tell you.'

'Thank you.' She forced a smile.

'You will have to be patient a little longer,' he told her. 'I appreciate it is hard for you, but in this game waiting is over half our work and it's the most difficult. It is essential that we don't make a false move and let the Russians or their friends know that you are here. I want you to go back to your flat, keep a low profile and I will keep my promise to find out what has happened to your friend and get you away from here as soon as I can. You must on no account come here again. Take this money. Please go now. Lie low and wait.' He gave her a reassuring smile, took her by the arm and led her to the door.

Lisl smiled bravely, 'I will do as you say,' she replied. 'But please remember, I must have news of Colonel Ivanov urgently.'

'Yes, I understand. I'll also arrange to get you away from here, but I have to receive instructions from London and those are what I'm waiting for.' He took her to the hall, where the porter showed her out.

A few days after Lisl's visit to the Embassy, James received a message from London informing him that John Harcourt had replaced Ron Fenton in Trieste and was now the co-ordinator for all Intelligence from the Balkans, Austria,

Albania and Italy. That he should report to Harcourt as soon as possible. That a safe route to London for 'Charlie' would be notified later. That the Russian defector Ivanov was dead.

James read the message through twice, then he looked across the room to where Radu Negulescu was sitting at his desk in the far corner of the room, working away quietly. 'A message from London,' said James. 'Ivanov is dead, there are no details. Here, read it for yourself,' and he strode across the room and handed the message to Negulescu.

The elderly Romanian shook his head. 'How shall we tell the Baroness?' he asked.

'We shall say nothing for the time being. I have to go to Trieste to see Harcourt. I'll then find out all the details. It's best for her to live in hope for the time being.'

'Perhaps I should tell you I am getting a little worried about the way I am being followed,' admitted Negulescu hesitantly. 'It has intensified during the last week and my contacts tell me that you too are under constant observation. I know you are always careful, but I beg you to take extra care now.' He blew his nose with care.

'Have you any idea why the Russians should have increased their surveillance of us now? Have we been careless in some way?'

'The only reason I can think of, Mr Wilson, is that Madame la Baroness disappeared from Vienna at the same time that her cousin took up the appointment as Ambassador here. They will connect her with the defection of Colonel Ivanov.'

'You may be right,' said James thoughtfully. 'We must get her out of this country as soon as possible. I will talk to Harcourt when I am in Trieste and see if things can be hurried up.'

4

John had slept badly and was feeling every one of his twenty-eight years as the train crossed the frontier into Italy. He was looking forward to all the delicious Italian food, but in the pit of his stomach there was a feeling of apprehension that refused to go away.

June is one of the most beautiful months in Northern Italy; although hot, there is still a freshness that is invigorating; the green of the trees and grass was as yet unbleached by the sun.

The railway wound along the lovely coastline, with the sea on one side and steep, rocky crags on the other; the carriage was often plunged into darkness as the train travelled through small tunnels. It was like getting fresh glimpses of heaven each time the train emerged into the breathtaking, sunny scenery.

On the right-hand side, just before Trieste, was the very old, romantic castle of Duino, perched on a rocky crag high above the sea; it was well preserved and still habitable; then, a little further on, the cursed castle Miremare and, round the bay, Trieste railway station.

As the express came to a halt with the inevitable jerk, the normally quiet railway station came to life; there were people trying to get on before those who were on could get off. John squeezed off the train, carrying a canvas bag, the only piece of luggage he had.

'Taxi?' asked the first driver of the only two taxis waiting.

'Excelsior Hotel,' said John, getting in.

The Excelsior Savoia hotel was palatial, luxurious and elegantly furnished. It stood on the seafront overlooking the bay. Directly in front of the hotel was a wide boulevard with tree-lined pavements on either side where people promenaded, relaxed and looked at the sea. Between the pavement and the sea was a double railway line where engines pulled long lines of goods wagons at infrequent intervals to the fish market and the port.

John was shown into a large and comfortably furnished bedroom on the third floor with a telephone and french windows that opened on to a balcony that overlooked the bay. Leading off the bedroom was a spacious bathroom with a large white marble bath and two washhand basins set in white marble.

He gave the porter a generous tip, took off his jacket and went on to the balcony. He leant on the parapet, gazed at the shimmering sea and wondered why he lived in London. He noticed the balcony was large and pillared and curved round connecting three rooms. The middle room was his, which had two windows and the french window on to the balcony; the other rooms were on either side of his room and appeared quite small, having only a french window on to the balcony. He wondered if these two rooms were occupied, and by whom.

This was not John's first visit to Trieste and he looked forward to revisiting many favourite haunts. Feeling restless, he decided to go into town and look around.

After leaving the hotel, he turned right and walked to the Piazza del l'Unita, a large and attractive square facing the sea. On the right was the magnificent Lloyd Triestino building, on the left the Palace of the Government and, at the far end of the square, the imposing town hall. This square had been the scene of riots and unrest, but now all was peaceful with colourful chairs, tables and sunshades outside the cafés, where early-morning customers were already drinking coffee.

John crossed the Piazza and walked up the Corso to the via Carducci. Here he entered a gentlemen's outfitters; he bought a summer suit, a good selection of casual wear and everything else he needed, down to the smallest detail. He then took a taxi back to the hotel, where he showered and changed into the clothes he had just bought.

The Italian sun streamed through the large windows of the hotel restaurant where John was having lunch. He would spend the afternoon picking up the threads where Ron had stopped. He would have to tread warily or he might easily end up with the same fate as Fenton; he knew there always had to be a certain amount of luck not to get caught out.

That evening he decided to visit the Rouge et Noir nightclub belonging to the Excelsior Hotel. From the reception hall he went down the marble stairs where the central part is covered with a deep rose-pink stair carpet to the exclusive nightclub.

It was a romantic place, with the seating arranged in two tiers around a highly polished, brass dance floor. It was dimly lit by crystal wall lights with pink shades; the walls were covered in pink damask, it was carpeted throughout in deep rose-pink and the pink sofa-like seats for two were placed far enough apart to ensure privacy.

John went to the bar where three women, belonging to the establishment, were sitting. He ordered a drink and said to the barman, 'I am looking for Mr Fenton. Do you know him?'

'No, signor. I do not know Mr Fenton.' The barman continued to polish a glass and did not look up.

'Well, that's disappointing, because I haven't seen him for a long time and was looking forward to meeting him again. 'What is your name?'

'Alberto,' replied the barman.

John smiled at the women and asked, 'What would you ladies care to drink?'

'Grazie, signor.' They smiled at the young Englishman.

'Alberto!' called John. 'Please give the ladies a drink.'

They raised their glasses towards him and smiled. John sat on a bar stool and studied the people sitting at small tables around the dance floor and on the second tier just two steps higher. All was deep-rose plush velvet and gold. The lights, small crystal chandeliers and candles, were reflected in the mirrors, making everyone and everything look shadowy. There were a number of couples, mostly older men with very young and attractive women, and a number of men sitting alone.

'Tell me, Alberto, why are there so many men in here alone? Is this usual? I had always thought that Italian men were fond of the ladies!'

'You are correct, signor, but the Trade Fair is now open in Belgrade and many men are on their way there or on their return and are enjoying an evening of relaxation.'

Two of the ladies from the bar had now joined one of the tables where two men had been sitting alone. The band was playing a soft Neapolitan tune and most couples were dancing with the men having both arms around their girl-friends and the girls' hands clasped behind their partners' neck. They were dancing cheek to cheek with their bodies pressed closely together.

John turned to the woman sitting at the bar. 'May I invite you to dance?' he asked.

She put her glass on the bar and smiled at him. 'Grazie, signor,' she replied, going with him to the brass dance floor.

Holding her closely, he asked, 'Do you know Mr Fenton?'

'Yes, but he is dead, signor. I am sorry. He was often here. He was very nice man.'

'Why did he die?' John asked her; they were speaking very quietly.

'No one knows. It is big mystery. One day he is alive, the next day dead. Some people say he was murdered, poisoned. Poison is terrible death, signor.'

They returned to the bar and John bought his partner a drink, thanked her and moved away to be alone. He noticed a man sitting alone at a small table nearby. His face seemed familiar to John, but who was he and where had they met? The man sat there completely relaxed, smoking a cigarette in a holder; just sitting, with a preoccupied air.

'The same again.' John said to Alberto, pushing his empty glass towards him. Then he asked, 'What is the name of the man sitting alone at the corner table?'

'I am sorry, he is new here.' Alberto busied himself about the bar.

John thought Alberto unusually uncommunicative for a barman and made a mental note to make some enquiries about him.

He decided that nothing further would be gained tonight so he finished his drink and went to his room; he felt tired and knew he would fall asleep immediately.

It was late when John awoke, with his bedside light still on and the book lying on his chest; the air was full of bustle and noise; cars hooting, things banging, church bells ringing and the hundred odd sounds that are all part of daytime in an Italian town.

A hurried shave and shower, then out into the bright sunlight and a table in the Piazza Del l'Unita d'Italia, where he ordered coffee. The tables were filling up and a man accompanied by a young woman asked if they could share his table. The man was about fifty with thin, receding, dark hair; a round, pallid face, dark brown eyes and heavy eyebrows. He was of medium height. He smiled at John through large spectacles with heavy, tortoiseshell rims.

'Bon journo, signor,' he said, 'I trust we do not disturb you.'

'No,' John assured him. 'On the contrary, I'm delighted to have company. I came to Trieste hoping to meet an old friend, but, alas, I can't find him.'

'This is my niece, Anna.' They shook hands and, while they were giving the waiter their order, John noticed with pleasure that Anna was really beautiful. She was of medium height and her bones were small and fine. She had dark Mediterranean colouring, with large, black eyes, high, wide cheek-bones and black hair dressed high at the back of her head, which was poised perfectly on a long neck to show a fine jaw-bone. Her mouth was curved and full but her expression was sad and unsmiling. She was wearing a sleeveless, pale blue dress of soft material that clung to her body, showing the curves of her bosom and the shape of her thighs. She had a string of white beads around her neck; a white bag and sandals completed the picture.

'My name is Aleco Yanakopolis,' said her uncle. 'May I ask where you are staying?'

'Certainly. In the Excelsior Hotel.'

'So are we!' he said. 'That is splendid, then we shall see each other again. I have a shipping line and I need to come to Trieste from time to time and find the Excelsior Hotel quite the quietest and the most comfortable. Do you plan to stay in Trieste long?'

'I'm a journalist,' John explained. 'I spend most of my time writing and I also enjoy the lovely climate. I shall probably be staying some time.' He made his excuses and left them.

As he turned away, he noticed a man sitting at a nearby table reading a newspaper. This was the same man who had been sitting alone in the Rouge et Noir the previous evening. Was this accidental? he wondered. It was quite possible; nearly everyone sat in the Piazza del l'Unita once every twenty-four hours. He carried on across the Piazza to the Corso, but still could not remember where he had met this man before.

'Hello! How good to see you,' said John, holding out his hand and smiling.

A large man with a sultry complexion hidden behind heavy sunglasses, wearing a brightly coloured, short-sleeved shirt stopped and grasped John's hand.

'Well, well,' he drawled in his Southern American accent. 'Fancy seeing you here!'

'Come and have a drink,' John urged.

'I can't stop now,' he said, and strode away.

John had known Pete Mason on and off for five years. He was a CIA man; efficient, quiet and a good linguist. Was there some urgent job that kept him so preoccupied and in such a hurry, or was he avoiding him?

There were so many ifs and buts; nothing concrete to go on and certainly no lead. There was just one man who might be able to help. He walked to a telephone kiosk and rang the Yugoslav Consulate and asked to speak to Mr Stanko Logar:

'John Harcourt here.'

'This is a pleasant surprise! Where are you?'

'Here in Trieste. Have you time for lunch?'

'For you I have always time,' came the smooth reply.

'Good, then the Excelsior Hotel at one.'

Stanko Logar arrived promptly, looking smart and full of self-confidence. Of medium height, he had a thin face with prominent cheek-bones, a slight figure in a light-weight, grey suit with a pale blue shirt. His shoes were a little pointed.

He walked quickly towards John with his arms outstretched, a smile lighting up his pale face and his eyes
twinkling with pleasure and shook John vigorously by
the hand.

'My friend, how good to see you! And what brings you
to our lovely Mediterranean?' he asked.

They found a table by the window and ordered escallop
of veal with a bottle of Chianti. John waited until the waiter
had left them, then going straight to the point, he asked, 'do
you know who killed Ron Fenton?'

Stanko looked straight before him. Eventually he spoke.
'I thought you had asked to meet me for a purpose,' he said.
'I do not know who killed him, but there is one thing I know
for sure and that is that my country is not responsible in
any way for the death of Ron Fenton. You know he was
poisoned?'

John nodded.

'Ron often visited the Obelisco Restaurant at Opicina and
that is where he was last seen alive. The last evening he was
there with a lady friend. I have been told that they both ate
the same meal and were served from the same dish. Also the
coffee they drank was poured from the same coffee pot. The
girl suffered no ill-effects that I heard of.'

'Do you know the girl?'

'I have seen her but I do not know her. I do not believe
her to be involved. I have heard that the Russians know a
very subtle method of poisoning: they treat the cup with
a poisonous substance. They use one substance that kills
immediately, one that causes a coma and then death later;
and a third that is delayed a few hours then causes paralysis
and death.'

'This is news to me,' said John. 'It could tie in with the
report we received from the Italian officials. The poison had
first paralysed and then killed Ron.'

'There you are, my friend. Be careful. I do not want you to finish up the same way.'

'Have you any idea *why* Ron was killed?' John asked.

'No, I have no idea. As you know, Trieste is the meeting of the ways for East and West. The town is full of people and organisations trying to find out something, or trying to stop someone from finding out something. You and I work on behalf of our countries, but here there are some who are working for themselves.'

'We know that Ron was involved with most espionage organisations within the Balkan countries, and that he had an important defector he was debriefing. The defector was found hanged. Perhaps you knew about this.'

'Yes, I had heard.'

'Do you think Ron was poisoned to keep him quiet?' asked John.

'Certainly,' replied Stanko. 'If you could find out what he knew, then you would know who silenced him. Were the Italian police helpful?'

'Not very,' replied John, thinking he would keep this information to himself. 'You keep your ear very near to the ground,' he added, flatteringly.

'We do our best,' replied Stanko, likewise giving nothing away. 'Why not have dinner one evening in the Obelisco Restaurant and make a few discreet inquiries,' he suggested.

'Thank you. I shall take your advice.'

'It has been good to see you and I wish you luck. Thank you for lunch. We must meet again soon.'

They parted; Stanko returning to the Yugoslav Consulate, no doubt to report John's arrival in Trieste and their conversation. Although Tito had now broken away from Moscow, John knew that if Stanko decided to tell him all he knew about Ron's death, he would have to be prepared to repay him in some way, for one could never expect something for nothing; that was not their way.

That evening, as John entered the lounge of the Excelsior Hotel, he saw the beautiful Anna sitting in a large armchair, looking through a glossy magazine.

He walked over to her and noticed her long neck bent over as she was reading, and the thick, black hair coiled on her head.

'Good evening,' he said. 'I see you are alone. May I join you?'

'Yes, my uncle is not feeling well, so he will remain in his room this evening.'

'In that case would it be possible for you to have dinner with me tonight?'

Smilingly, Anna thanked him.

'Then I'll be in the Rouge et Noir at eight o'clock and wait for you.'

Promptly at two minutes to eight that evening John was sitting at a table in the nightclub bar, awaiting Anna.

He saw her first as she came in. She was wearing a black dress; her arms were bare, and as she walked her long earrings swung backwards and forwards like pendulums.

He went towards her. 'Would you like a drink here, or . . . ?'

'Let us go somewhere else,' she replied.

'The Castello San Guisto?'

'Perfect,' she replied.

They went by taxi along streets crowded with people promenading in the cool of the evening.

The castle of San Guisto is on a hill in the centre of town and the taxi wound its way up and round, through fortifications, into small dark tunnels and on through the main castle gate.

An atmosphere of quiet elegance engulfed them, but they chose to dine in the restaurant on the roof looking out over the battlements at the magnificent view of the town below, a mass of twinkling lights spreading out all around, disappearing into the night.

John ordered apéritifs and turned all his attention to Anna. She sipped her drink, gazing into the distance with sad, liquid eyes. How lovely she is, he thought. What more could a man desire than to be sitting with a beautiful girl in this romantic setting on a balmy June evening?

'Do you always travel with your uncle?' he asked her.

'Oh, no!' she replied. 'I work in Trieste, but when my uncle is here he feels very responsible for me. You understand?'

'So your name is not Yanakopolis.'

'My name is Anna Marieva. My father was Russian.'

'Is your father here also?' he asked.

'No,' she replied. 'I do not know where he is. My mother escaped from Russia when I was six years old and we have stayed with my grandparents in Greece ever since.' My mother is there now.'

'How many years have you lived in Greece?'

'Sixteen,' she replied.

He made a quick calculation. That would make her twenty-two. At that moment the waiter arrived with giant scampi on skewers, grilled brown and with a delicious, piquant sauce to dip them into. Ever since he had known he was coming to Trieste, John had looked forward to eating scampi again, cooked as only Italians can cook them and, as always, the actual taste was far better than he had remembered.

They danced slowly, romantically. When they sat down John asked Anna how she came to work in Trieste.

'I came with my uncle for a visit,' she explained, then

I met someone and fell in love and decided to stay. You understand?'

He nodded.

'My uncle found me work in his office and pays for me to have a room in the Excelsior Hotel—' Suddenly Anna became silent and introspective. Then, without looking at John, she whispered, 'It is all over now and I don't know what to do.'

Slowly, very slowly, large tears rolled down her face and fell on to her lap, while not a muscle of her face moved; the atmosphere was charged with tragedy and now John realised why she looked so sad and seldom smiled. He couldn't decide whether she looked even more beautiful when she was weeping. Silently he handed her his handkerchief and she dabbed ineffectively at her tears.

The waiter arrived with the main course and the wine. Anna sipped some wine but only toyed with the food. In order to give her time to control her emotions, John ate his meal slowly while talking about a holiday he had spent in Corfu. She gave him back his handkerchief; he held her hand for a moment and smiled at her.

'I'm sorry,' she whispered. 'Please forgive me.'

'It's all my fault for asking so many questions,'. he replied. 'I promise to ask no more. It's you who must forgive me. Come and dance.' He took her hand.

The sky was clear and star-lit with the moon coming up. He now knew a little more about the beautiful Anna and all the male protectiveness welled up in him as he held her close and tenderly in his arms. They did not speak. There was no need. They just moved in unison to the romantic melody under the stars with the battlements outlined darkly against the sky.

After he had taken Anna back to her room and given her a chaste kiss upon her brow, he returned to his room and stood on the balcony gazing over the darkened sea. He was physically attracted to Anna but knew he must steel himself against becoming emotionally involved. In this sort of job one was always questioning, doubting.

Was Anna's story true?

Was Aleco Yanakopolis really her uncle?

Had she still contact with Russia?

The next three days were unfruitful and frustrating. John avoided the Rouge et Noir. He avoided Anna. He spent the entire time walking the streets of Trieste, refreshing his memory of every street and alley and drinking more coffee in bars than was good for him. Although he had covered much of the town and chatted with many waiters and barmen, nothing of interest had come to light and he went to bed waiting for fate to give him a break.

5

Today was a day of action. John rented a furnished three-roomed flat on the top floor in a block of flats in the via Carducci and engaged an Italian woman of about fifty as a daily help to shop, cook, clean and generally look after him. She was the motherly type, of ample proportions, with a flowing Italian vocabulary, dramatic gestures and a good sense of humour. Her name was Marta.

John spent the morning buying small necessities for the flat and generally settling in. He also bought a car.

That evening he went to the Rouge et Noir hoping to see Anna. He sat on a bar stool and, finding Alberto as uncommunicative as ever, he sat in deep contemplation, drinking whisky.

'Hi there! What are you drinking? Whisky?' It was Pete Mason and his good-natured exuberance brightened up the place.

'Good to see you, Pete. Perhaps you will have dinner with me?'

'Not tonight,' he replied. 'But I've a better suggestion. A round of golf tomorrow morning at nine o'clock. How about that?' and Pete looked at a table nearby. John looked in the same direction and noticed a man sitting alone, reading a newspaper. This was the same man he had seen here before alone and also in the Piazza Unita.

'So long,' drawled Pete, pocketing John's telephone number. He downed his whisky and strode off.

Surreptitiously John studied the lone man and tried to remember why there should be something familiar about him and he wondered if Pete's glance in that direction had meant anything or not.

He was about forty-five; his own height, but with broader shoulders. His dark hair was combed straight back from his forehead and thinned out on the back of his neck as if it could grow no further. He had heavy features and the skin under his lower jaw was beginning to sag a little. The skin of his face was covered in marks rather like overgrown freckles; usually caused by exposure to extremes of climate. His face and body had a certain squareness and determination which indicated a forcefulness of character. The shoulders of his jacket were well padded and his clothes looked expensive. John wondered who he was and what he was doing in Trieste but knew better by now than to ask the uncommunicative Alberto.

It was a hot evening so he decided to drive up the hill to Opicina, which is a thousand feet up, and to take Stanko Logar's advice and make some inquiries in the Obelisco Restaurant about Ron Fenton. He parked in the hotel car park; before going into the hotel he walked along the road built by Napoleon and stood gazing at the fantastic view of Trieste and the sea.

The atmosphere in the hotel was relaxed. John went into the restaurant, ordered a bottle of wine and some food; the Yugoslav waiter was friendly. He enjoyed the meal, but refused coffee and spent most of the time studying the other diners; they were laughing and talking and eating with relish. He thought of Ron and hoped he had been equally happy during his last meal.

He paid the bill, tipped the waiter generously and mentioned that he was a friend of Mr Fenton. The waiter's face lit up with pleasure.

'Mr Fenton very good man,' said the waiter. 'He come much here, but now he come not here.'

John produced more money and asked if Ron came alone or with companions.

'Often a beautiful girl; often men.'

'The last time he came here, can you remember who war with him?' asked John.

'Si, signor. Same beautiful girl. They sit there,' He pointed to a table, 'and go home not late. Finish coffee, then go home. Three, four days after many police here ask questions, many questions about Mr Fenton and look everywhere in kitchen. All from restaurant must go to police in Trieste. They not kind. Ask many, many questions.'

'Did you serve Mr Fenton that evening?' John asked.

'No. Ricardo serve him.'

'I should like to meet Ricardo. Which waiter is he?'

'No, sorry not possible. Ricardo never come back again, that is last day here. No one see him again. He come from Roma and only work here six weeks. What happen Mr Fenton? We hear much stories, but nothing sure.'

'He's dead,' said John. 'Poisoned.'

The waiter went deathly white, a look of anguish contorted his young face and he placed his hand on his heart.

'I promise you, signor, I know nothing.' He looked furtively around as if afraid of being overheard discussing this subject.

John left the restaurant. Just as he was getting into his car the waiter suddenly reappeared, whispered ,'Sokolov,' and disappeared.

Back in his flat John went straight to the telephone directory. There were three listings of that name in Trieste and the area around; which one would it be? It was too late to ring tonight, it would have to wait until tomorrow.

His mind was full of poison, Ricardo, coffee cups. He stood up and stretched, putting his hands high above his head; he touched his toes; he flexed his muscles. All was well. He added up difficult numbers; he wrote down his mother's telephone number and signed his name; he sang a few lines of 'Rule Britannia'. All seemed well with his mind and body. He had not drunk coffee tonight at the restaurant. He decided to push aside all thoughts of poison and to have a good night's sleep.

Next morning John met Pete as arranged. Walking down the fairway Pete said, 'Good to have you here, we can now talk freely. I never trust bars or telephones. You settled in all right?'

'Yes, thanks. I've a small apartment in the via Carducci. I expect you know why I'm here.'

'Sure,' replied Pete. 'If I can help, just let me know.'

'Did you see much of Ron?' John asked. 'Can you tell me who he mixed with and why someone killed him?'

Pete looked thoughtful, selected a number five club, addressed his ball with great concentration and played it beautifully on to the green.

'If I could answer those questions, there sure would be no need for you to be here. I liked Ron – we got on well together and helped each other when we could. But naturally, we were not seen in each other's company very often. He had a steady girlfriend, Anna Marieva and—'

'Anna Marieva!'

'Yeah. You know her?'

'Yes.'

'Well, I'll be damned!'

'She and her uncle are staying at the Excelsior. I had no idea it was Ron. She told me about someone she loved and that it was now over. She was very distressed.'

'Sure. She was with him and ate the same food and drank the same coffee as Ron did. She must have been very shaken. The police questioned her.'

'Do you think Anna Marieva is involved in any way?' asked John.

'I work on the principle that *all* women are dangerous, especially the attractive ones,' Pete replied. 'Ron was on to something. You knew Ron. Always seemed so casual, relaxed and vague. As if he had all the time in the world and nothing important ever came his way. While behind that facade a quick intelligence was usually one jump ahead of anyone else, and when necessary he could move with lightning speed. Well, Ron had been particularly casual recently. That's how I knew he was on to something really big.'

'Does the name Sokolov mean anything to you?' John asked.

'Sure. He's a Russian refugee who did a lot of work for Ron. You'll find him in the bar Roma in the via Carducci at one o'clock most days. He's about twenty-five, slim with fairish hair and a pale complexion.'

'Thanks.'

They concentrated on the game.

John left Pete, drove back to the via Carducci, where he parked his car outside his flat, and walked to the Bar Roma. He could see no one looking at all like Pete's description of Sokolov, so he sat at a table facing the door and ordered whisky and soda.

Although his eyes were on the door, he couldn't stop thinking about Anna. So she had been Ron's girlfriend. She and her uncle had made his acquaintance on his first day in Trieste. Had this been chance? Whatever happened he must not become emotionally involved with her. He decided he must see her soon, and alone, to discover all she knew about Ron.

A slim young man entered the bar. He ordered coffee and sat alone at a small table. John took out a cigarette, felt in all his pockets, then stepped across the room and asked the

51

young man if he had a light. The young man took out his lighter, flicked it on, then held it for John, who sat down opposite him and thoughtfully blew smoke into the air.

John Harcourt only took action when he got a certain feeling to do so; it was a kind of intuition which never let him down; in fact he knew he owed his successful career to this.

And he had that feeling now.

'Would you be Mr Sokolov?' he asked.

'I don't think I know you,' replied the young man cautiously.

'My name is John Harcourt. I knew Ron Fenton very well. He was one of my best friends.'

The young man's face revealed nothing. 'How long have you been in Trieste, and who told you about me?'

'I arrived a short time ago,' John replied. 'An American friend of mine told me about you.'

'Ah!' It was slow and thoughtful.

Sokolov was old before his time. Pete Mason had said he was about twenty but he looked at least thirty-five. He had an intellectual air and looked in need of a good, square meal and some new clothes. He was a secret sort of fellow; John studied him closely.

'Meet me in the Bar Al Pescatori in the Viale Miremare at nine o'clock tonight,' Sokolov whispered.

John nodded.

Sokolov stood up and, with a slight inclination of the head, walked away.

John wandered off to the Piazza Del Unita to have something more to drink and a snack in order to kill time until nine o'clock. He looked around to find an empty table and to his delight saw Anna Marieva sitting at a table alone. He sat down in a chair opposite her.

52

She smiled at him.

'I've been wanting to see you – may I order you something?' he asked.

He ordered coffee for her and Campari for himself. He waited until they had been served before asking her the question uppermost in his mind.

Very gently he said, 'I believe you knew Ron Fenton.'

It was as if he had struck her. She became rigid.

'How did you know?' she whispered.

'Forgive me, but it is true, isn't it?'

She nodded.

'He was a great friend of mine,' John told her. 'I'm also sad that he is dead – I came here hoping to see him. I would like to talk about him if you feel able to do so.'

'Where shall I begin? I had only been in Trieste a few days when I met Ron. My uncle knew him and introduced us. I fell in love with him at once, immediately, at our first meeting. I had never met anyone like him before and I knew he was the man for me.' She began to cry softly, but continued between sobs, 'We met whenever we could, but sometimes he could not see me for many days at a time. He said he had urgent work to do and I must trust him and realise that it was work alone that kept him from me; there was no other woman in his life.'

'Did he ever talk about his work?'

'No, it was always a mystery. I asked him often, but he always said that serious subjects like work did not suit me and that I was his relaxation and must not remind him of work.'

'When did you see him last?' John asked as casually as possible.

'We had a wonderful evening together and had dinner in the Hotel Obelisco. Immediately we finished coffee, a waiter handed Ron a note. He read it, frowned, and said he must take me back to my room straight away because some work problem had cropped up and he would have to do something about it. I cried. I begged him not to go. But when Ron had made up his mind nothing could change it, you understand?'

'Yes. Then what happened?'

'On the way back he kept opening and shutting his eyes and stretching a leg or an arm. What is the matter? I asked him. It is nothing he replied. When we reached the Excelsior he leaned heavily on me and had difficulty going up the entrance steps. He said, "Forgive me for not seeing you to your room. I'll be in touch." That was the last time I saw him.'

'Did Ron get in touch with you again? Or send you a message?'

'No,' she replied. 'Nothing. The next day, the day after, the days after that were terrible days. No Ron, no message. Then the police came and asked me many, many questions.' She began to sob again. 'They seemed to think I had killed him. I wanted to kill myself. My uncle stayed with me all the time. He said I must forget all about Ron and start a fresh life. But I can't forget. Such a terrible death.'

She was now weeping uncontrollably and John realised that further conversation was impossible.

He took her back to her room and left her to her grief.

Her uncle knocked on her door. 'And how do you like your new friend?' he asked. 'Why all these tears?'

'I like him, but he's not Ron. Ron I loved,' she sobbed.

'You are young,' said her uncle soothingly. 'Time will heal and then you will be happy again. You may not think so now, but you will be in love with someone else one day – this is life.' He put his arms around her and drew her towards him, kissing her wet cheeks.

'Perhaps you should go back to your mother,' he then suggested. 'Just for a little holiday.'

Anna stopped crying. 'Please don't send me away, dear Uncle Aleco,' she entreated. 'Just a little more time, but if you mention Ron that makes it worse.'

'All right, I will not mention the subject again and you will not cry any more. Is that a bargain?'

She smiled through her tears and kissed him good-night.

At nine o'clock precisely John Harcourt entered the Bar Al Pescatori. He looked around and saw Sokolov already there. He ordered and sat down at the same table.

'Good evening. I hope you haven't been waiting long for me.'

'No. I have only just come myself.'

'Good. You've found a quiet corner, I see.'

'Yes,' explained Sokolov, 'you must excuse me that I first had to check with Pete Mason. He has confirmed that I can tell you all I know. I worked for Mr. Fenton. He was good to me and paid me well; he warned me never to talk to anyone about him or the work I was doing for him.'

'Good, tell me all you can. Who you are, how you came to work for him and about the work you did.'

'I am Russian. I worked for Mr Fenton as an interpreter. I live in the refugee camp here. In Russia I was a teacher of English and a writer. I could no longer accept the way of life in Russia, with the restrictions on what I could write and the ideologies I must accept, so I escaped through Romania to Yugoslavia. They kept me in prison in Yugoslavia for a year and questioned me and beat me every day. At last they let me out of prison, but I must live in a camp and report to the police every week. Then I managed to escape and come here. I was put in a camp and interrogated and that was how Mr Fenton heard of me. That was three years ago. I worked for him ever since.'

'So you just worked on Russian translations and interpreting?'

Sokolov nodded agreement.

'Were you busy recently?' John asked.

'Yes,' Sokolov continued, 'a Russian MGB officer with the rank of Colonel defected. His name was Aleksandr Petrovich Ivanov and he came from Vienna, where he was working as head of Intelligence at the Russian Embassy. When he reached the Italian frontier he asked for Mr Fenton, who went to the frontier post with the chief of police. Colonel Ivanov asked for political asylum in England. Mr Fenton brought him to Trieste and took him to a "safe" flat, but the Russians discovered where he was and tried to get him.'

'What exactly happened?'

'One evening, just as it was getting dark, someone rang his doorbell. The Colonel looked through a window and saw three men with their hats pulled down on their heads. He knew they were Russians. They kicked and hammered on the door and shouted in Russian, 'Open the door Aleksandr Petrovich, it would be better for you to co-operate.' They tried to force the door but it is specially strengthened. 'We shall get you!' one of the men shouted through the door. The Colonel rang for Mr Fenton, who came immediately with Italian police. Mr Fenton arranged for Colonel Ivanov to move to a single cell in the main Trieste prison, as the safest place.'

'Was he locked in his cell, and where did the interrogations take place?' John asked.

'The cell was kept locked for his own safety but he was given a comfortable chair and some extra bedding. He was made as comfortable as possible. We had the use of an office in the prison for interrogations. There were less risks that way.'

'Can you tell me about the interrogations?'

'Certainly,' replied Sokolov. 'Mr Fenton questioned him for many hours and many days and sent a report to London. In my humble opinion the Colonel was an honest defector.'

'Where was Colonel Ivanov before he went to Vienna?'

'Before going to Vienna, Colonel Ivanov was working in the headquarters of Military Intelligence in Moscow, dealing with Russian agents in the West. He would be able to supply a list of these agents, but he also said he had information of the greatest importance to the British Government that would shake the top people. He said that he would supply the list of agents and this important information only when he was granted asylum and was actually in Britain. Mr Fenton asked London to grant asylum and to say how the Colonel should travel, and by what route. London agreed to grant asylum, but before travel arrangements were made, he was dead.'

'Tell me what happened.'

'Even when the interrogation was finished, Mr Fenton visited Colonel Ivanov. He would take him cigarettes or newspapers or some fruit. I often went also to help with conversation. Mr Fenton was a kind man, he thought the Colonel might be lonely. Then one morning we went to the prison after nine o'clock, the Governor called Mr Fenton into his office and told him that the prison guard had found Colonel Ivanov hanging in his cell and had cut him down. He was dead.'

'How did it happen? Please try to remember every detail.'

Sokolov continued:

'Mr Fenton was very angry. White and silent, he strode in haste to the cell, with the Governor trying to keep up and the guard with the keys almost having to run. The guard opened the door and we went in. Colonel Ivanov was lying on the floor just as he had fallen when he was cut down. The guard had taken him breakfast at eight o'clock and found him hanging by a rope, which had been fixed to one of the bars protecting the windows.'

'Had you seen any rope in the prison?' John asked.

'No. Never. And there was none in the Colonel's cell. I can swear to that.'

Sokolov hurriedly made the sign of the cross. 'Mr Fenton had searched him himself. Why to kill himself? The day before he was making plans for the future. He was happy. Mr Fenton was certain it was not suicide and insisted he and the Governor interview all the prison staff immediately. They admitted nothing. They were also certain that the keys were always with them and that no one from outside had entered the prison. They all had alibis.'

'What do you think yourself, Mr Sokolov?'

'There is no doubt in my mind that it was murder. You see, Mr Harcourt, his hands were tied behind his back with a piece of twine. The noose had been placed round his neck, probably slipped over his head, then he was pulled up about six inches from the floor and the free end of the rope was fastened round the other bars. His neck was not broken. The noose had tightened with the weight of his body, and so he suffocated to death.'

'Did anyone look for fingerprints?'

'Yes, but there were none. Whoever did it wore gloves.'

'Then a few days later Mr Fenton was poisoned. Do you think it was the same murderer?' asked John.

'Yes, I do,' replied Sokolov. 'Mr Fenton told the police that although they were hushing up the whole affair, he would be asking the Foreign Office to make diplomatic representations at the highest level.'

'You think Mr Fenton was murdered to prevent him from following up the murder of Colonel Ivanov?'

'That is possible,' agreed Sokolov. 'But there is another possibility. He may have been murdered because of what he had learnt from Colonel Ivanov. The Russians may have thought he told us more than he did.'

'You mean that perhaps they didn't know that the most important information was only going to be told when the Colonel reached London?'

'You understand, Mr Harcourt, that I am now nervous and, although I need the money, I do not wish to be seen with you or anyone else connected with intelligence. After Mr Fenton's death, I am afraid.'

'Have a cigarette,' said John as he offered one from his silver case. Inside were two cigarettes, and a tightly folded wad of Italian money. Sokolov's eyes met John's; John inclined his head a fraction and Sokolov took a cigarette and the notes. He fumbled in his pocket for a light, put the cigarette in his mouth and walked out of the bar while lighting it.

John immediately left the bar and walked to his flat. What neither of them noticed was the dark figure of a man standing outside the bar, who followed Sokolov.

In his flat John found a message that James Wilson would be arriving on the Orient Express in three days time.

6

In Istanbul, two large, thick-set men boarded the Simplon Orient Express. They were both wearing wide-brimmed black trilby hats, square-cut jackets and trousers on the baggy side with rather wide legs. They had on heavy, round-toed shoes and were carrying briefcases. Their broad faces were pale and their eyes were small. Their hair was close-shaven and they neither smiled nor spoke. They were Russian and members of the MGB.

They didn't have sleeping berths, but settled themselves into corner seats nearest the corridor, opposite each other. The compartment already had two other occupants who wanted to sleep, a young man and a young woman, who hung their coats on a hook on the wall above their seats and sat with them hanging over their faces and bodies. This was in order to block out the light; it also gave a feeling of privacy and security.

The train chugged on and on; day turned into night and the two MGB men dozed with their hats tipped well forward over their faces.

Late afternoon the next day the train stopped at Bucharest. Here the platform was crowded with Russian soldiers, Romanian police and some passengers. The soldiers and police were armed and they immediately boarded the train, checked all travel documents, insisted that all suitcases were opened and the contents inspected. This was carried out in an unfriendly and discourteous manner greatly resented by the passengers. They also checked the amount of money carried by each passenger. Some *Securitate* boarded the train and searched every nook and cranny for escapees, while others walked along the rail with their Alsatian dogs sniffing out for anyone brave enough to try to escape from behind the Iron Curtain by travelling on the axles between the wheels.

The grey-haired, bespectacled sleeping-car attendant was standing on the platform with a list of passengers who had booked sleepers.

James Wilson walked up to the attendant, gave his name and produced his ticket. The attendant smiled courteously, picked up James's luggage and led him to a luxurious, single sleeping compartment. He enjoyed travelling by train and usually found good company on the Orient Express. He unpacked his pyjamas, slippers, sponge bag and dressing gown and stowed his suitcase away tidily; he always began by being tidy but somehow things never stayed that way.

That evening, when he went along to the dining car he found it almost full. He was shown to a table for two, the other seat being already occupied. Ah! he thought, just what I was hoping; to share a table for two with an attractive woman.

'Good evening,' he ventured in English, 'may I join you?'

'Of course!' the voice was deep, husky and mid-European. She looked about thirty, very much at ease and sure of herself. Her hair was naturally auburn with red lights and her eyes were golden brown. She had not yet ordered and was still studying the menu.

James smiled, 'May I get you a drink?' he asked.

'Thank you, how kind,' she drawled, 'I only drink champagne.'

James beckoned the waiter and ordered a bottle of champagne and a whisky and soda for himself. He was glad he had brought plenty of money with him.

He discovered that his dinner companion was Hungarian. She told him that she was returning from a visit to her parents, who lived on the outskirts of Budapest, and was now on her way to rejoin her husband in Paris, where he was the Ambassador. She was good company and the hours just flew by as they finished the bottle of champagne. She asked him where he was going and he explained that he was only going as far as Trieste.

From a gold cigarette case she took a long, black, Russian cigarette and placed it with care in a long, tortoiseshell cigarette holder. She offered James one but he refused, preferring his own. He had tried them once and found them too strong.

As they sat there smoking and talking, James's eyes wandered over the other diners. They looked the usual sort one met on these journeys; quite an assortment. The clientele had changed since the war. Then he noticed two heavily built men sitting side-by-side facing him, at the far end of the dining coach; from time to time they looked his way and once their eyes met.

James wondered . . . but no, one must guard against imagining things; they were probably just Bulgarians on a business trip. He looked back to his table companion and gave himself up to enjoying her company for the rest of the evening.

When he eventually returned to his sleeping compartment, it was with a feeling of weariness but also with a feeling of having wined and dined well. He made sure the door was locked and tucked his money, passport and revolver under his pillow.

When James came to with a start he wasn't sure if something had awakened him, or whether it was the heat. He always found he was either too hot or too cold in a sleeper. Now he was too hot, so he slipped on his dressing-gown and went into the corridor to get some fresh air and to smoke a cigarette. He stood looking out of the window into the passing blackness and could see here and there a single twinkling light or a cluster of lights, showing that there was life out there somewhere. He drew deeply on his cigarette.

Then he saw them. Instinctively he knew this meant trouble. One came from the right and one from the left, fast and silently. He tried to get back into his compartment but there was no time; the two men had him in a vice-like grip. He dropped his cigarette. He felt so vulnerable in his pyjamas and was furious with himself for having left his revolver under his pillow. He recognized the men as the two he had seen in the dining car.

They didn't speak but held him in a vicious grip with his arms pinned painfully behind him; they were powerful and knew their job. James struggled to free himself, he knew he was fighting for his life. The taller of the two struck James a skull-splitting blow on the head with a blunt instrument; at the same time the other man gave him a mighty punch in the solar plexus.

James did not see the blunt instrument but he felt it. The pain was instant, sending out a dozen streamers of searing pain. It was strange how he could see the pain, like strands of steel; it had never happened before. Shining bright rays of pain travelled from where the blow had come to his teeth, his nose, his temples, his eyes and the bones of his face. He was certain he could go mad with the intenseness of the pain, then suddenly before his eyes was a wall of red. James felt no more. It was all over.

This had taken place in a few seconds, but to James, absorbed in pain, it had seemed much longer. The two men looked at the crumpled figure on the floor, pulled him into the sleeping compartment and shut and locked the door. The smaller man picked up James's tie, made a slip knot, put it round his neck and pulled it tight using all his strength and held it so for a few minutes. The other man nodded, satisfied that James was dead.

The men looked at their watches; they drew aside a corner of the curtain and peered out of the window with their hands cupped round their eyes. They waited without speaking. Suddenly they moved; all was well, the train was now going through a tunnel, just as they had planned it would. They left the compartment quickly and quietly; one went to the right and one to the left. The sleeping car attendant was sitting on his chair in his corner sleeping peacefully; there was no movement along the corridor.

The two MGB men returned to James's compartment and, making no sound, picked him up like a baby and carried him along the corridor to the outside door. They pushed down the window and bundled his body out. They closed the window silently and returned to the compartment, where they made sure that they had left nothing behind and that everything was as they had found it. They shut the door quietly behind them and went back to their seats without disturbing the sleeping attendant. Once in their seats they pulled their hats over their faces and went to sleep. Professional men who had completed their mission.

7

It was a warm, balmy night so John Harcourt decided to walk to the railway station to meet James Wilson. He had never actually met him but had had countless telephone conversations since their work had often overlapped. He had always found James ready to help and was certain they would get on famously; in fact it would be good to have someone to discuss things with. He wondered what brought James on this journey; it must be something too important to refer to on the telephone or to send by a coded message.

He crossed over the road and walked along under the trees, with the sea on his left looking dark and lonely, but lit up by long rays of rippling lights, where the lighted windows and street lamps cast their reflections.

John looked across to the Piazza d'Unita still full of people either sitting at the tables or just strolling about. He continued walking beside the sea, past the Grand Hotel; then he bore round to the left to the railway station. This was a grand building. The high walls were as long as the platforms and the whole was enclosed by a high domed roof. This gave a feeling of great spaciousness. There were three wide platforms well lit by high wrought-iron lamps.

John looked at his watch, then checked it by the station clock. It was 11.05 p.m., and the Simplon Orient Express was due to arrive at 11.15, so he had only ten minutes to wait. Quite a number of people were on the platform. John began studying them. This was automatic and routine; part of his training, to observe everything and everyone but never to be seen to be looking. Obviously some were meeting friends off the train, they had no luggage and were wandering about looking anxiously down the line. Others were all set for the journey, some with mountains of luggage and some with just one or two suitcases.

Looking down the track, John saw two lights approaching. The express was on time, puffing into the station. The moment it stopped all was bustle and noise. Doors were flung open, people pushed their way off the train; all was activity, shouting, people and luggage.

John walked up the platform to the sleeping car and watched those alighting, looking for James. Those getting off were mostly greeted by friends or relations, or they left the platform with no hesitation, knowing where they were going. John looked up and down the platform. Had he missed James? Surely not, but there was no one standing about looking lost and there were no more people getting off the train.

The sleeping-car attendant was standing on the platform surrounded by a small group of people. He was checking in new arrivals and taking them to their sleeping compartments. John considered that James might have fallen asleep and not realised that the train had reached Trieste, so he went up to the attendant, told him he had come to meet Mr Wilson, and asked for the number of his sleeping compartment.

The small, elderly, grey-haired attendant looked at John and shook his head. His pale blue eyes looked tired and worried through the gold rimmed spectacles.

'Monsieur Wilson is not in 'is compartment. 'E 'as slept in 'is bed but I 'ave not seen 'im since last night. I went to warn 'im we are in Trieste but 'e is not there.' The agitated attendant continued in a strong French accent, ''is *luggage* is there but *'e* is not.'

'Show me his compartment.'

The attendant led the way, opened the door and stood to one side.

John entered the compartment and looked around. The bed had been slept in; otherwise the place was tidy. James's suit was hanging on a hanger; his underclothes were folded on a chair and his shoes were by the bed. John pulled back the bedclothes and picked up the pillow. Under the pillow was a wallet, a revolver and a British passport.

John picked up the passport. The name 'James Wilson' was written there clearly; he checked the photograph and personal details.

'Is this the man who got on the train in Bucharest?' John asked the attendant, showing him the photograph.

'Oui, monsieur. That is the man,' replied the attendant, watching John carefully and looking even more worried.

John opened the suitcase. There were shirts, socks and underclothes, but no pyjamas and no dressing gown.

'Have you searched the other compartments?' John asked, beginning to feel anxious, but determined not to show it.

The attendant went allong all the sleeping compartments, knocking, apologising, explaining; but there was no trace of James and no one had seen or heard anything unusual.

The attendant returned to James's compartment and turning to John said, 'Last night I saw 'im return from the dining car and go alone into this compartment – 'e was wearing these clothes,' and he put his hand on James's suit.

'Did you see him at any time today?'

'No,' replied the old man thoughtfully. 'I do not recall seeing 'im today. 'E was not in 'is compartment when I bring the tea this morning, so I am not able to ask if 'e wants the bed arranged for the daytime or does 'e want to sleep again, so I do nothing. Please excuse, I must find the Station Master, the train will be delayed.'

They went together in search of the Station Master and found him talking to the engine driver. When he heard that an English passenger was missing, he threw up his hands.

'What can I do?' he asked excitedly. 'Find the guard and search the train. Hurry! The express cannot be delayed.'

The train was searched from end to end. There was no sign of James and no clue. The platform was now becoming crowded with passengers who were leaving their carriages to find out when the train would be departing. They protested that a delay would cause loss of connections in Paris; that important appointments would be missed. The Station Master did his best to calm them.

'Please, please have a little more patience! The train will not be delayed much longer.'

He went to his office and telephoned the police.

John Harcourt slipped quietly out of the station and made his way quickly to his flat. He contacted the British Embassy in Bucharest who confirmed that James had left as planned. John informed them that he had not arrived in Trieste. He then sent a message to Hugh Compton in London.

8

After leaving the Bar Al Pescatori, Pavel Sokolov decided to walk back to the refugee camp. He left the viale Miremare and cut through the via Geppa; it was a quiet street at this time of night with only one or two cars about.

Suddenly a large, black car was on the pavement beside him, the door was open and strong hands dragged him inside the car, which didn't actually stop. It was all so quick. He struggled, but it was useless. The two men in the back of the car were strong, brutal and silent. They thrust him, face down, on the floor, pulling his arms behind his back and tying his wrists together. They seemed to take pleasure in stamping on him as he lay there and digging the heels of their shoes into his back.

Sokolov made no sound; he was petrified. This is what he had always dreaded and since Ron Fenton's death he had lain low and given his intelligence connections a wide berth. He had made this one exception and had met John Harcourt only briefly. Now he feared he would suffer the same fate as Mr Fenton. Worse even than death, Sokolov feared pain. In the refugee camp the hours were often whiled away with stories of man's inhumanity to man. He knew the worst that could happen to him.

The car stopped. Although the journey had seemed interminable, because of the discomfort, Sokolov knew that they must still be somewhere within the city's boundary. He was blindfolded, dragged from the car and frog-marched between the two men down some steps. He felt a change in the air and knew they were now inside a building and the floor beneath his feet felt hard, like concrete.

They flung him to the ground. It was very hard and he hit

his head against a wall. A door banged, it was bolted and he heard the men's footsteps receding. He lay there with a splitting headache.

Some time later the door was opened and for the first time he heard the men speak; to his amazement it was in his native tongue, Russian. There were three voices, but one spoke with authority and the other two just awaited his orders.

The man in authority was speaking, 'Tell me what you were talking about to Mr Harcourt tonight. If you do not tell me we shall make you speak, so start talking now.' And, as if to enforce his words, they put the boot in without warning. Sokolov's hands were still fastened behind his back so he had no way of protecting himself. 'We know you were working for Ron Fenton, and you know what happened to him, so be sensible and save yourself trouble.'

Sokolov was thinking frantically. If only his head didn't hurt so much it would be easier. If he told them the truth they would be furious to learn that he had helped in an interrogation by the British of someone of his own nationality. It would be counted as treason. On the other hand he did not think he could stand too much torture. Already his body was one big ache from the kicks he had just received to his head, his back and, most sensitive of all, his groin.

'Mr Harcourt searched me out because he hoped I could tell him how Mr Fenton was killed. He said he knew it was poison, but he did not know who had done it or how. That was all we talked about.'

They picked him up and flung him down again with great force; he had difficulty in getting his breath and oh, the pain in his head!

'What information did Colonel Ivanov give Mr Fenton?' demanded the boss Russian, while his two subordinates landed well placed kicks.

Sokolov was shaking uncontrollably. 'He told Mr Fenton that he had important information he would only disclose when he was in England, and only after he had been granted political asylum. That is the truth. That is all the Colonel would say. He was interrogated many times, but he said nothing and then he was dead.' Sokolov stumbled over the words, now sobbing with fear, pain and emotion.

'Lock and bolt the place,' commanded the interrogator. 'He will keep,' he added and strode away.

When they had gone, Sokolov lay on the hard, cold floor, sobbing. His hands were still tied behind his back and he was still blindfolded. He was very thirsty and knew he could not take much more.

9

Hugh Compton awakened with a start. 'Not again!' he said, struggling to open his eyes.

He and Julia had been peacefully asleep in their large, double bed, curled up together happily as they had slept for the last twenty years, except for the times when they were apart because of his work. Before their marriage, Julia had been in MI6 herself; that was how they had met. The telephone went on ringing relentlessly.

Hugh disentangled himself, turned on the bedside light and looked at the clock; it was 3.15 a.m. Lying on his back he picked up the receiver.

It was Basil Simmons, the Duty Officer:

'Message from Harcourt, sir. James Wilson is missing from the Simplon Orient, he should have reached Trieste 11.15 p.m. tonight. His compartment was undisturbed and his luggage and day clothes were there. Only his night clothes were missing.'

Hugh sat up in bed. Somehow it seemed easier to take things in when sitting up. 'Thanks for letting me know,' he said. 'Carry out the procedures as laid down, but also inform Interpol and ask them to check the track. It won't be easy, but see what they can do. They are usually most helpful, but if you have difficulty, ring me again. I'll see the report in the morning. O.K.? Good night.' And he replaced the receiver.

He lay back and turned out the light. 'Anything important?' asked Julia sleepily.

'No,' he replied, 'I'll tell you in the morning. Try to sleep again.'

Julia, who had been bargain-hunting in Harrod's sale all day and was exhausted, fell sleep again almost immediately.

Hugh was now wide awake and wondering what had happened. This was a bit of a shock; first Fenton dead; now Wilson missing; and both with a Trieste connection. Also Ivanov was dead; again Trieste.

And what was this 'very important information' that Ivanov would only disclose after he had been granted asylum in England?

Hugh's mind went round and round. He knew there must be a key to these killings, but for the moment it was eluding him. He would have to see the Chief immediately he arrived in the office.

Sir Gerald Oxborough Downey, known to his staff as GOD, was in charge of MI6 and was generally known as the Chief, or *C*. He had direct access to the Prime Minister. He was tall with greying hair and his brown eyes were always a little bloodshot. Educated at Eton and Cambridge, he had gone straight into the Foreign Office (his father had been a career diplomat) and, after having worked in various departments, he joined the Intelligence set-up. He was now fifty-five and was made a knight in last year's Birthday Honours.

He seldom smiled and when he did it was with only one side of his face. He spoke within his mouth in clipped phrases and his staff had to listen carefully to hear what he was saying. He had an autocratic manner and would brook no arguments with his subordinates. He was respected but not loved. The skin of his face was stretched tightly over his cheekbones and there were fine red veins on his nose and cheeks. He dressed in the height of sartorial elegance and walked with the confidence of the well bred. His marriage had not been a great success, but she had the money and was an excellent hostess. In fact she was essential for the success of his position. They had no children and this made him feel strangely deprived; he had always wanted a family. They had a country house in Kent and a flat in Kensington.

Hugh Compton was in his office early. He read through the Duty Officer's report and decided to see the Chief without delay.

Sir Gerald Downey had an office on the top floor with a view over St James's Park. Although well furnished, the room conveyed a feeling of space. His large desk was uncluttered. A green leather-bound blotter with a matching tray for pens and pencils and a silver-mounted inkwell, a present from his wife, were all that was on it.

He arrived punctually at 9.30 each morning, having walked from their flat in Kensington Close. He looked forward to these brisk morning walks and always followed the same route: along Wright's Lane, right into Kensington High Street, across into Hyde Park, where there were only a few people, some exercising their dogs and some enjoying a canter in the Row. Finally St James's Park and into Birdcage Walk. He now felt braced for whatever the day might bring.

The doorman saluted and opened the lift door. Sir Gerald strode into his office and flung open a window; it seemed so airless after his walk. He hung his black furled umbrella and bowler hat on a hook behind the door, then walked over to his desk, where he read the report from the Duty Officer. He sat looking out of the window for a moment before glancing through the morning's mail. He put the mail in the top right-hand drawer of his desk. Only the paper relevant to what he was dealing with was on his blotter.

His P.A. rang through to say that Hugh Compton was waiting to see him.

'I was expecting you,' said Sir Gerald, picking up the report. 'I've just read this message about Wilson.' He motioned Hugh to a chair.

'Yes, sir. That's why I wanted to see you. I'm worried.' Hugh sat in one of the large green leather armchairs and continued, 'Firstly, Colonel Ivanov was hanged in a Trieste prison – he didn't kill himself, it was murder. Secondly, Fenton was poisoned before he had a chance to find out who hanged Ivanov and we have no idea who killed Fenton. Thirdly, Wilson was on his way to Trieste to see Harcourt and now he has disappeared mysteriously from the Orient Express. All these events have happened in the space of four weeks. They *must* be connected.'

Sir Gerald listened intently to what Hugh was saying. He was sitting at his desk with his elbows on the arms of his chair and his fingertips pressed firmly together. His eyes were downcast, looking past his fingertips to his blotter, while his body swayed backwards and forwards in a slow rhythmic movement.

When Hugh had finished speaking, Sir Gerald stopped swaying and raised his bloodshot eyes. 'You may be right,' he conceded. 'On the other hand it might just be coincidence. We must have more facts, Hugh. It is your staff who should be supplying these. For God's sake, tread warily. Whatever happens, I don't want the press to get wind of any of this. We can't afford to lose any more good operators, so you will all have to be more careful. Above all be discreet – don't stir up a hornet's nest. And report to me the moment you discover anything significant. I have to see the P.M. later today, so I had better just mention about Wilson being missing in case it gets into the foreign press.'

Hugh looked into the bloodshot eyes and wondered what was going on behind that impenetrable gaze. He got up. 'Thank you, sir. I will keep you informed.' He closed the door quietly behind him, smiled at Gerald's secretary and returned to his office deep in thought. He hadn't received much help from that quarter, so the ball was still firmly in his court.

Interpol had wasted no time and had organised a search of the route followed by the Orient Express before reaching Trieste, including an area of fifty yards on either side of the railway line. There were teams with strong torches checking through the tunnels. They were checking with police stations and hospitals.

It was midday when a team searching a tunnel found the body of James Wilson lying beside the railway line clad in dressing gown and pyjamas. These garments were torn and soaked in blood. He had been badly battered and bruised with cuts on the head, shoulders and legs.

One of the men made a sketch of the body, showing the position in which it was lying in relation to the railway line. They were well prepared and had with them a light-weight canvas stretcher. They put on rubber gloves and lifted James on to the stretcher; his feet dangled over the end.

The two men now had to retrace their steps through the tunnel, carrying the stretcher between them. This was no simple matter. They were far into the tunnel and there was no light whatsoever. It entailed holding the torch and the stretcher shaft in the same hand which limited the arc of light. They swore as they stumbled over railway sleepers and had numerous rests before emerging into the fresh air.

The body was taken to the nearest police station where fingerprint and forensic experts were called in. Interpol informed the Foreign Office in London, gave a description and asked for someone to come and identify the body.

Big Ben was striking four o'clock when Hugh Compton received the news that the body of a man, answering the description of James Wilson, had been found. The man had been strangled before being thrown out of the train. Someone would have to identify the body. Hugh replaced the receiver.

The door opened and Jenny, his typist, brought him a cup of tea. He thanked her automatically as she put it on his desk. She went out as discreetly as she had come in. He noticed the two lumps of sugar in the saucer and, as usual, the tea had spilled and had turned the sugar brown.

With a spoon and two fingers he got the sugar into the cup without the lumps breaking. Slowly he stirred the tea. How he disliked the feel of the cheap spoon and the thickness of the cup. The tea was awful; it always was, but there was something comforting about this mundane cuppa.

It proved that the ordinary things of life continue, regardless of murder and other horrendous happenings. He was thinking of James; young, fit, happy and with so much more he could give to life. He drank the tea.

Sir Gerald listened attentively as Hugh informed him of Interpol's findings. Not a muscle of his face moved. There was not a flicker of emotion. 'You had better go yourself to identify Wilson,' he said. 'Better give some other reason to the staff and to his family; an accident of some sort. Give it thought and make it foolproof. The fewer people who know when we lose any of our own people, the better.' His tone was dismissive. 'Is there anything else?' he asked.

'No, sir,' mumbled Hugh. 'Nothing else.' As he left the Chief he realized once again how suited Sir Gerald was to this job. Unhampered by personal feelings towards his staff, he looked at them objectively, used them and, if necessary, discarded them and went on to the next item on the agenda without so much as a backward glance.

Hugh was glad to get home that evening. He poured his wife a gin and tonic and himself a whisky. He was going to talk the whole thing over with Julia; it would help, it always did. She was a good listener. She did not interrupt him and by the time he had finished telling her about Interpol finding James Wilson's body, her glass was empty.

He refilled it.

She wrinkled her nose, a habit she had when she was thinking. 'And then there were seven,' she said. 'It's just like the ten little nniger boys. Who will be next? Is this casualty rate only in Section B or are the other sections suffering similar disasters?'

'I have no idea,' Hugh explained. 'The trouble is that Gerald has insisted on utmost secrecy: strictly need-to-know basis. I haven't been able to talk about this with anyone.' He couldn't remain sitting still a moment longer, he felt too agitated and began walking about the room.

Julia had kicked off her shoes and was curled up comfortably on the sofa. She put her half-finished glass on the small table beside her and looked up at Hugh. 'There are times,' she said, 'when one has to stretch a point and this is one of those times. Why don't you have a word with the other section heads, one by one, and impress on them the need not to betray your confidence.'

'Julia, darling, I believe you're right. I would then have the overall picture. I'll ask Dick to join me for lunch tomorrow. Will you ask Bill and Cathy for drinks in the evening?'

'Fine,' agreed Julia. 'And when will you be seeing Tony?'

'Section D is always so busy. Tony usually starts work at eight in order to get an hour's work done before being interrupted by people and telephones. I'll set the alarm for six-thirty and disturb Tony's peace just after eight. I'm sure I can rely on their discretion. The next day I have to fly to Milan to identify poor old James. We don't have any engagements, do we?'

Julia shook her head. 'No,' she replied. 'I try to keep the weekdays free, because I never know what time you will be home.'

'I'm worried about John Harcourt,' Hugh said, 'I don't want to lose him. If only we could discover who we are up against.'

'Hugh, darling, do stop worrying. You know as well as I do that John is capable of dealing with any situation, even the most unexpected. If he senses that you're worried it will tend to undermine his confidence in himself. That might prove fatal. Tomorrow, after you've talked with the other three, you'll feel quite different. Let's have dinner with a bottle of wine.'

Hugh willingly agreed and went off in search of a corkscrew.

10

Time passed slowly for Pavel Sokolov. He had no idea how many hours he had lain on the cold, concrete floor. His head still throbbed mercilessly and his body ached all over. It was worse when he tried to move. Eventually he managed to free his hands and remove the handkerchief from his eyes.

Slowly he pushed himself into a sitting position with his back against a wall and his knees bent. It was dark. He felt for his watch but it wasn't on his wrist; it must have been wrenched off somehow, he thought. Very slowly he began crawling around the floor feeling for his watch, but it was all too painful and his head was pounding. He slumped back against the wall and felt the tears run down his face. He now gave himself up to the luxury of weeping.

He wallowed in self-pity for several hours. Why had this happened to him? He had always hated violence of any kind. That was how things had gone wrong for him in Russia. He had written an article against violence. Against beatings-up; against violence during interrogation; against violence in prisons and against the violent actions of the MGB.

A friend had taken the article and read it out at a meeting. He had been warned that he would be arrested, and his parents had pleaded with him to leave the country and to tell the world the truth about Russia.

He had gone into hiding, moving from place to place, planning and scheming, until at last he managed to escape. He had been hungry and tired ever since leaving home and he couldn't take it much longer. He had never wanted to get mixed up in intelligence, it was not up his street at all. And now here he was – caught by the long arm of the MGB.

Exhausted, Sokolov slept for a time. When he awoke he

was instantly aware of pain, cold and stiffness. He clawed his way up against the wall, straightening himself slowly and with difficulty. He tried walking around. No bones had been broken and slowly he began to move a little more easily.

'Pavel,' he said to himself, 'pull yourself together, you have not come all this way to give up without a struggle, to fail now. Survival is everything, fight to survive, you are not dead yet, have courage.'

He turned with his back to the door and faced the corner of the room where there would be an icon in every Russian household. He closed his eyes and imagined his family's icon, the one he and his parents had faced every time they entered their home. He stood there praying and, as he did so, he grew calmer and more resolute.

Suddenly he heard noisy footsteps running down steps and the door was flung open. Two heavyweight men grabbed hold of him.

'Tidy yourself,' one of the men told him, speaking Russian and handing him a comb. 'Come with us. If you try to get away or make one false move, you will be dead.' He held Pavel's arm with his left hand, keeping his right hand in his coat pocket, holding a gun.

'Follow him,' said the man shaking Pavel by the arm and nodding his head towards the other Russian. 'Remember, I shall be just behind you.'

Pavel felt his newly found confidence slipping away. He stumbled out of the room and up the stairs. One of the Russians was in front of him and the other behind, pushing him roughly in the back. When they reached the street, Pavel felt the warmth and noticed there was no one about.

Siesta time, he thought, as he was shoved into the back of a large, black car and pushed to the floor so he could not see where he was going.

After about twenty minutes, the car stopped. One of the men climbed out. 'Get out!' he snarled at Pavel while the other man kicked him to encourage him to move more quickly.

With aching head and limbs Pavel struggled out of the car. When he stood upright he found he was standing in a garage. He was led through a door directly into a house and found himself in a pleasant room overlooking the Adriatic.

The two Russians frog-marched him to a room in the far side of the villa where steep cliffs were only about a foot away and towered higher than the window, excluding the light and giving the room a claustrophobic atmosphere.

'Leave him here and wait outside the door,' commanded a man sitting behind a desk with a bright light on it. The man had black, penetrating eyes set far apart in a flat, expressionless face. His eyes pierced Pavel.

'Sit down,' he said, motioning to Pavel to sit on a chair on the opposite side of his desk. 'I am the head of Russian Intelligence for this area. I have had you watched ever since you arrived at the refugee camp. We have our system, and it is not possible to avoid us. We know you are a writer of some distinction but you have used your talents to spread dis-information about Russia. From now on you will work for us. Is that understood, comrade?'

Pavel felt himself choking. He could not bear to look at that expressionless face any longer. He lowered his eyes. 'It must be a mistake,' he said, 'I am totally unsuited for this type of work.'

The Russian gave Pavel a hard, cold stare. 'We never make mistakes, comrade. You settled down very quickly when Mr Fenton asked you to work for him. You *will* work for us. You have no choice.'

Russian methods were well known to Pavel. He knew that if he did not co-operate, his parents, who were still in

Russia, would be arrested and ill-treated. There were also his grandparents. Nothing must happen to them, they could never stand it, they were now so frail. He loved his family so he must do all he could to protect them. He thought he was going to be sick. The thought of working for Russian Intelligence filled him with horror, but this was nothing compared to the fear he felt at the thought of what would happen to him if he refused.

Pavel sat, swallowing hard and clenching and unclenching his cold, clammy hands while his mind went round, as if in a maze, trying to find a way out, knowing in the end he would have to agree in order to save himself and his family.

'So that is agreed. You are a Russian and you will be working for Russia. If you try to doublecross me, I shall know.'

A young man came into the room. He was a stocky five feet six inches with well padded shoulders. 'This is your contact. You will know him only as "Mario",' said the head of Russian Intelligence. 'I want you to keep in contact with Major Harcourt. Work your way into his confidence. Report who he sees, where he goes, if he has liaisons with men or women – all his habits. Nothing can be too trivial. Remember, we shall be watching you and you will be silenced for ever if you give me cause to doubt your loyalty to Russia. Go with Mario.'

Pavel got to his feet and staggered from the room. Mario led him into a small, bare office, furnished with only a wooden table and two hard chairs. Mario told him to sit down and put a sheet of writing paper before him. 'Write your full name and address, the names and address of your parents, the names and address of your grandparents and sign the paper "Bianco",' Mario ordered.

When Pavel and finished, Mario read it slowly and

carefully. 'Good,' he said. 'I just wanted an example of your handwriting.' Mario gave him the address of a flat where he could be contacted or a message left, then took him to the car and told the driver to drop him off somewhere near the refugee camp.

11

John Harcourt was perplexed.

So far he had no lead on who was responsible for the poisoning of Ron Fenton and the hanging of Colonel Ivanov. Now James Wilson had been found strangled and thrown off the Orient Express. Did they all know something and have to be silenced, and was there a connection between the three? He decided to seek out Pete Mason. Perhaps the CIA network had heard something that would be worth following up? He drove to the golf club.

Sure enough, there was Pete sitting outside the club-house with a glass of beer in his hand.

'Hullo,' said John, sitting beside him. 'There's something I must talk to you about. James Wilson, one of our people in Romania, was strangled and thrown off the Orient Express.'

Pete blew through threw his teeth, 'Well, something's going on,' he drawled. 'You can bet your shirt on that and I should think something pretty big. My guess is it's the Russians. What do you think yourself?'

'My reason says it is the Russians, yet I have a nagging feeling it's someone else,' replied John. 'But I don't know who. One should go on reason. I shall have to dig around and see what comes up.'

'Good luck. I hope you come up with something soon. Now I have something difficult to say to you, John. This morning I received instructions from Washington to avoid all contact with you and not in any circumstances to give you information of any kind, and to make sure that you do not discover the identity of any of our agents. I'm sorry about this, John, but orders are orders. You understand I have no choice, I have to carry them out. You'll know it's nothing personal – just carrying out Goddamned orders!'

John looked shaken. He put the glass of beer he was drinking on the table and asked, 'What have I done? You must tell me.'

'You can take my word for it that it's not you. My guess is that those guys in Washington are nervous about all the people you're losing and fear it might be contagious. Give them a few months and it'll blow over and we'll have a good laugh about it over a bottle of bourbon.'

'Damn them,' muttered John. 'I shall miss you.'

Pete stood up. 'I must be going,' he said. He grasped John by the hand and pumped his arm up and down. 'Good luck and take care. So long.' He strode away.

For the first time John understood what it meant to be on one's own. Pete was the only person in Trieste he could talk to as a friend and now that was at an end. He would send a message to Hugh Compton letting him know of Washington's attitude.

He drove back to his flat feeling in need of company, so telephoned Anna and suggested he would call for her and they would have a drink together later.

Sitting at a table opposite Anna, John sipped a martini and recovered his usual high spirits. On an impulse he asked her if she knew any Russians.

'I only know two,' she told him. 'I met them with my uncle. They are businessmen. Why do you want to know?'

'I'm writing an article where I have to refer to life in Russia. It's only a passing reference but it would be helpful to meet them, if that's possible.'

'Of course.' Anna looked at her watch. 'They usually go to the Nettuno in Sistiana. Why don't we go there now and if we find them I will introduce you. You would like that?'

'Yes. Very much,' replied John getting to his feet. 'We'll drive there now.'

They drove out of the town and took the coast road past Miremare, where the delicate pink flowers of the tamarisk trees lined the route. The beaches below were crowded with bathers and people lying in the sun.

They passed Grignano and San Croce, where the calm sea was dotted with sailing boats, looking like white ducks on a pond. They left the main road and drove down the narrow, stony, winding lane to the tiny village of Sistiana nestling in the bay beside the sea.

About half the tables in the hotel Neptuno were occupied. John and Anna sat at a large, round, wooden table which had a bowl of pink roses in the centre. Anna looked around, but the Russians were not there.

'Perhaps they come later,' she said hopefully.

John stretched his arm across the table and took her hand.

'I don't mind if they never come,' he said, smiling at her and squeezing her fingers gently.

She smiled back into his eyes and for the first time since they met she looked really happy. 'You look more beautiful than ever,' he said softly. She looked down and a slight blush crept into her cheeks. She looked up past him and pulled her hand away.

'They have just come in,' she said.

John looked behind him and saw two men entering the room.

Anna went quickly to the door and invited them to join John and herself at their table. The men glanced at John.

'Mr Harcourt is a journalist,' Anna explained, 'and he is anxious to meet some Russians in connection with his work.'

One of the Russians was about forty with raven-black hair

combed straight back from his high, rounded forehead. His black, penetrating eyes, set far apart in a flat, expressionless face, held John in their gaze. He held out his hand.

'Pleased to meet you, Mr Harcourt,' he said. 'It is a pleasure for me to meet an Englishman. There are not very many here. My name is Boris Molohovski.' They shook hands. 'This is my colleague, Nicolai Petrov.'

Mr Petrov was much shorter, squarer and younger. They sat down and John ordered wine for everyone.

The moment Boris Molohovski had entered the restaurant, John had recognised him as the man he had seen sitting alone in the Rouge et Noir nightclub and also in the Piazza del l'Unita. When they had shaken hands he remembered why his face had seemed familiar; he had been shown a photograph of Molohovski by Hugh Compton before he left London to go to Trieste. He was sitting face to face with the head of Russian Intelligence for Italy, Austria and the Balkans. He felt the adrenalin flowing. He had been well briefed on Molohovski and had read up his dossier. John knew that here was a ruthless, intelligent and successful operator.

'Have you been here long?' John asked the Russians.

'From time to time,' explained Molohovski. 'We run an import-export business and have our headquarters here.'

'What do you deal in?'

'Mostly powdered milk at the moment, but we are always prepared to vary our items according to the needs of our country. We find the free port here convenient. May I ask what brings *you* to Trieste, Mr Harcourt?'

'I am a journalist,' replied John casually, 'but I have come here to find out what happened to my old friend Ron Fenton. He was such a pleasant fellow, I cannot imagine why anyone should want to kill him.'

The silence lasted just too long as the two men sat looking at each other.

Anna was worried. She had not expected the conversation to take this turn.

Molohovski recovered and said, 'I heard a rumour that an Englishman had been killed, but since I did not know him I took no further interest. Have you been to the police?'

'Of course. That's where I began my enquiries. The police will only say it was poison, but can give no lead as to who killed my friend or the reason. I can't rest until I find out. Should you ever hear anything in this connection, I trust you will contact me. Here's my card.'

Molohovski took the card, glanced at it, smiled politely, put it in his inside jacket pocket but did not offer his own card or telephone number in return.

'What work was your friend doing here?' he asked.

'That's the funny thing,' replied John. 'It was also import-export.'

'Amazing!' Molohovski stood up and held out his hand to Anna. 'I am afraid we must go. We have a business appointment.' He turned to John, 'Forgive us for leaving so soon, perhaps we can meet again and continue this interesting discussion about your friend,' he said smoothly, as he bowed slightly and walked towards the door followed by his colleague.

John looked across the table at Anna. Frowning slightly, she was obviously anxious. 'What sort of import-export company did Ron have?' she asked. 'My uncle knows all the businessmen here and he had no idea what Ron was dealing in.'

'Shall we eat?' asked John. 'I'm famished!' He summoned the waiter and discussed the meal at length. He then took her hand and said gently, 'Shall we make a pact never to talk about Ron again – since it makes us both sad?'

Anna nodded her head in agreement, but her eyes were full of tears.

The atmosphere had been spoilt and the evening was not the success it had promised to be, so John suggested they made it an early night on the pretext of a busy day tomorrow. He thanked Anna for introducing him to her Russian acquaintances and told her he felt sure he would have a lot in common with them. He took her back to her room, kissed her gently and promised to see her again soon.

Back in his flat John fell on the sofa in his favourite thinking position, with his head on one end and his feet up on the other. He let his mind run back over the events of the past few weeks; the stranger in the night who had warned him not to investigate Ron's death; that Boris Molohovski was obviously watching his movements; that Molohovski would have been briefed about him and knew exactly who he was. This charade must go on for a time; he would shatter it only when it suited him; he felt sure the Russians would not wish to show their hand.

How much did Anna know and was she working for the Russians? Was her uncle working for the Russians and was he directing her without her knowing about it? He could not decide, but one thing he knew was that the Russians looked upon his arrival in Trieste as of sufficient importance to bring Boris Molohovski out of his lair to have a personal meeting with him. His instinct, which had never let him down, warned him not to underestimate Molohovski.

He swung his feet off the sofa and sat upright. Perhaps he would be the next. He was damned if he would let them get him; he would be vigilant as never before. He didn't feel like sleeping but sat on into the night deep in thought, sipping whisky and soda from time to time. When would these murders end? All had been fairly quiet until Colonel Ivanov had been found hanged. Then Ron had been poisoned; and now James. There had to be a connection; he must find the key to this mystery. There was also the fact that Pete Mason had been ordered to avoid him. Perhaps if he read again the last report Ron sent to London just before he was killed, he might find a clue.

Ron had never left anything lying around. He stored away every detail in his excellent memory, had sent all the interrogation reports to London, and had kept no copies. John had read all the recent reports before coming to Trieste, but he now decided to look at these reports again. Perhaps he had overlooked something. He would ask Hugh Compton to send him copies as soon as possible.

It was some time before John Harcourt found Pavel Sokolov. He had not been in any of his usual haunts, but by chance he bumped into him on the corner of the via Dante and the via Mazzini. John hardly recognised him: he looked so ill and his face was badly bruised.

'Just the person I'm looking for!' exclaimed John, barring his way. He took Pavel by the arm and said, 'Come and have a drink in the bar across the road. I have something to ask you.'

The bar was fairly empty, so they were able to choose a table where they could not be overheard.

'Are you all right?' John asked anxiously. 'You look pretty awful. What happened to your face?'

'I had a little accident the other night – fell down a flight of stone steps. I was trying to find my way back to the Camp, but it was a dark night and there was no lighting. I hit my face on a stone post at the bottom of the steps. It looks much worse than it really is.'

John noticed that Pavel seemed to have shrunk. He was altogether smaller and sat looking at the table. If his eyes met John's accidentally, he immediately looked away. Something very unpleasant had certainly happened since they parted that dark night. It was equally clear that

Sokolov was not going to tell him about it. Ron had trusted him, thought John, so surely he was reliable. But then again, how could he be sure? Actually, there was little choice, Sokolov was the only person who could tell him about the interrogations of Colonel Ivanov.

'I need your help,' John began, leaning across the table and forcing Sokolov to look him in the eye. They were such worried, frightened eyes. 'I want you to tell me everything you can remember of what Colonel Ivanov told Mr Fenton. Every little detail. And if there are two ways of translating what he said, then please tell me both translations. This is very important and very urgent because innocent people are being killed.'

Sokolov sat looking at the table; his mind was in a whirl. Should he tell Mr Harcourt that he had been forced to work for the Russians and to spy on him on threat of death if he refused? No, he dare not. They might find out; he shuddered to think of what would then happen. No, he was not brave; he would play along with Mr Harcourt and would also report to his Russian contact, Mario.

He must survive somehow.

As they sipped their coffee John questioned him painstakingly, making him go through each day's interrogation. Questioning him on each point that might bring forth something new, asking if he was sure that the meaning had been correctly interpreted. Digging, questing; John felt sure the clue was somewhere here.

John ordered lunch for them both; he thought a good meal was probably what Sokolov needed badly. He waited until they had finished their meal before pressing for more information.

'Did Colonel Ivanov give the name of any of his contacts in Austria? Did anyone help him to decide to defect? Think carefully. Did he ever mention any name at any time, no matter how unimportant or unconnected it may have seemed to you.'

'We often worked late into the night,' explained Pavel wearily. 'Mr Fenton received questionnaires from London. They were long and technical and went into great detail. We all three got very tired. One night we had to stop and Mr Fenton poured us all a glass of whisky to restore us so that we could carry on. That was the only time I saw Colonel Ivanov relax; he began talking about his plans for the future. He was sad to have left his children, but he had made his choice so must make a new life in the West. He asked Mr Fenton if it would be possible for him to contact a friend in Vienna, but Mr Fenton said it was not allowed to contact anyone until he was in England.'

'Did he mention the name of this friend?'

'No, and he never spoke about anything personal at any other time. He would never give any information about friends or acquaintances, he did not consider that to be part of the deal. But one thing always interested me and that was that when Colonel Ivanov was writing his reports he drew designs or shapes all around what he had written, there was never a clear piece of paper left. Mr Fenton called this "doodling".'

John nodded and Pavel continued.

'On each piece of paper somewhere in the doodling there was always a small landscape drawing with the figure of a young woman walking away into the sunset. Colonel Ivanov was an excellent artist and they were perfect in every detail. Amongst the many doodlings was the face of a woman, always the same face from different angles, almost hidden by the other drawings.'

'What has happened to these handwritten reports?' interrupted John.

'I translated them into English and after Mr Fenton had

sent his reports to London, we burnt them. Mr Fenton often asked Colonel Ivanov who this young woman was, but he remained silent. One day there was a larger portrait of this young woman, very beautiful. It was lying on the table when Colonel Ivanov went to the toilet. I cleared up all the papers to translate, I put this drawing amongst them and took it as well. Later Colonel Ivanov asked me where it was and I told him I had destroyed it – but I kept it. It was too good to destroy.'

'What did you do with it?' demanded John.

Without speaking, Pavel put his hand into his inside coat pocket and drew out a shabby, brown wallet. It was full of old, mostly dirty, pieces of paper and photographs. Slowly he selected the cleanest piece, unfolded it with care and smoothed it out on the table.

John picked it up and, the moment he saw it, he recognised it. His heart missed a beat but not a muscle in his face moved.

'She is certainly beautiful,' he said evenly. 'Do you think she is his wife?'

Pavel shook his head. 'No,' he said thoughtfully. 'The way he spoke about his wife was as if it was in the past. Having decided to begin a new life in the West, his private life in Moscow had been put behind him. This is only my opinion and could be wrong.'

Colonel Ivanov was an outstanding artist if his work could be judged by this portrait, which was the head and shoulders of a young woman in her early twenties. Her eyes were large and set far apart in an oval face; her hair was off her face and rested on her shoulders where it curled up at the ends. Her nose was small and her mouth had the merest suggestion of a smile. It was the eyes that held you. That was where the smile was and from where the whole expression radiated.

'May I keep this?' John asked, folding the paper and putting it in his wallet.

A frown was on Pavel's face, he looked upset. 'It is British government property, strictly speaking,' joked John. 'I promise to take good care of it.'

John had immediately realised that this was a portrait of Lisl von Althof. He had been briefed in London that she was working for British Intelligence in Vienna and would be reporting to him shortly when she had information on the disappearance of another agent. They had shown him photographs of her and he had no doubt that this was the same person.

He slipped an envelope of banknotes into Sokolov's hand and left the bar.

Back in his flat, he immediately contacted Vienna and asked for news of Lisl, to be told she had gone into hiding in the safe house in Bucharest because somehow the Russians had discovered that she was working for the British.

He next sent a message to Romania asking if anyone had yet seen Lisl. When the reply came that the last person to have seen her had been James Wilson, he sat up with a jerk. What a fool he had been running around in circles in Trieste! He must cast his net wider and include Austria and Romania.

He took out of his pocket the folded paper and studied the portrait again. He must find out the relationship that had existed between Lisl and Ivanov. Ron had been killed after he had met Ivanov; James was killed after he had visited Lisl. There *was* a connection, and somewhere here he would find the clue to all these murders.

John guessed that either he or Lisl was at risk of being murdered next. He sent a message to Bucharest telling them to get Lisl out of Romania immediately.

Back came the reply. 'Too ill to move. Typhoid. Must have doctor. Will arrange.' Signed Negulescu.

John decided he must go to Bucharest and get Lisl out to a safer place. He knew he should keep London informed of his plans, but he decided to tell no one. He felt safer that way because he no longer knew who he could trust.

During the morning another message arrived from Bucharest. It read:

NEGULESCU DEAD. SHOT
THROUGH THE HEAD IN BED.

John relayed the message to London. That would be his last communication until he had moved Lisl to safety.

Radu Negulescu had been a quiet, hardworking and loyal member of the staff of the British Embassy. James Wilson had held him in high esteem. Where would this end? John asked himself. The CIA must have smelt that something was very wrong and wanted to disassociate themselves from the British. John recalled that the message that Lisl was ill had been signed by Negulescu. He would have visited Lisl and arranged for a doctor to see her. With James and Negulescu dead, Lisl would be very vulnerable. All this confirmed his decision to rescue her himself, and he must act quickly.

Time was running out.

12

The other heads of sections were pleased to talk to Hugh. It was a relief all round. Section *A* had lost one man – drowned in mysterious circumstances – while Section *C* had two suicides quite out of character. All this within the last three months. Only Section *D* was unscathed. They had all been warned by Downey not to discuss these deaths for fear the press might find out and splash it across the front pages. The Secret Service preferred to keep their failures and successes to themselves.

Section heads were all concerned for the safety of their agents and urged Hugh to discuss the problem with GOD.

Never one to let the grass grow under his feet, but careful not to let slip his discussions with the others, Hugh sought an immediate interview with the Chief.

'Good morning, sir. Thank you for seeing me straight away,' said Hugh as Gerald waved him to a chair. Hugh sat down and continued:

'We have just received information that Radu Negulescu, a Romanian who worked with James, is dead. He was shot in his bed. The previous day he had visited Lisl von Althof, who is ill, and arranged for a doctor to visit her.'

The head of Intelligence frowned. 'Four killed in a matter of weeks. This is *bad*.' He pulled a pristine handkerchief from his coat sleeve and blew his nose noisily. 'Our intelligence service must have been penetrated either in Bucharest or Trieste. I will arrange for a special investigation. Find out what young Harcourt is up to in Trieste and keep me informed.'

'Yes, sir. As soon as Lisl von Althof is well enough I'll get her out of Romania.'

'No,' replied Sir Gerald testily. 'Leave her where she is for the moment. We must not lose anyone else. I will get the investigation under way immediately and let you know when to move the Baroness.' He stood up and Hugh knew the interview was over.

Back in his office Hugh telephoned the other heads of Sections and told them that GOD was initiating an immediate investigation. This was reassuring but they wanted to know who would be heading the investigation.

'They will probably send someone from MI5,' Hugh suggested.

The trouble with the Chief, thought Hugh, was that one could never have a heart-to-heart with him; there was always a barrier. He only loosened up when he had drunk too much; he liked to drink and habitually drank a great deal. Then he would become amorous in an unattractive way and be difficult and unpleasant. Hugh dreaded office parties and had only had him home for dinner once, after which Julia had declared *never again*; once was enough.

13

This was the moment Sokolov had feared. The message had just been:

Come immediately. Mario.

It had been agreed that Sokolov would contact Mario only when he had information for him. The trouble was, he had none. The Russians were probably becoming impatient. Sokolov felt himself sweating.

He rang the doorbell.

'Come in,' said Mario, and led the way into a large, modern room with a balcony.

'What have you been up to since we last met?' he asked roughly.

Sokolov shivered, although it was not cold. He swallowed, cleared his throat and said, 'I have done very little because I felt ill after leaving here.' Sokolov saw that Mario was not alone; his large friend was sitting on a table, swinging his legs and picking his nails.

'Don't waste my time!' shouted Mario angrily, moving towards him. 'We have been watching you. You had a long, cosy chat with your friend Mr Harcourt and you did most of the talking. We got tired of waiting for you to come and tell us all about it.'

'I was coming to report when I felt better.' Pavel's mouth was dry and it felt as if his stomach was in his throat. He stumbled on, 'it was not an important conversation. We went over a little of the interrogations but I told him nothing of importance. We were talking mostly about life in the camp here.'

'We will soon find out,' said Mario, as the other Russian came over to where Sokolov was standing. He bent down and with a knife ripped open the bottom of Sokolov's left trouser leg and removed a small bugging device. Sokolov just stood there completely shaken. He felt caught in a net from which he could not escape.

At this moment Molohovski came into the room reading aloud from a typescript paper. Sokolov had heard these words before. They were word for word what he had told John Harcourt. He closed his eyes but Molohovski continued to read, relentlessly. Sokolov heard himself telling Harcourt about how he had kept the drawing of the girl. Now he realised some of the implications that had not occurred to him before. They had listened to and recorded every word.

He groaned within himself; what would they think? What would they do? How would he make them understand that he had done his best and that this sort of thing was new to him. He would do better next time.

They had left him standing in the middle of the room. Feeling unbearably weak, he moved towards a chair to sit down, but Molohovski stepped in front of him.

'I consider you a risk, comrade Sokolov,' he said, 'and we cannot afford to have risks.' He nodded to Mario, 'You know what to do.' Then he left the room.

Pavel Sokolov knew instinctively what this meant, but somehow the full realisation had not yet affected him. He was surprised at how he felt nothing, neither fear nor hope. He was just numb and seemed to be a spectator looking at what was befalling him in a completely detached way.

Mario nodded to his burly companion.

They frog-marched him from the room, down two flights of stone steps into a small cellar. They tied his hands and feet and pushed him roughly on to an old chair. He did not try to resist, he knew it would be useless; he accepted the inevitable and tried not to think about what was happening.

He thought about his home and his parents who loved

him so much; then in his mind he saw the icon in the corner of the living-room. This icon had always comforted him through his childhood disappointments. He now concentrated all his forces on it. Clearly he saw the ageless face of the Smolensk Mother of God, with her large eyes, long straight nose and small mouth. It had been in his family for as long as any of them could remember. The Christchild was small, with the face of an adult man, sitting perched high on the left arm of the virgin. She had a small, bright star on her right shoulder.

Mario unlocked a cupboard and took a Tokarev TT33 pistol from the top shelf. He loaded it in a leisurely fashion while his companion tied Sokolov securely to the chair. Mario walked over to the chair with the pistol in his hand. No one spoke.

Sokolov did not look at Mario. He shut his eyes and forced his mind to think only of the face of the icon back home. In this way he was only aware of the face of the Mother of God looking down on him as she had done all his life. It was like having a friend present. And there was the face of the little grown-up child. Their faces had nothing to do with human emotions or passions; their serene eyes were looking into eternity.

He was hardly aware of the pressure of cold steel on his right temple; then it was all over. He had gone off with the Mother of God.

The two Russians untied the body, pulled a tarpaulin from the bottom of the cupboard, wrapped the body in it and loaded it into the boot of a large black car. They drove to the villa on the edge of the bay where they had taken Pavel for his first meeting with Boris Molohovski. Here they put the body into a powerful speedboat, untied the boat, started the engine and roared forth into the night with the spray glimmering as it was thrown back out of the path of the boat.

About a mile out in the Adriatic, Mario cut off the engine and, with the help of his companion, tipped the body into the sea, having first tied a large block of concrete securely round the feet. They watched as the body sank.

Boris Molohovski felt pleased with the way things were going. He listened twice more to the conversation between Harcourt and Sokolov. He smiled to himself; this would please his Chief. He sent a transcript to Moscow with his recommendations and asking for instructions. He saw Elizabeth von Althof as the one remaining danger; the only person left who could know what Aleksandr Petrovich Ivanov knew. It was known they had been lovers.

He did not have long to await the reply from Moscow. When it came it was clear and precise:

Apprehend von Althof immediately; interrogate her thoroughly, then dispose of her.

That was what Boris liked. Clear instructions for him to take straightforward actions.

He lost no time in sending out instructions to his own agents, knowing that Moscow would already have alerted their people in other European countries. It would not be long before the Baroness would be found and this episode closed.

14

John Harcourt planned his trip to Romania with meticulous care. He went to his housekeeper.

'Marta,' he said, 'I have to go to England. My father is very ill.'

'I am so sorry, signor,' she replied, looking as if she would burst into tears at any moment. 'When will you return?'

'It depends what happens, Marta. I have no idea. But I must leave immediately, so why don't you take a holiday, and I'll let you know when I get back.'

'Grazie, signor. I will go to my sister in Milano. She needs some help. Already with five children, and now a new baby.'

'Good idea. You can go now, in fact. I shall be leaving myself as soon as I've packed. Here is money for one month. If I'm away longer I'll pay you the extra when I return.'

A great smile spread across her round face, as she clutched the money in both hands. Grazie, grazie,' she kept repeating. 'I wish you a good journey to England. Goodbye, signor.'

'Goodbye, Marta.' They shook hands. 'Have a good holiday.' John saw her to the door then returned to the living room, sat down and mentally went over his plans again.

He would travel to Bucharest as Carlo Parravani. A false Italian passport had thoughtfully been provided by administration in London, as had also black hair dye and horn-rimmed spectacles with clear glass. They always provided their agents with a package of aids for deception. London had also given him the name and address of an excellent forger of passports and other official documents, should he need one.

He slipped on rubber gloves and began the messy job of colouring his hair black, taking care not to splash the dye on anything around. He was meticulous in dyeing the hair on the rest of his body the same colour as the hair on his head.

He had a light canvas bag into which he stuffed some shirts, underwear, socks, razor and toothbrush. He wore a holster with his pistol, a Beretta ·380, tucked snugly under his left armpit. The spare ammunition was distributed in the pockets of the clothes in the canvas bag and in the pockets of what he was wearing.

Kneeling in front of the oven, he tore his British passport into small pieces, struck a match and set light to them, watching them burn on the bottom tray in the oven. The hard cover took a long time but finally it was ash also. He picked up the oven tray and carried it to the lavatory, taking care that the ash did not blow away, and tipped it into the pan and flushed it twice.

He studied himself in the mirror and was satisfied at the likeness with the photograph in the Italian passport.

All was ready. He picked up the small canvas bag, slinging the strap over his shoulder. As he did so he felt the Beretta against his body; it was loaded. He only had to flick the safety-catch off, which he could do with his thumb as he took aim.

He slipped quietly out of his flat into the warm, sultry night and walked to Valentino's home.

What John Harcourt had not noticed was a figure in the shadows outside his flat who watched him leave and duly noted that at a quarter to ten that night a young man with an athletic bearing had left John Harcourt's flat; that he was probably upper-working-class Italian. He was carrying a canvas bag that seemed to be of no weight. The observer noted the direction in which he walked, but was unable to follow because his job was to watch, follow and report on the movements of John Harcourt. He had seen Harcourt go into his flat and he must wait there in case he came out. The lights were still on in the flat and his car was outside.

This was one of Boris Molohovski's men and he would hand in his report in the morning.

Valentino Cavalli lived with his family in a small house in the outskirts of Trieste; he was unmarried and his mother, a widow, enjoyed having her eldest son at home. She had six children and spent all her days cooking, washing, ironing and caring for her family, which included taking them to mass and making regular confessions.

John pressed the doorbell and after what seemed a long time standing there in the dark, he saw a light go on which shone through the glass panel of the door. When the door was opened, John was relieved to see Valentino's large frame and ample proportions outlined against the light. He was wearing a white, open-neck shirt and light trousers.

'Valentino, I need help,' John whispered, as Valentino drew in a startled breath and John continued before he could speak. 'It's John, I'm in disguise, my name is now Carlo Parravani. I must get to Bucharest immediately.'

'Ho! ho!' laughed Valentino. 'Up to your old tricks, eh? I must say you make a good Italian – I didn't recognise you!'

'Seriously, can you help?'

'As usual the gods are with you, my friend. I leave at three o'clock in the morning with a load of perishable fruit for Romania. See? The truck is already loaded.' Valentino gestured towards a large refrigerated lorry standing on a piece of waste-ground next to the house.

'Come in, come in and meet the family.'

'Remember, *Carlo Parravani* is now my name,' whispered John anxiously.

'Trust Valentino. You can always trust Valentino. He asks no questions.' Valentino was smiling as he led John into the living room.

John knew he could trust Valentino with his life. They had worked together previously when he was on a temporary job in Italy.

'Mamma,' shouted Valentino, 'this is my old friend Carlo. He is coming with me on this trip. I told him he could sleep here for a few hours before we leave.'

Mamma smiled and his brothers and sisters beamed their welcome. They all shook him by the hand. Mamma explained that they were just about to have their evening meal and invited Carlo to join them.

It was eleven o'clock by the time the heap of pasta, with a delicious Bolognaise sauce accompanied by green salad, had been eaten. The meal had been silent because everyone was intent on the serious business of eating. Mamma glanced around occasionally and pride glowed across her face as she saw the pleasure the meal gave to her family. When the plates were cleared away the talking and laughter began again.

Because they were going to begin their journey in a few hours time, Valentino suggested that he and Carlo should go to his room and get some sleep. They went upstairs and John stretched out on a mattress on the floor.

The church clock was striking three when John climbed into the passenger seat of the refrigerator lorry. He was relieved to be on his way as he peered into the darkness of the night. A shudder went down his spine; he found the hour before dawn sad and unfriendly. He looked sideways at Valentino and was comforted to watch him settling down to what was for him a routine drive.

15

Lisl was grateful to Mr Negulescu for sending Doctor Ionnitiu to her; she had never felt so ill before. He was wearing a beige linen suite; his curling, dark hair had receded from his forehead. He stood quietly beside the bed with his stethoscope dangling round his neck. He had just given her a thorough examination and was looking down at her through his gold-rimmed spectacles with kindly brown eyes.

'You have typhoid fever,' he said gently, 'you must remain in bed for three weeks, eat only boiled rice and drink only boiled water; you must not eat anything else or you may pierce the walls of your intestines: this illness makes them very thin. Also I have no drugs to help you, those I had are finished and there have been no further deliveries to this country. I will come and see you again this evening and will bring you rice. My wife will cook it for you.'

Lisl watched him walk over to the tap, fill the saucepan with water and put it on the electric ring. He was a middle-aged man with a dark complexion and small bones. He moved quickly and surely and was quiet both in his speech and his actions. When the water boiled, he poured some into a cup and looked for a jug. But there was none, so he stood the saucepan on the floor beside the bed.

'Drink this water and sleep,' he said. 'Are you expecting anyone to visit you?'

'Not today,' replied Lisl.

'Mr Negulescu impressed on me the need to keep your door locked, so I shall take the key, lock it and let myself in this evening without disturbing you.'

He went out, locking the door behind him, and Lisl heard his footsteps going down the concrete stairs. The tears ran down her face. She didn't know why she was crying, but she felt depressed, alone and desperately unhappy.

As the hours passed she felt worse; the sheets became sodden rags and her nightdress became like a wet shroud; perspiration ran in streams over her forehead and down her face; she closed her eyes to stop the water going into them and lay on her back gazing up at the ceiling. The ceiling was white and there was a fly on it immediately above her head. Lisl gazed up at the fly; mostly it remained stationary but from time to time it took a little walk. It seemed to mesmerise her. Nothing else mattered; she felt compelled to watch that fly; everything else seemed hazy and of no importance.

Lisl head Doctor Ionnitiu saying, 'I have brought you boiled rice and water, I want you to eat and drink.'

She tried to say 'Good evening' but the words would not come out. It seemed so rude when he was so kind. She tried again; but she just lay there quite motionless, gazing at the ceiling, watching the fly.

He laid his clean, white, folded handkerchief across her forehead to keep the perspiration from her face. He leant over her bed, 'Listen carefully,' he was saying. 'I am going to put this in your mouth, it is made of glass. You have a very high fever, if this breaks, don't swallow it.'

He had been speaking in French and, although Lisl understood, she was unable to make herself speak. She could still see the fly and it hadn't moved.

Doctor Ionnitiu put some object into her mouth; her brain didn't register what it was because she was drifting away.

She had no idea how long it was before she came to. It felt like a lifetime. She remembered she had felt very ill, but she didn't feel ill any more. She opened her eyes; the room looked different. Then she realised she was lying with her head at the foot of the bed. She shivered with cold;

the sheets were cold and wet. Somehow she felt different; strangely purified and so very, very tired.

She looked round the room and was surprised to see Doctor Ionnitiu sitting on the chair.

'At last!' he said, standing up. 'I have been with you all night and all day. The crisis is now past. You have been very ill and should have had your mother with you. You are tired and weak. I want you to sleep and when you awake I want you to eat and drink.'

She was shivering all over.

'I am so cold,' she murmured.

The Doctor removed the top sheet and covered her with blankets. 'It is an exceptionally hot evening,' he said. 'It is a tropical summer's night and yet you need these blankets!'

It was then that she noticed how tired he looked and how furrowed and pale his face had become. His tie and coat were over the back of the chair and his whole appearance was crumpled. A dark stubble showed on his chin.

He was saying, 'Sleep. I will return when I can. There are so many people waiting for me,' he added wearily.

Lisl fell asleep immediately and didn't awake until noon the following day. She felt hungry and thirsty and thankfully drank the water and ate the rice the doctor had left for her.

She thought gratefully of the kind doctor who had cared so well for her, a foreigner and a complete stranger.

Each day Lisl grew stronger and the kind doctor visited her bringing boiled rice and water. She began to weary of this rigid diet so one day the doctor, beaming broadly, opened a small parcel. 'This is from my wife,' he said. 'Give your stomach a holiday, and have some bread and jam.'

Never had bread and jam tasted so good.

Doctor Ionnitiu never asked Lisl any questions except medical ones. He would talk about his wife and talk about the weather. One day he mentioned that he was the official doctor to the British Embassy. Although he said so little, Lisl found herself looking forward to these visits.

Most of her hair had fallen out and this upset her; she knew it was just a matter of time and it would grow again. Slowly she regained her strength and each day she felt brighter.

Suddenly she was awake. The door was flung open and in burst four men; two of them were pointing automatic pistols at her. Lisl sat up, clutching the bedclothes around her, feeling frightened and vulnerable.

They pulled her roughly from the bed. Her heart was pounding, then she thought it had stopped altogether; but no, there it was again, pounding away. She felt dizzy, the room swam. Two men held her tightly between them. The other two were collecting up her few possessions and stuffing them into a sack. It was all over in a few minutes and Lisl was being dragged towards the door clad only in her nightdress. One of the men grabbed a blanket, wound it tightly around her and slung her over his shoulder.

She was no longer afraid; she was past fear and now expected to die. She was ready for total oblivion and thought no further. Every step the man took as he staggered down stairs jolted her body painfully. She just wanted it over.

'What are you doing? Where are you taking her? She is very ill, she has a fever!' demanded Doctor Ionnitiu, on his way upstairs to visit her.

He stood in front of them and tried to bar their way. One of the men flung him to one side, grabbed him by the throat and banged his head against the wall, then punched him hard in the stomach and ran to join the others who had now reached the street.

They rushed across the pavement, bundled her into a large

black car which still had its engine running and which drove off as soon as the men had clambered in.

Minutes later Doctor Ionnitiu sat alone in his car. He was sure nothing was broken, but he had an almighty headache. What should he do? What *could* he do? Those men looked like Russians, and what could one do against an occupying force? He recalled that it had been Mr Negulescu who had asked him to visit Lisl and that he had been killed only a short time ago. It would be no good going to the authorities or doing anything official. Somehow he must get word to the Austrian authorities that this Austrian lady had been kidnapped. He would have to work in a roundabout way, in order not to get involved.

He began to feel sick and distinctly unwell, so he drove home.

16

Valentino chose to cross the frontier into Yugoslavia at Sezana. Their papers were in order so the guards waved them on. The truck was noisy, which meant they had to shout, so they tended to drive in silence, just helping themselves to what seemed to be an endless supply of tinned beer from the floor of the cab. The empty tins were thrown out of the window.

They went by way of Lublijana and Zagreb to Belgrade. The road was good, with scarcely any traffic in either direction. They stopped briefly from time to time but pressed on until Belgrade. Valentino stopped the truck outside a small café on the outskirts of the town. The area looked uncared-for and depressing; most of the brown paint had peeled off the window frames and the words *CAFÉ PETRONI* painted in bold capitals across the top of the windows looked uncertain, with the *R* and *N* missing.

It was evening but still stifling, with a hot, dry breeze stirring the dust. The sky, that had been vividly blue all day was now pale, streaked with pink; the sun would soon be setting.

They walked through the open door into a small room with bare floorboards, scrubbed tables and wooden chairs. Valentino was well known, this was one of his routine stops and they were soon enjoying a simple meal of fried pork, boiled potatoes and red cabbage.

John walked outside to stretch his legs but was soon joined by Valentino, who was anxious to get going. They drove into the centre of the town where a number of shops were still open. There were a few cars and some lorries that shook, made a great deal of noise with black smoke belching from their exhausts and looked as if they would break down at any moment. The buildings showed the effects of war and the whole town was in need of a facelift.

They drove a short way down the road that would lead to the Romanian border town of Turnu Severin and, just outside Belgrade, Valentino parked the truck on the side of a deserted mud track and settled down to a few hours sleep.

John walked about in the wooded area nearby, enjoying the exercise in the cool of the night. Then he climbed back into the truck and was also soon asleep.

A sudden jolt awakened him. Valentino had started up the engine and they were now on their way again. Dawn had not yet broken, but they made good speed in the darkness down the deserted, wide road which the Germans had built during the war.

They soon left the main autoroute and headed down a much smaller and less well maintained road towards Romania. They breakfasted at Pozarevac on black bread, goats cheese and black coffee. As they journeyed on, the sun rose, casting its strong bright light over the plain.

On the left were the waters of the Danube which spread out over the flat countryside forming a long, broad stretch of water for about eighty miles.

It was tiring driving along this road, full of pot-holes, with the sun shimmering on the vast stretch of water. The entire area was deserted, the only traffic being one old lorry limping along. At Sip the river narrowed and a bridge spanned the Danube, on the far side of which was the Romanian frontier. They drove over the bridge and stopped.

'Good morning! How are you?' shouted Valentino to the Romanian guards. 'This is my co-driver – he keeps me awake,' he joked.

They obviously knew Valentino and, although they glanced at the passports and papers, they returned them while still joking and waved them on their way.

Valentino turned to John. 'You see what it is to be known and trusted, my friend,' he said smiling. 'We are now in Romania with no trouble at all.'

'Well done. I knew you led a charmed life. I just hope some of it rubs off on me,' replied John.

'Valentino never let his friend down. Valentino asks no questions. While Valentino is here everything is OK,' and Valentino began singing.

So they drove on to Bucharest, stopping on the way for a good meal and a rest at Craiova.

'I am going to the warehouse on the outskirts of Bucharest,' explained Valentino. 'Where do you want to go?'

'You can leave me at the warehouse,' replied John. 'I shall be staying with a friend and can find my way to her house. I should like to come back with you but I've no idea when I shall be returning. It all depends on how long her husband will be away.'

Valentino gave John a big smile and a knowing wink. 'Ah!' he said. 'You are a lucky one. Romanian girls are . . . ' Then words failed him, so with hands and face he made John understand what he meant. 'I do this trip every ten days,' he continued. 'On the return journey I stop at the abattoir in Craiova and fill up with carcasses of beef and lamb. There is a good market for cheap meat in Trieste. So, my friend, if her husband returns you will know where to find me. And whatever you are up to, Valentino is happy to have your company. You are my friend.'

'Thank you, Valentino. Keep a lookout for me. I may well need you.'

'OK, OK. You can rely on Valentino!'

Valentino drew up outside the warehouse, they both jumped down and shook hands warmly, then John walked off towards the centre of the city.

17

In Bucharest most people spoke French. Paris was their cultural Mecca and they left the working-class to speak Romanian. Now that the Iron Curtain was in place across Europe and communism had taken over, all this was changing, but so gradually as be hardly noticeable.

John had lived in France and spoke French like a Frenchman. His plan was to contact Edwin Hobbs, who had just been sent out to replace James Wilson. He couldn't simply walk into the British Embassy because he didn't want anyone except for Edwin to know he was in Romania. And he needed his help to find Lisl. Edwin and he had both been at Charterhouse and in the same house, but Edwin, being sixteen months younger, had been in a lower form.

After leaving Valentino John had walked towards the centre of the city and when he reached the Calea Victoriei he went into a café and ordered coffee. He knew the address of the Embassy and discovered from the waiter that it was not too far. The coffee was bitter; he left it.

It had taken him two hours from leaving Valentino at the warehouse to find the Embassy. The sun was now high in a cloudless blue sky and was already powerful. He found a large, shady plane tree from where he could watch the main entrance to the Embassy. He was in need of a rest and leaned against the trunk.

Nothing seemed to be happening except that a Romanian policeman came out of the building from time to time and held lengthy conversations with a Romanian soldier, armed with a rifle, who stood under a magnificent lime tree just outside the main doors of the Embassy.

The soldier was young, relaxed and looked bored. He

was whistling gently to himself. A Russian army truck went noisily past with about a dozen soldiers, all armed with rifles, in the back. John had already noticed that the town was full of Russian soldiers, either walking about in groups or in army transport. The soldiers all had rifles slung across their backs and the NCOs and officers had revolvers in holsters at their waists. Most of them were extremely young and they looked lean, fit and alert. This was Josef Stalin's army of occupation.

John was struck by the difference between the Russian and Romanian soldiers. The tall, blond, athletic, young Russians with shaven heads and well scrubbed faces; their long-sleeved grey tunics, buttoned to the neck, were pulled in at the waist with wide, black leather belts; their trousers were tucked into high, black, leather boots which were well-worn and unpolished.

By contrast, the Romanian soldiers looked more in keeping with a Gilbert-and-Sullivan opera. Their hair was a good length and black; their caps were large and flat; their uniforms were brightened up with wide, bright stripes, colourful cords with tassels.

The Romanian sentry leant against the tree and lit a cigarette. His rifle fell to the ground; he left it there and a smile spread across his swarthy, gipsy-like features as he watched the smoke curl upwards.

A Rolls Royce, flying a Union Jack, came round from the back of the building and stopped at the front door. John watched intently from under the shadow of the plane tree. The sentry picked up his rifle, snuffed his cigarette, put the stub in his pocket and stood sloppily to attention. A uniformed chauffeur got out of the car and opened the back door. The main doors of the Embassy opened, the policeman came outside, stood to one side and saluted as a tall figure in an immaculate cream linen suit ran quickly down the steps

117

and into the waiting car. The sentry saluted, the chauffeur closed the door, got into the driving seat and the car moved smoothly and silently away.

There was no mistaking the tall, slim, slightly stooping figure, the thinning grey hair and clean-cut features of Sir Rupert Neville, the British Ambassador. John had met him a few years ago in Whitehall.

Putting a few cigarettes loose in his pocket and holding one in his hand, John walked over to the sentry and asked for a light. The sentry gave him a box of matches and, as he handed the box back, he gave him the loose cigarettes from his pocket. In 1949 a Romanian would sell his soul for a packet of cigarettes.

The sentry slipped them into his pocket and was eager to talk, so John led the conversation to discover the address of the Ambassador's residence. He also found out that all the Ambassadors spent the summer months in their villas beside the lake at Snagov. The largest one belonged to the Russian Ambassador. All the gardens went down to the water's edge and each one had its own motor boat.

John found a taxi and was driven to Snagov, where he paid off the taxi and had a simple meal. He ordered a bottle of the local wine and mixed it with a lavish amount of soda water; he had not realised how hungry and thirsty he was until he sat down in the restaurant, which was small with scrubbed wooden tables and chairs; it was used mostly by locals and was only half full. Feeling much refreshed, John generously tipped the waiter (he thought he was probably the owner) who told him how to find the British residence on the lake.

An inferior dust-and-stone road encircled the lake. The entire area was wooded and wild except where magnificent villas overlooked the water. They were hidden from the road by mature trees and the gardens around each villa were landscaped right down to the water's edge; some were more ornate than others.

John enjoyed walking along the leafy road, listening to the country sounds and smelling the summer scents. After twenty minutes' brisk walking he saw the entrance to the British Ambassador's summer home.

Two Romanian soldiers were standing at the entrance talking together, they had not seen him so he quickly stepped into the trees on the land beside the grounds of the British villa. This large area seemed to belong to no one and was thickly wooded and overgrown. Painstakingly he made his way through the undergrowth; all was so dense and wild that it seemed almost impossible at times to make any headway. He was careful not to tear his clothes or to become too dirty, because that would look suspicious, especially in Bucharest. Hot and scratched, he eventually reached the lake and fell thankfully on to the grass.

Some small boats were moving about on the far side of the lake, but they were too far away to make out much detail. It was a large lake and he was prevented from seeing all of it because of the trees. The part of the lake immediately in front of him and stretching away to the right towards the Ambassador's house, was a mass of lotus flowers, their heads just above the water; pink perfection.

The flowers reminded John of his school days and the interminable lessons on the Ancient Egyptians and how they worshipped the lotus flower and designed the capitals of the columns for their temples to represent lotus flowers wide open or in bud. It was late afternoon and the sun was still hot. It was very quiet, there had been no traffic on the road and, lying there on the grass under the trees, John fell asleep.

When he awakened it was dusk and much cooler. He stood up, stretched and walked over to the high wooden fence surrounding the British residence. He climbed on to the fence, dropped down lightly on the other side and found himself among small shrubs. He could just see the outline of the villa across the grounds. A well kept lawn stretched down to the lake where the Ambassador's launch was moored at the jetty. The evening air was heavy with the scent of tobacco flowers from the flower beds.

He must be careful not to make a false move. He had broken all the rules by entering the country on a false passport, without the knowledge or consent of the Foreign Office, his superiors had no idea what he was doing and he was now in the private grounds of the British Ambassador's residence without an invitation. It would be wisest to keep the Ambassador out of this. Sir Rupert was a stickler for protocol and the correct channels; *always play safe* had been his rule.

Well, John mused, that was probably how one became an Ambassador.

A car door banged. John stood still in the shrubbery, listening. Another car door banged; there were voices, a man's and a woman's. He didn't move, but looked towards the villa which was now ablaze with lights. There was a rustle in the bushes behind him. He froze. He pulled out his knife and peered into the undergrowth over the fence. All was dark and silent; it could have been a bird or animal, he thought. He heard the sound of more cars arriving and could hear voices, as people greeted each other before going into the house.

He picked his way carefully through the shrubs, darted across the lawn, avoiding the flower beds, and reached the building. He stood in the shadow getting his bearings. From where he was standing he could make out the massive outline of the villa; it was both elegant and grand.

It was a hot summer night, lights were on in most of

the ground floor rooms and in some on the first floor; the windows were wide open to let in the air and the sound of voices came floating out into the grounds.

John knew that in the Balkans ambassadors spent most evenings entertaining themselves or being entertained by other ambassadors. Cautiously he crept round the house, keeping close to the building until he reached the window of a room from where the sound of voices came. Being careful not to be caught in the reflection of light, he peered into the room. The Ambassador was entertaining at home and his guests were just entering the dining room. He saw a colourful collection of ladies in long, flowing summer dresses being escorted by gentlemen in dinner jackets or uniforms.

He could only see a portion of the room from where he was standing, but how inviting it all looked! The crystal chandeliers; a centrepiece of summer flowers on the table flanked by silver deer on either side; the crystal and silver on the table shining. There were large trailing flower arrangements on pedestals around the room. When everyone was seated, the white-jacketed waiters, wearing white gloves, walked quickly around the table without ever getting in each other's way.

There must be eighteen or twenty people, John thought, as he peered into the room. He studied those facing him; there was no one he recognised. Some of the women looked lovely, wearing décolleté dresses showing their bare shoulders, with jewels flashing in the lights and exotic hair styles and colours. He could see the Ambassador sitting at the head of the table, where the conversation was loud and vivacious with much laughter.

John crept along to the next window in order to see the rest of the room. At the end of the table a middle-aged woman sat bolt upright in her chair wearing two rows of pearls on a midnight blue dress. She wore her greying hair in a bun. He had never met her, but knew this must be Lady Neville.

Suddenly John saw him! His luck was in, because seated nearly halfway down the table was Edwin Hobbs, holding his chin up as if the collar of his dress shirt were two sizes too small. He was short and stocky and his mouse-coloured hair fell untidily over his forehead, which gave him a schoolboyish appearance. He was laughing and seemed to be enjoying himself immensely. How could he get Edwin's attention without being seen?

The dinner went on interminably, one course after another. At last dessert was passed round and champagne glasses filled, so he knew dinner was drawing to a close.

Lady Neville rose to her feet, looking regal and elegant in the simplicity of her dress. She smiled round the table at the ladies; the gentlemen stood up and the ladies withdrew.

After the ladies had left the dining room, the men lit up cigars and cigarettes and continued to drink. John was desperate to contact Edwin; somehow he had to get him alone.

He crept round the house to where the cars were parked. The drivers were all in the cars; some were asleep. John remained carefully in the shadows since the drivers were sure to be paid informers of the communist regime.

It was then that he thought of the lavatory. At this stage of the evening, when the ladies had left them, the gentlemen would take the opportunity to relieve themselves and were usually shown to a cloakroom not far from the dining room. He worked himself back round the house, looking for drains, pipes and windows. Then he found what he wanted; a small window with opaque glass and with a narrow window at the top which was slightly open. John returned to the window from which he could see Edwin and waited, willing him to use the lavatory.

A gentleman sitting with his back to the window got to his feet. He was short and fat with podgy hands and black hair that shone like a raven's plumage. He spoke to a waiter and they left the room together. John watched as a light came on in the room with the opaque glass window; the curtains had not been completely closed. He was now certain that this was the lavatory.

John took up his position again in the shadow and continued to watch Edwin through the dining-room window. Round again went the port; Edwin filled his glass and passed on the decanter. John waited. The fat gentleman returned, went to his place and sat down. How much longer will they sit here? he wondered.

Then the Ambassador rose to his feet, the butler pulled the chair back and Sir Rupert led the way from the dining-room to join the ladies in the drawing room. John was despondent as he watched them all following. Suddenly he noticed Edwin detach himself from the others and leave the room by the other door.

He crouched down and darted back round the house. The light was shining through the opaque window. Perhaps it had been left on by the fat gentleman; perhaps it was one of the waiters. He had to risk it – this might be his only chance.

Standing right up against the wall, with his head tilted backwards, he called in the direction of the open window, 'Edwin! Edwin!'

He held his breath and listened. He only heard the sound of running water. He had his knife in his hand. He called again, louder and more distinctly.

'Edwin! Edwin!'

There was a moment's silence, then came the one English word, 'Yes?'

'It's John Harcourt.'

'Oh, my God!' came the reply. It was Edwin's voice.

'Must see you alone. No one must know I'm here.'

'Will return one hour after all the guests have left. Meet me on the road half a mile further on towards the village. Will switch headlights on and off four times.'

Relief swept through John. He darted across the lawn, into the shrubbery and scaled the wooden fence. He breathed more easily on the other side as he plunged into the undergrowth. Well, he thought, so far so good.

It was a light moonlit night. He peered up through the trees to the starry sky. Slowly he picked his way through the tangled wood, making as little noise as possible, until he finally reached the road. He walked down the deserted road for what he judged to be about half a mile, then crept back into the woods well hidden from the road and sat down to await Edwin.

The Ambassador's dinner party finally broke up. Edwin had to wait until all the guests had left before he could leave. His was now the only car in the drive and he found Franz, the driver, fast asleep over the driving wheel. The moment Edwin opened the back door Franz sprang out, 'Pardon, monsieur,' he mumbled, closing the door.

They drove back to Bucharest in silence, Edwin deep in thought, and when they reached the house Edwin told Franz to put the car in the garage and to give him the keys because he wouldn't be needing him for the next couple of days, so he could go home for a short holiday.

Edwin walked restlessly around his sitting room. What was Harcourt up to and what was he letting himself in for, he wondered. He must give Franz time to get clear of the area.

The Russians had a strict rule that all foreigners should ask permission in writing to travel outside Bucharest and this included all western diplomats. Diplomats were, how-ever, allowed to go to their villas at Snagov.

Edwin slipped quietly out of his front door, locking it behind him; he got into the car and drove down the road as quietly as possible; he had no wish to draw attention to himself. It was a quarter past one in the morning and at this hour every sound was magnified. Once clear of Bucharest, he put his foot down and drove as fast as he could to Snagov.

When he reached the dusty road around the lake he slowed down and, after passing the Ambassador's villa, he drove on for a bit and then flashed his headlights on and off four times as arranged. He peered into the woods on either side but could see no one. He drove on slowly, fearing that something had happened to Harcourt. He continued driving down the road, flashing his lights at intervals. Then he saw a figure come out from the bushes on his right. He reached for his pistol. Was it Harcourt? He couldn't be sure in the darkness. The man ran to the car. 'Thanks for coming,' he said, getting in.

Edwin recognised the voice and put his gun away. He put his finger on his lips and gave John a meaningful look. He drove on until he could find a place to turn the car and then drove back to Bucharest as fast as he could. Neither of them spoke.

Arriving back in the house, Edwin drove the car into the garage, locked it and entered the house. Switching on the light, he turned round and regarded John's disguise with amusement. He again put his fingers to his lips and wrote on a large piece of paper:

'Don't speak. We can't be too careful. This place is bugged. So is the car, and the Russians search the house when no one is in. The servants are paid to report the smallest detail to the Securitate.'

125

John nodded that he understood.

Then Edwin scrawled, 'Why are you here arriving like this? What are you up to?'

John smiled. It was his turn to write, 'What news of Lisl von Althof?'

Edwin sighed, but John was writing again, 'Have you a drink?' then he added, 'I'm also famished.'

Edwin motioned him to a side table on which stood a tray of drinks and a selection of glasses. John helped himself to a gin and tonic while Edwin went to the kitchen and returned with a loaf of bread, the remains of a cold chicken, a bowl of cold rice mixed with peppers, a bowl of yoghurt and some local cheeses. He put the tray on the table and returned to the kitchen for a plate, knife, fork and some spoons.

John drew a chair up to the table and began eating immediately. He had a good appetite and went on the principle that it was wisest to eat as much as possible in these circumstances, since it was uncertain where and when the next meal would be. He ate rapidly and with obvious enjoyment until there was little left. During this time Edwin had been writing. He now pushed the paper across the table. John picked it up, walked over to the drinks tray and poured himself another gin and tonic. He sat down again and studied the paper.

Edwin had written that from reliable sources he had discovered that Lisl von Althof had been taken forcibly from her room. Four or five men, certainly Russians and probably MGB, had rushed up the steps to the top floor and had come down almost immediately carrying a young woman wrapped in a blanket. They had all crowded into the same car and driven off at speed. He had done all he could to find out where she had been taken, but without success.

John just managed to hold back an exclamation. How he longed to talk, to go into details, to ask questions and to discuss the whole problem with Edwin. Writing on pieces of paper was frustrating.

He picked up a pencil and wrote down his conviction that Lisl held the key to the recent killings and that his fears that she was in danger had now been confirmed. It was even more essential that no one should know where he was or what he was doing, not even the Ambassador. The utmost secrecy must be observed until the person responsible for the killings had been caught.

They sat for a while in silence then Edwin wrote, 'Negulescu sent a doctor to Lisl, his name is Ionnitiu. He is trustworthy, being the Embassy doctor. Tomorrow morning I shall have diplomatic stomach pains and send for him. He might know something. No one will search the house while I am here; help yourself to anything you may need. You will have to sleep in the attic and remain there while I am away. I shall lock you in and take the attic key with me.'

The attic was low, unbearably hot and airless. John found a small window and flung it open. Edwin came in with sheets, pillows, towels and a blanket and dropped them on the small single bed. A little later Edwin locked the attic door and slept for what was left of the night.

Next morning, when the servants arrived, they found him screwed up with severe stomach pains. Each one gave him different advice; the cook maintained that it was caused by bathing every day.

Edwin rang Doctor Ionnitiu. There was no reply, not even from his wife or servants. A shudder ran down Edwin's spine.

18

The car journey was unbearable.

Lisl sat shaking all over wedged between two large, rough men; their clothes and bodies smelt foul. She felt ill, weak and quite unable to cope with the situation. She realised they were driving out of Bucharest; then one of the men caught hold of the end of the blanket, that was wrapped around her and put it over her face and head. She was now shaking uncontrollably. The men were making coarse jokes in Russian and were smoking strong-smelling, black cigarettes.

It seemed to Lisl that they had been travelling for about forty minutes when she felt the surface of the road change and become much more bumpy. The driver decelerated and they continued at a much slower pace. The car then swung to the right and stopped; there was a quick exchange of words in Russian with someone outside; then they drove on over a smooth surface for a short distance.

When the car stopped, Lisl was dragged out with the blanket still over her head and nothing on her feet. She was petrified and her legs felt like jelly. Someone picked her up, carried her down a number of steps, walked into a room, put her down and let her fall. Her head struck the wall and she passed out.

When she regained consciousness, she was lying on a low, narrow, wooden bed, in a small windowless room with a bare electric light bulb high in the ceiling. Painfully she recalled the past events and pulled the blanket more closely round her. She had no idea how long she had been lying there nor whether it was day or night.

A young Russian soldier came in and handed her a mug

of soup and went out without speaking. He banged the door shut and locked it noisily.

The soup was grey, watery and tasteless with pieces of cabbage floating about in it. She was thirsty, so drank it thankfully, then lay back on the hard wooden bed. There was no pillow and her head ached mercilessly; in fact, she ached all over. She wondered if she was being left to die and a great fear welled up inside her. She just lay there with her eyes closed and let time go by.

A key turned in the lock. Lisl opened her eyes and watched a pale young man in his mid twenties enter the room. He was slightly built, of medium height, with small dark eyes and thin hands. He wore a lightweight, dark suit that was shiny in places. In his long, thin fingers he held a piece of cardboard with some paper clipped to it.

He walked over to a wooden, upright chair and sat facing her. 'We know who you are,' he said, speaking Russian. 'I want you to tell me everything that Aleksandr Petrovich Ivanov told you. You must remember every word.'

His voice was cold and matter-of-fact. There was no expression in his thin, sallow face; his eyes, seen through his rimless spectacles, looked like small, dark pebbles. While Lisl lay looking up at him, she realised that no matter how ill she felt, no matter what they did to her, she could never betray Sascha. All the principles she had been brought up to believe in, her love and respect for him and her loyalty to those she was working for, were all too powerful a part of her. She could never live with herself if she betrayed them.

'I am waiting.' said the Russian in his toneless voice. She forced her mind to work; what should she do? What could she do? Perhaps it would be best to say something.

'We spoke often,' she began weakly. 'It is impossible to remember every word. He told me about his childhood in the Caspian port of Krasnovodsk, where the harbour was so enclosed that there were no sea breezes and the land rose high round the town so that the summers were hot, humid and unbearable. Aleksandr Ivanov and his two brothers would sometimes take the train around the harbour of Belek, a small town at the foot of the Balkan mountains. They would take a tent with them and some bread, goat's cheese and water and climb until the air became dry and a breeze blew on their faces. They immediately felt invigorated and happy. They would stay on the mountain for as long as the food lasted, then return home tanned and tired.' Lisl stopped. Her thoughts were with those carefree children; it would have been better if Sascha had stayed in Krasnovodsk and become a fisherman like his father, she thought.

The young man had remained motionless. 'We know about his childhood,' he said, in his expressionless way. 'What did he tell you about his work just before he came to Vienna and while in Vienna?'

'We were lovers,' she said quietly, 'and lovers do not talk of work.'

He fixed her with his small, dark eyes. 'You were working for British Intelligence,' he said, 'reporting to a man in Trieste, called Fenton. We know you contacted the British here. You are intelligent and we have ways of making you talk, so why not help yourself and tell me whatever Ivanov told you of either military or political matters. It would be best for you if you could remember now. Time is short.'

'There is nothing to tell,' she whispered. 'I am ill, I am cold and I am very tired.' She shut her eyes and remained silent.

She heard the door shut and the key turn. She opened her eyes and looked around the room. She was alone.

19

Having failed to get a reply from Doctor Ionnitiu during the morning, Edwin got out of bed, dressed quickly and ran downstairs. He told the servants the stomach attack had gone as suddenly as it had come and that he was now hungry and ready for lunch.

As soon as he had finished lunch, he dismissed the servants, telling them he would be out for dinner, then quickly piled food on to a tray with a bottle of wine and took it to the attic. Here he found John prowling about like a caged lion. Edwin held up his hand to caution him not to speak and put the tray down on a small table in the room.

He handed John a note telling him there had been no reply from Doctor Ionnitiu, that he had been trying all the morning without success, that he was off to the Embassy and would be back as soon as possible. He made a 'thumbs up' sign, smiled encouragingly and went out of the room, locking it after him. He put the key in his pocket.

Anger and frustration took hold of John. Anger at his helplessness; frustration at his inactivity. He opened the bottle of wine and drank two glasses quickly. He then sat at the table and ate the food furiously. After lunch he sat there thinking of every possibility for finding Lisl and finally he had to accept that he would have to rely on Edwin. But would it be in time?

When Edwin reached the Embassy it was deserted because it was the siesta hour; this suited him admirably. He arranged for one of his contacts to find an agent codenamed 'Omega' because, when all else failed, he was their last resource.

Mihai Popescu was a student of French literature. He

had been studying in Paris before the Iron Curtain put a stop to that, so now he had to study in Bucharest. He had a passionate hatred of communists in general and of Russians in particular. He possessed an innocence that was disarming and could charm both old and young; he was also an Anglophile. He spent most of his time talking to anyone who would listen, particularly Embassy staffs; he would visit the kitchens where the cooks took pity on his youth and would give him some delicious morsel.

Edwin was walking up and down his office when 'Omega' arrived.

'Sit down,' he said impatiently. 'I need your help.'

Mihai smiled. 'Yes, what can I do for you?' he replied eagerly, running his fingers through his thick, black hair.

'Listen carefully,' explained Edwin. 'I want you to find out where three people are. Baroness Elizabeth von Althof, who was removed forcibly from her flat. She has been ill and was in a very weak condition. The other two are Doctor Ionnitiu and his wife – we can get no reply from them. First go to the Doctor's house, speak to their servants and neighbours; tell them that he is the British Embassy doctor and that they can get a message to us if they know anything. There will be a reward.'

'I know Doctor Ionnitiu. I will go there straight away.'

'There is something else I want done as well and this is very urgent,' continued Edwin, looking intently at Mihai to make sure he understood. 'I want you to whisper around domestic staffs of all foreign Embassies that a substantial reward will be paid by the British Embassy to anyone who can tell us where the Baroness is. Begin with the Russian Embassy, including their Residences at Snagov and Brasov.'

'I will do all I can,' replied Mihai, his large, brown eyes shining.

'You may need this,' said Edwin, holding out a wad of notes. 'There will be a reward when you report back. Now go, and do all this as quickly as possible.'

Edwin returned to the house, went directly to the attic and gave John a written account of what he had arranged with Mihai, including the fact that he had alerted other agents with contacts in the military and police to look for Lisl.

John read the paper and nodded. Edwin picked it up and held it by one corner over a large ash-tray. Using his cigarette lighter he lit the bottom corner and watched the flames devour the paper, until he was forced to drop it. He carried the ash-tray carefully to the bathroom, emptied it into the lavatory basin and pulled the chain. He had carried out this ritual each time they had written down anything.

John went into the kitchen and had something to eat while Edwin dressed for dinner; he had been invited to dine with the Bulgarian Ambassador. When he went out he locked John in the attic again.

A passage ran the length of the attic, with three doors leading off it. One was to the room with the bed where John slept, one was to a small room with a wash-hand basin, and the third was to an even smaller lavatory. It was all very basic. There was only cold water and the lavatory needed a great deal of persuasion to make it flush. John strode up and down this attic passage to help pass the time until Edwin's return.

The Belgian Ambassador and his wife stood at the top of the stairs that led from the hall to the drawing room, receiving their guests. The Ambassador was middle-aged with a full figure; the button of his jacket was decidedly strained and his face was florid. He grasped Edwin by the hand and shook it vigorously. 'Good evening!' he shouted, patting him on the back and handing him on to his wife. Madame

Zhivkov nodded her head and smiled but said nothing. Her well corseted figure was erect, swathed in scarlet, leaving one rounded shoulder bare; on the other shoulder was an arrangement of black imitation flowers. Her hennaed hair was piled loosely on her head.

Edwin bowed, smiled and made way for the next guest to be received.

He glanced quickly round the room. He knew them all; the usual diplomatic gathering. A waiter held a tray with a selection of drinks; Edwin took a whisky and soda. Nearby he saw Radka Antonov with her large, easy-going husband. She was wearing a soft, clinging, sleeveless, emerald-green dress, scattered with sequins; her chestnut hair curled on her shoulders and from her ears hung diamond pendants, swinging like chandeliers.

She left her husband, came quickly over to Edwin, clutched him by the arm and said, "'Allo darleeng, 'ow are you, you naughty Breetish boy?' Radka was her usual effervescent self. 'I 'ave a letter for your Ambassador. Eet was geeven to me as I was leaving my 'ouse.'

'Who is it from?' Edwin asked.

'I 'ave no idea. My butler, Ludovic, gave eet to me. Per'aps we could open eet and see?' she joked.

'You are a wicked girl. Do you always open other people's letters?' he asked while taking the letter from her and putting it in his pocket. He had glanced at the envelope and noticed the uneducated handwriting and the poor quality of the paper. They were joined by other guests and the conversation became general.

They went in to dinner and after they were seated Edwin noticed two empty chairs. Just then the butler entered the room and spoke quietly to the Ambassador, who announced, 'I am sorry to tell you that we shall be without two of our guests tonight. I have just received a message that Monsieur

Nicoliev and Madame Nicolieva are unable to be with us. Monsieur Nicoliev has been unavoidably detained.'

The butler was busy removing glasses and place settings, while there were raised eyebrows among the guests. Dimitri Nicoliev was Edwin's opposite number at the Russian Embassy and something of importance must have occurred for him to have sent an excuse at the last moment. There was much 'Russian watching' being done by Western diplomats so gossip would be rife after dinner.

Edwin was already speculating that Dimitri's absence might just possibly be connected with the arrest of Lisl and the disappearance of the Ionnitius. This made it difficult for him to concentrate on what the lady on his right was saying. She was the Dutch Commercial Attaché's wife and she was telling him about the exploits of her children.

As soon as the senior guests had left, Edwin made his farewells and drove home as fast as possible. He put the car in the garage and locked the door. As he turned round a figure came out of the shadows.

'Who is it?' he asked tensely, his hand in his pocket holding his pistol.

'Omega.'

Edwin relaxed. 'Come with me,' he said, and led him to the bottom of the garden, where he was sure they would not be overheard.

'I have done everything you said.' Mihai was breathless and in a hurry to pour out his information in a young, excitable way. 'I went to Doctor Ionnitiu's house. It was locked and empty. The neighbours would not speak. They are afraid. So I wrote notes about the reward and put these through the doors of all the houses in the area.'

'Splendid, but what have you done about Baroness von Althof?'

'I have been from one Embassy to the other and told my

friends about the gossip I had heard and about the reward. Some of them laughed, because you know there are so many rumours, but I told them that I felt this to be more than a rumour. I had some good food in the Russian kitchen at Snagov. You know how we Romanians hate the Russians, so the women and men servants are always ready to talk about what is going on – their pay is bad so the reward may help.'

'Thank you, Omega, that was quick work,' said Edwin, 'The next time we meet I shall have the books you want for your studies. Well done. Now disappear for a time. Lie low. Remember, I shall deny ever having seen you, spoken with you and certainly anything to do with Baroness von Althof. You know what happens to people who cannot keep quiet. We have our ways.' Edwin strode up the garden and into the house.

Omega stowed the money away and melted into the shadows.

It was just after midnight when Edwin let himself into the house. He went to his study, picked up the telephone and spoke to the Duty Officer at the British Embassy; they were both guarded in their speech.

'If you're not busy, shall I come round and keep you company for a while?'

'Marvellous idea, come as soon as you like,' came the reply.

They hung up, and Edwin ran upstairs to unlock John who immediately thrust a piece of paper into his hand. Edwin read it and shook his head. It told him that John had heard someone moving around in the house about forty minutes before he returned.

They went downstairs together. Edwin studied his desk; it looked just as he had left it. He looked in the drawers;

everything was there. The rooms looked undisturbed. He went into the bedroom; all seemed well. He looked round the bathroom; lying in the washbasin was a black hair. It was not his; his hair was much lighter. A professional job, he mused, someone who knew what he was doing had made a thorough search; probably the MGB, waiting for that human error. He was always careful to leave nothing that could be of use or might interest someone. He would have had no evidence that anyone had been in his house had it not been for the one black hair.

He took the envelope that Rodka had handed him out of his pocket and studied it. It was a small, cheap, buff envelope and written in an uneducated hand were the two words: *Ambassadre Ingleterre.*

Followed by John, Edwin went into the kitchen to steam open the envelope. Inside it was a scruffy piece of lined paper, which looked as if it had been torn from a note book and was written on both sides. Edwin and John sat side by side at the kitchen table trying to make out what was written. It was in Romanian.

When Edwin had finished reading, a look of satisfaction spread across his face. He signed to John not to speak, led him out of the house, locked the door and drove to the British Embassy.

At the Embassy the Duty Officer let them in and handed Edwin a handful of papers.

'These are telephone messages,' he said. 'They are all local and here are two letters just handed in.'

'Thank you,' Edwin took the papers. 'We shall be in my office if any more messages arrive.' He and John went upstairs two at a time.

Once inside the office Edwin shut the door and flung off his coat. 'Make yourself at home,' he said, waving towards an armchair. 'At last we can talk freely.'

'Thank God!' John sank into an armchair.

'We may be getting somewhere,' continued Edwin, reading the messages and letters. He was having to decide which messages were worth following up and which could be discounted. John couldn't help him because they were all in Romanian. 'Listen to this one!' Edwin exclaimed suddenly.

The letter was from the Ionnitiu's maid who was in the house when the doctor returned in an agitated state; his wife had rung for tea and cake and when she took the tray in she heard the doctor say to his wife, 'they have taken her off in a car down the Strada Popovich, they turned left at the end of the street. She is very ill and the Austrian authorities should be told that she has been kidnapped.' Then his wife said, 'if it is the Russians it will be dangerous to get involved.' The doctor replied, 'that is likely, but I am a doctor and she is my patient. She is ill and in need of medical care.' In the night the Russians broke into the house and took the doctor and his wife away.' The letter was signed 'Elena Ceseanu'.

'That sounds authentic,' John said. 'So we can now be almost certain that it is the Russians who have Lisl.'

'Yes. I'll arrange for Elena Ceseanu to get a reward. Tomorrow morning I shall have to see H.E. and tell him about the Ionnitius. He was a good doctor and now the Embassy is without its medical adviser. We shall probably never hear of them again.'

'But can't H.E. do something about them?' John asked.

'He will protest to the Russians and to the Romanians, but it never does any good, the Russians will flatly deny it. I shall also have to mention about Lisl being kidnapped and suggest to H.E. that he informs the Austrian Ambassador.'

'You won't mention me to H.E., will you?' John asked anxiously.

'Have no fear. You can rely on me to say nothing,' Edwin reassured him.

'What about the letter we looked at in the kitchen?' John reminded Edwin. 'What did it say?'

Edwin took it from his pocket. 'I hadn't forgotten it,' he said. 'It's our best lead,' and he translated it into English as he read:

'I am the butler of Madame Antonov. I am from Transylvania and my wife Rosika comes from Konrat in Russia. She is a good woman and a good cook. She cooks for the Russian Ambassador when he is at Snagov. She does not live in the house but has a room in a long wooden building in the grounds away from the house with the other servants. Servants cannot live in the house. Only Russian soldiers sleep in the house. My wife she knows something but better you talk to her. Today is her free day. She is with me in the Antonov residence. She leaves here at six in the morning. Ludwic.'

John's face was alight, 'I vote we go there now and find out what Rosika has to tell us.'

'Right,' agreed Edwin.

The Duty Officer let them out and locked the door behind them. They got into Edwin's car and drove to Strada Eliza Filipescu, where the Antonov residence was. Edwin parked the car in the shadows on the left-hand side of the road. They left the car, crossed the road and walked back to number four. The large iron gates were open, so they went quickly inside and stepped on to the lawn on the left-hand side of the drive.

Before them stood a substantial two-storey house that had been built about eighty years previously. There was an imposing front door with a porch supported by pillars in either side. The gravel drive went to the front of the house with a large parking area, and there were lawns on either side of the drive. Round the back of the house were shrubs and two mature lime trees, their scent filling the night air.

It was after one in the morning and lights still shone from windows on the ground floor and some from a room above; all windows had balconies. The Romanians were late retiring, and late rising.

John and Edwin went into the shrubbery at the side of the house and then crept round to the back where they found a flight of steps leading to the cellar, so Edwin felt certain that was where they would find Ludovic and Rosika. They did not wish to be seen by Radka and her husband.

At the bottom of the steps was a door. Edwin tried to turn the handle; the door was locked. He knocked, waited, then knocked again, this time a little louder. They heard noises from within and a light shone out from under the door. A man's voice called nervously in Romanian from the other side of the door, 'Who is it? Who is there?'

Edwin replied in Romanian, 'This is Monsieur Hobbs of the British Embassy. I am a friend of Madame Antonov.'

Nothing happened for a moment or two, then a bolt was pulled back and the door was opened just enough to allow the thin, pale face of Ludovic to peer out.

'Ah! Monsieur Hobbs,' he said, holding the door open. 'Come in, please.'

'This is a friend of mine,' explained Edwin, nodding towards John.

They went into the basement room where a small woman was standing nervously rubbing her hands together. She was wearing a long white cotton nightdress, high at the neck with long sleeves; she clutched a black shawl around her shoulders. Her black hair hung lankly down her back and her dark eyes were fearful as she looked searchingly at the visitors. She was also pale and thin and wore nothing on her feet.

'This is Rosika,' said Ludovic. He wore trousers under a crumpled white nightshirt; his feet were bare.

Rosika curtseyed. 'Kiss the hand,' she murmured, with downcast eyes. She continued to fidget with her hands.

'Good evening,' replied Edwin, 'My friend and I came here because of the letter you wrote to our Ambassador. We apologise for calling at this hour but we didn't want to miss you. Thank you for writing and we are most anxious to hear what you have to tell us. May we sit down?'

'Please,' said Ludovic apologetically, fetching two wooden chairs and placing them side by side. Edwin and John sat while the other two remained standing.

'Rosika,' said Edwin, smiling, trying to put her at ease. 'We need your help. Someone has been kidnapped and we are trying to find her. If you can help us, there will be a good reward. Please tell us what you know.'

Rosika looked at them both, her eyes wide and dark; she looked from one to the other. Ludovic had spoken of Monsieur Hobbs, she recalled, and said he was a kind man. Should she tell them all she had heard? Could she trust them? She thought of the reward. Her mother was ill and needed medicine and food; Lodovic was not strong, he had a weak chest. If he was ill and could not work, she would not be able to keep them both on the little she earned. They needed money desperately. She looked at her husband.

His eyes pleaded; his whole body pleaded. 'Please Rosika,' he whispered, leaning towards her and taking her hand.

'It was three days ago,' she began, hesitatingly. 'I was at Snagov and had just gone to my room in the shed to take my shoes off and sit down, because my feet hurt from the stone floor in the hot kitchen, when Doru, who does the garden, came in. He said he did not like something he had seen. He had been working in a thick clump of bushes on the right side of the house when a big black car drove in. Instead of stopping at the main door, it drove round to the side of the house, near to where he was working. He was afraid and hid in the bushes, but he could see through the bushes what went on.'

Edwin nodded and Rosika continued:

'He saw two men get out of the car. Doru said they were Russians. They dragged someone out of the back of the car. There was a blanket over the head, but Doru said the person looked like a woman because she was wearing only a thin nightdress which clung to her body. She could not walk, so one of the men picked her up, threw her over his shoulder and carried her down the stone steps and into the basement. Then the door banged, the two men ran up the steps, got into the car and they drove away.'

She stopped as if she had been talking too much and looked anxiously at Ludovic. He looked appreciatively at her and nodded approval. He knew just how desperately they needed money. He smiled, the high cheek-bones accentuating the hollows in his cheeks.

Rosika continued, 'Doru was so upset, he was worried about the woman. I told him to forget it. We have to look after ourselves and that is difficult enough these days. Anyway, people disappear every day and are shot every day, so why bother about this one? I told him I did not want to know about it and I sent him away.' Tears were now running down her face.

'Thank you for telling me all this,' said Edwin encouragingly. 'Can you think of anything else that might have a connection with what Doru told you? Even if you think it is not important, please tell me.'

'I did not want to know about this woman. It is too dangerous,' continued a tearful Rosika. 'Terrible things happen to people these days.'

Edwin nodded his head in agreement and translated all that Rosika had been telling him to John.

'Well, the very next day a soldier came into the kitchen, picked up a tin mug belonging to one of the soldiers and told me to fill it with soup. From the look on his face I dared not speak. He took the soup down to the basement. To begin with I could not think why he went there. Then I thought, that must be for that poor woman Doru saw.'

'Ah! Yes,' said Edwin, quickly translating for John. 'Have you seen or heard anything else? Think carefully.'

Rosika opened her mouth as if to speak and then shut it again. Ludovic, who had been standing beside her while she had been speaking, now turned to her anxiously.

'I understand how you feel,' Edwin said soothingly, 'but you can trust me. No harm will come to you. If you tell me everything, you will be well rewarded.' He took two thick wads of notes from his pocket and held them in his hands.

They watched him.

'Yesterday at Snagov there was much activity,' she said. 'Gospodeen Nicoliev told Madame Olga – she is the house-keeper – to prepare the best guest rooms for two very important people. She heard the Ambassador mention a plane from Moscow. Olga heard all this and she told me because she is my friend.'

'What else do you know?' asked Edwin encouragingly, turning over the wads of money.

'I have to be back early this morning because Madame Ambassador will explain what I have to cook. It has to be very special. They have arranged the dining table for two extra people. The very large entrance hall has been cleared of everything except for a table which has been put right in the middle with three chairs on one side and one on the other. The room looks very empty.'

'Have you heard who is going to sit on these chairs?'

'I do not know,' replied Rosika, shaking her head. 'But Madam Olga was watching over the furniture that the soldiers were moving under the direction of Gospodeen Nicoliev and Gospodeen Lopatin, and she heard Gospodeen Nicoliev say, "She must sit here." He was holding the chair that was by itself facing the three chairs.'

Edwin had been busy translating it into English, when John asked, 'How large is the hall?'

Rosika look perplexed. 'I am not good at sizes, but I guess about seven or eight metres. It is almost square.'

'You have done very well,' said Edwin.

John interrupted, 'Did you hear anything about what is happening after the guests arrive? Any little detail?'

Edwin continued to translate.

'Only that all the servants have to be in their rooms and stay there from five o'clock in the evening and we shall be told when to go back to work. We must not go outside our rooms. This makes it difficult for preparing food. It must all be ready and on the dining table before then. The soldiers will have to be smart and clean. They will be inspected at ten o'clock in the morning.'

'How many soldiers are there?' asked John.

'Six.'

'Where are they and how are they armed?' John inquired.

'They all have rifles,' Rosika replied. 'One stands at the entrance gate, one is on the steps of the house by the main door and one stands by the lake. The other three are resting until it is their turn to be on sentry duty. They usually lie about on their beds. They are not allowed to wander about the house or grounds, they have to stay in their room.'

'Are there any steps up to the main door?' asked John.

'Yes, that is where the soldier stands.'

'How many steps are there? Are they wide or narrow? Is

there a porch? Are there any pillars? I need to know every detail,' there was urgency in John's voice.

Edwin translated.

'I think there are about eight stone steps, but I cannot be sure. They are wider than the big double doors, but not much. There is no porch and no pillars. It is plain-looking although it is the largest villa in Snagov.' Rosika was now anxious to tell all she knew.

'You said there are double doors. How wide are they?

Rosika thought for a moment. 'I am not sure. It is difficult to say. Together they would be about two metres wide. Maybe a little more.'

Edwin leaned forward. 'Rosika,' he said earnestly, 'are you certain you have told us everything?'

'Yes, truly I have. There is nothing more.' She looked anxiously at Ludovic.

Edwin asked John if he wanted to ask anything more. He shook his head. Then Edwin turned to Rosika and Lodovic.

'I want you both to listen carefully,' he said, holding out the large wads of money towards them. 'Here is a lot of money. Do not let anyone see it or know that you have it. Do not buy anything expensive that would make people talk. Your rooms may be searched at any time so the safest thing is for you to bury it tonight in the garden here. Wrap it in something waterproof and put it in a tin and bury it under a shrub. Tend the shrub and be sure it does not die. You must tell no one and I shall deny that I have ever seen or spoken to you. If either of you talks, you know what to expect.' He drew his finger across his throat and looked from one to the other.

Ludovic wrapped the money lovingly in Rosika's shawl. 'Kiss the hand,' they said in unison. Rosika curtseyed and tears streamed down their faces. It was a pathetic sight with the two standing in their night clothes in the small, poorly furnished and dimly lit, cold cellar room.

John and Edwin slipped out of the door and returned to the car, making as little noise as possible.

Rosika just stood there. She took some of the money from Ludovic and held the bundles away from her as if they were red hot coals; she could neither move nor speak, she had never seen so much money before. She was afraid.

Ludovic broke the silence. 'Rosika! Oh Rosika!' he whispered, kissing her gently on her wet cheeks. Slowly she turned her head and looked at him. 'What shall we do with so much money? she asked, looking fearfully round the room.

'We must do as Monsieur Hobbs told us. We must trust him.' He was now smiling as he took the money from her. He took out two of the smaller notes and gave one to Rosika and kept one for himself. 'We must bury it now while everyone is asleep.' He gave her back the money, and together they stole into the garden.

The Duty Officer was surprised when Edwin returned to the Embassy for the second time that night.

'Suffering from insomnia?' he inquired.

Edwin laughed. 'Do you have any coffee?' he asked, 'We shall be working for the rest of the night.'

When they were alone in the office drinking the coffee, Edwin said quietly, 'We've been lucky tonight. Sometimes things happen like this, but not often.'

'We needed a break after all the disasters we've had recently,' John replied. 'I have a plan,' he added.

20

Sir Gerald Downey had just returned from a weekend at his Kentish home. He walked into Hugh's office, a thing he seldom did.

Hugh stood up.

'Good morning, Hugh,' he said briskly. 'Could you get all your chaps busy finding out where all our overseas agents are and what they're up to? I need the information by this evening.'

'Certainly, sir. Any particular reason?'

'No,' replied the Chief. 'Just that one must have a tight hold of the reins when things are going wrong. By the way, how is your wife? It's a long time since I last saw her, and I did so enjoy the evening at your place.'

Hugh felt he should not ignore such a hint. 'Why not join us for a meal tonight, sir? I could telephone Julia now.'

'Thank you. I'd like that, and then we can discuss over dinner what you have found out about our people on the Continent. What time shall I arrive?'

'About eight?'

'Fine,' replied Sir Gerald, and returned to his office.

Hugh picked up the telephone. He hoped Julia would be in and at the same time wondered how she would react. The ringing went on and on; then she picked it up.

'Hello! Surprise for you!' exclaimed Hugh. 'Gerald is coming for dinner tonight.'

'Tonight!' came the incredulous reply. 'Whatever for?'

'He really asked himself – nothing I could do. I realise it's terribly short notice, but it can be quite simple.' He paused, looking pleadingly down the telephone.

'I'm not a bloody wizard,' she replied. 'And I look a mess.'

'Darling, I think you're pretty miraculous and I'll come home as early as possible to help. Gerald won't arrive until eight. I'm sorry to do this to you.'

'Oh, all right,' she said, and put down the receiver.

That evening Hugh concentrated on being a good host, although he had received a disturbing telegram just before he left the office. He knew he would have to tell Sir Gerald, but he wanted to put it off as long as possible, and the Chief had shown no inclination to talk shop. Julia had produced an excellent dinner and he had been complimented on the wine. They went into the drawing room where he poured out cognac for himself and Sir Gerald while Julia went to the kitchen to prepare coffee.

The two men sat there cradling their brandy glasses in both hands. It was Courvoisier, a favourite of Sir Gerald's. To all appearances they were both at peace with the world.

Hugh felt this was the moment to tell the Chief the bad news. He fortified himself with a few more sips of brandy then said, 'Just as I was leaving this evening we received a telegram from Hobbs in Bucharest informing us that Lisl von Althof was kidnapped from our safe place in Bucharest at about four p.m. their time. They have no news of where she is but eye-witnesses say the men who kidnapped her looked like Russians. She has not yet recovered from typhoid fever.'

Julia had just come in with the coffee. 'Black?' she asked, looking at Sir Gerald.

'Thank you,' he replied, absently.

'Is anything wrong?' she asked, looking from one to other.

'I have just heard that a vital agent has been kidnapped,' Sir Gerald spoke through clenched teeth.

Julia looked at Hugh.

'Lisl von Althof', he said, then continued, 'but that is not all, sir. I got hold of Edwin Hobbs this evening and he told me that the Embassy doctor, Ionnitiu – who had been visiting Lisl – has been arrested. So has his wife.'

Sir Gerald emptied his brandy glass in a gulp. 'What a bloody mess! And what are you bloody doing about it? There will be no one left soon,' he snapped.

Hugh went scarlet in the face but before he had time to answer, the Chief continued tersely, 'What about the rest? What is Harcourt up to in Trieste?'

Hugh was pouring brandy into Sir Gerald's empty glass. 'I don't know. I'm afraid I couldn't contact him,' continued Hugh apologetically. 'I tried all day. I'll continue to try him later tonight and carry on until I succeed.'

'Let me know the moment you find out where he is,' barked Sir Gerald. 'You must have a tighter control of your operators.'

'Yes, sir.' Hugh knew the danger signs. To the world at large Sir Gerald Downey seemed aloof, restrained, unemotional and polished. But these days he became unreasonable when he had too much to drink – as if the pressure was too much.

Julia was sitting on the sofa outwardly relaxed but inwardly as taut as a violin E string. She decided it was best for her to remain silent.

Downey finished his brandy and stood up. 'I must be going,' he announced abruptly, and strode to the door.

'Good night,' said Julia standing up. She remained in the room while Hugh followed him to his car and watched him drive away.

'Thank God he's gone,' Julia sank back on to the sofa as Hugh returned. 'But no wonder he was angry. It is all rather upsetting.'

'How do you think *I* feel?' asked Hugh in a hurt voice. 'I don't enjoy losing people I know and like and for whom I am responsible! There is something uncanny about the whole bloody thing.'

'Let's leave the clearing up. I can do it in the morning,' said Julia soothingly. 'Come to bed and get some sleep. You'll need to be up early in morning.'

Hugh was in his office by eight o'clock. He had slept badly and was a bit on edge. He had just hung his bowler hat on the hook behind the door when Sir Gerald came in. He was his usual calm, smooth self; brisk and to the point.

'My sister's husband died last night. I heard early this morning. She lives in France, so I shall be away for about a week sorting things out. I have told Dick Reynolds, and he will be answering for me until I return. I've put him in the picture concerning your Section, so let him know what you manage to find out. Use all your contacts, even Interpol and the CIA. I have informed the P.M. that I shall be away.'

He turned on his heel and strode out of the room before Hugh had time to offer his condolences. Hugh wondered if he would survive in this job much longer.

During the morning a large, exquisite bouquet of flowers arrived at the house for Julia; it was from Sir Gerald. Attached was a card thanking her for an enjoyable evening.

Julia smiled, this was typical of Gerald, she thought. One had to forgive him. She rang Hugh to tell him. He just grunted and rang off.

Hugh walked down the passage to find Dick Reynolds; he had to talk this over with someone. He had a feeling in the pit of his stomach that made him restless and uneasy; he had a foreboding he was unable to shake off and was sure something sinister was going on; none of their agents was safe.

150

Dick Reynolds was a quiet, self-effacing, gentle intellectual with the gift of listening intently to what was being said. When he spoke it was usually to the point. He listened now without interrupting until Hugh had finished bringing him up to date on the latest events in Bucharest and telling him of his fears for other agents.

'One of the few people who knew the identities of all your recent casualties is John Harcourt,' said Dick.' 'It seems rather far-fetched, I know, but it has to be someone, and now you tell me that you are unable to contact him. Perhaps he is really on the other side.'

'Out of the question!' replied Hugh vehemently. 'I would stake my life on his integrity, and such a thought would never cross my mind.'

'Perhaps it should,' pursued Dick. 'When this sort of thing happens, suspect everyone. Remember, every man has his price. If you take my advice, you will investigate *everyone* and give your findings to the Chief to sort out.'

Hugh felt depressed at the thought of investigating his friends and colleagues. Sitting in his office, he decided to put out some feelers but to wait until the Chief returned before initiating investigations.

21

Boris Molohovski had been in a foul temper ever since his agents had lost track of John Harcourt. He had made them scour every inch of Trieste, the villages around and all the surrounding countryside. He had called twice at the Yugoslav Embassy and had long talks with Stanko Logar to discover if he had any ideas as to where Harcourt could be. He had drawn a blank each time.

While he was sitting in his office studying a map showing the routes across the frontier between Trieste and Yugoslavia, a clerk brought him in a message. His face brightened as he read it; he jumped up, knocking over his chair in his hurry, and flung open the door of the adjoining office. 'Ivan Aleksandrov, we have good news from Bucharest! They are holding Elizabeth von Althof.' He waved the paper in the air.

'Fantastic! Now she is safely in our hands it is not so important what Harcourt is up to. Who is going to interrogate her?'

'They will keep her there and carry out a full interrogation. Someone will be flying from Moscow to make certain we get all the information we want. Then that will be the end of the little Baroness. She was dangerous and the best agent the British had left. I shall send congratulations immediately – they have done well.'

Molohovski returned to his room in buoyant mood. He decided to keep up the pressure on finding Harcourt; he liked to keep tabs on all foreign agents operating in his area. He decided to dine tonight in the Excelsior Hotel and to go to the Rouge et Noir where Alberto would whisper the latest rumours – for which he would be well paid.

As he entered the hotel, he saw Anna sitting in the foyer reading a letter. He walked over to her. 'Good evening,' he said smiling. 'I hope I'm not disturbing you.'

'Not at all,' she replied, folding the letter and putting it in her bag.

'Perhaps that is a letter from our mutual acquaintance, Mr Harcourt?' he said encouragingly.

'No,' replied Anna. 'I have not seen Mr Harcourt for a little while. He has not been here or in the Piazza.' She turned large, liquid eyes on him.

'Did he give you any idea he might be going away? Perhaps just a little hint?'

She shook her head. 'No,' she replied thoughtfully. 'Nothing. And he never told me what sort of journalist he was. Perhaps I should have pressed him for more details, but he never talked about himself.'

'Do not concern yourself,' said Molohovski. 'I am sure he has come to no harm. As it happens, I was looking for him myself. Should he contact you, or should you catch a glimpse of him, perhaps you would be so kind as to let me know. I have some work for him.'

'Of course. I shall be only too happy to do that for you.'

'Then I shall disturb you no longer.' He went downstairs to the Rouge et Noir smiling to himself. He considered that, one way and another, this had been a satisfactory day.

Alberto confirmed that John had not been seen around for some time, and he had no other information of importance. Molohovski finished his glass of vodka and went into the restaurant for a quick meal. The room was almost empty, because it was still too early for Italians to dine.

On returning to his office he circulated a description of John Harcourt on the Russian Intelligence network to all countries in Europe and the Balkans. He also ordered his staff and agents in Trieste to double their efforts.

Boris Molohovski was an experienced and conscientious Intelligence operator and he was worried; he knew he would have no rest until he had tracked down Harcourt. He did not like being beaten. He had kept his superiors in Moscow informed of all he was doing.

That was the thing he had to remember; providing he informed Moscow of every action he took, nothing too serious would happen to him even if things went wrong, but if he failed to inform his Chief and they heard of it later, he would be recalled and have to prove that his actions were in the best interests of the Soviet Union and that he was not trying to deceive them.

Molohovski set up an operations office and arranged with Ivan Aleksandrov to have it manned twenty-four hours of the day. He had cast his net so wide that it was now just a matter of waiting. Moscow had a reliable agent in London and they had been assured that Harcourt had not set foot there.

22

John looked across the room at Edwin and said:

'The plan is clear in my mind, but I need your help. I must have a jeep with false Russian numberplates.'

'All right, I have one, but it is the *only* one I have, so I would appreciate having it returned when you've finished with it. The false numberplates are no problem. I take it you have a gun and sufficient ammunition. What else do you need?'

John thought for a moment. 'Six hand grenades and some smoke bombs might come in useful.'

'You may have them, but they must never be traced back to me. If H.E. ever got wind of this, I would be kicked on to the next aircraft to London in disgrace, my career in ruins.'

'You can trust me never to breathe a word. And believe me, I am truly grateful for your help. Could I also have a couple of blankets and some bandages, just in case?'

Edwin nodded. 'Everything will be ready for you by two this afternoon.'

'Any chance of you coming along yourself? It may be difficult driving the jeep, rescuing Lisl and fending off unwanted attention.'

'Much as I'd like to, it's out of the question. But I have an idea. There is just one person who might jump at it – and whom I can recommend – if he can come at such short notice. His name is Nicolai Vascescu. About our age, strong as a horse and fit, if a bit overweight. He's a Romanian who has somehow managed to keep hold of enough of his private income to live well without working. Something of a play-boy, but an excellent horseman and, from what I hear, a good lover – he only ever shaves at night! He is a practised marksman with handguns, since duels are still the accepted way of solving a dispute. He is a happy extrovert and easy to get on with. I feel sure you would like him – he also has a great sense of adventure.'

'But what are his politics?'

'He's an Anglophile and altogether anti-Russian. They harass him constantly: whenever he gets a car, they just confiscate it.'

'All right. Find out if he will come, but impress on him total secrecy, and this includes his mistress.'

'Very well. I'll go and sound him out. Meanwhile, you'd better stay here and get some sleep while you can. I have a camp bed and will bring something for you to eat before you leave. Help yourself to a drink. What time will you set off?'

'Just before dark. I'll need the cover of darkness for the attack, which must be a surprise. Also for our getaway.'

'Right. Now here's a photograph of the Russian Ambassador's residence at Snagov. The drive is fairly long and there are some trees partially obscuring the house. Here you can see one side of the flight of steps leading to the front door.' Edwin handed John the photograph. 'I only hope your luck still holds. There are so many uncertainties and details we cannot check.'

'I agree,' replied John, 'but there is no time to be lost or Lisl will be either broken or shot, or both.'

Edwin left John to sleep. It was now nine o'clock in the morning, so he decided to leave at once, to seek out Nikki Vascescu.

Nikki lived in a large house in the Strada Paris, not far from where Draga Sankov lived. He parked the car in the drive and pushed the door-bell; he heard it ring loudly within the house. The heavy door was opened by an ageing manservant.

Edwin handed him his card and asked if he could see Monsieur Vascescu, apologising for calling at such an early hour.

He was invited in and offered a chair in the grand entrance hall while the servant departed, carrying Edwin's card on a silver salver.

After a considerable wait, Edwin was rewarded by the sight of Nikki coming downstairs, clad only in a red silk dressing-gown, below which were substantial, hairy legs and bare feet. He looked larger than ever and as if he had only just awakened.

Edwin stood up. 'Good morning, Nikki,' he said, holding out his hand.

Nikki pumped it vigorously, towering above him.

'My dear chap! You are most welcome as always,' he replied, running his fingers through his thick, black hair. 'Come in here and we will have some coffee,' he led Edwin into a small reception room, charmingly and expensively furnished.

The coffee must have been made already because the servant brought it in immediately. Nikki dismissed the servant, picked up the gleaming pot and poured steaming coffee into two blue-and-gold Sevres cups.

Edwin drank the coffee gratefully. 'Delicious!' he murmured.

Nikki sank into a large armchair. 'Now tell me,' he said, 'why have you come to visit me at this hour? I am intrigued. I cannot wait to hear,' and his dark eyes looked keenly at Edwin.

'I need your help, but first I must be assured of your complete and total secrecy – both now and always.'

'I promise,' replied Nikki. 'Here is my hand. I swear to keep your secret.' He then put his hand on his heart. '*Never* will I betray you,' he added dramatically.

'I knew I could count on you. The problem is this:' explained Edwin, 'a good friend of mine needs someone to help him. You'll have to be prepared to go off with him today, and I cannot say when you'll return. It may be a matter of days, or it may be weeks. You will need a pistol and plenty of ammunition. It will be dangerous.'

'Would I be correct in guessing it will be against the Russians?'

'Yes.'

'Wonderful! I can't wait.' Nikki's eyes were gleaming, he was now wide-awake and alert, his face shining at the thought of adventure.

'This is a most serious affair,' stressed Edwin, leaning forward and looking earnestly at Nikki. 'No one must know you're going off on anything unusual. Your life and my friend's life depend on this. It will be tough and there may be shooting. My friend is brave and trustworthy, his name is John and you must do whatever he says without hesitation, and see that no harm comes to him. Are you willing to go?'

'Go? Just try to keep me away! You are lucky, having such work. Imagine what it is like for me. I have never worked except being in the Cavalry for a year. I only ride, avoid being arrested by the Russians on some made-up charge or other, and while away my time with romantic adventures.'

Edwin nodded and said:

'A car will arrive here at four o'clock this afternoon precisely to take you to the British Embassy. Press the bell three times and wait. You will be expected. Wear dark clothes – nothing white or light coloured. Something for travelling by day and night in an open jeep, and suitable for action. John will outline the plan to you before you leave and tell you himself what he wants you to do.'

158

'Right, I'll be there,' said Nikki, jumping up from the armchair and walking around the room.

Edwin walked towards the door. 'Remember, Nikki, not a word to anyone.'

'Trust me!' replied Nikki, smiling as he let Edwin out of the house.

John was in Edwin's office finishing a substantial meal that Edwin had provided for them. He felt refreshed after his sleep and was anxious to get started. All this inactivity did him no good and made him feel like a caged lion. He knew that caution during the investigation and planning stages was essential and that he could not afford to overlook any detail or it might mean death for himself or for someone else. He sensed there was danger hanging over him but he had no idea where that danger was.

He had spent those long hours in Edwin's hot attic trying to work it out, but had made no progress; he only knew that the best British agents – and he had known them all – were losing their lives at a frightening rate. He had also been pondering Pete Mason's remark. What did the CIA know that caused them to forbid Pete to communicate with him?

The Embassy doorbell rang three times. Edwin looked at his watch. 'That will be Nikki,' he said. 'I'll go and let him in myself.'

When Edwin returned with Nikki, John jumped up to meet him. Here was someone much heavier and broader than himself. His dark hair was swept back from a swarthy face where the features were rounded and aristocratic. He had a good-natured smile and his brown eyes had humorous creases around them.

'This is Nikki,' said Edwin, as they entered the room.

John walked towards him and they clasped hands firmly,

159

looking searchingly into each other's eyes. They both knew instinctively that they could trust one another.

'Sit down,' said John, pointing to a chair on the other side of the table, 'and I'll tell you what we have to do.'

Edwin settled into a large, comfortable armchair from where he could watch Nikki's face. He wanted to see his reaction as John unfolded the plan he had made to free Lisl.

'You'll only be told what you need to know,' John explained. 'That's a strict rule in our organisation.'

Nikki nodded. His dark eyes fixed on John's face, concentrating on what he was about to hear.

'A young woman has been kidnapped by the Russians and our job is to get her back safely. She has just had typhoid fever, so may have no strength to walk. Her name is Lisl. She is about five feet five inches tall, with long, blonde hair falling over her shoulders. Her eyes are large, grey and set wide apart. She is of average build. She may have lost some hair with the fever and have lost weight—' John stopped. 'Have you got that picture firmly in your mind?' he asked.

'Yes,' replied Nikki. 'I picture her exactly. Where is she?'

'We believe the Russians are holding her in their Ambassador's house on Lake Snagov. Here is a photograph of the front of the house.'

Nikki studied the photograph carefully.

'The drive is quite long and winds through woodlands,' John continued. 'The house cannot be seen from the road. We know there is a Russian soldier at the entrance gates armed with a rifle. Then there is a second Russian soldier at the bottom of the flight of steps leading up to the front door. He is also armed with a rifle. A third Russian soldier, similarly armed, is beside the lake. There are three other Russian soldiers off duty. They will be in their quarters at the back of the house, since all the staff have instructions to be in their rooms. The servants are unarmed and unlikely to put up resistance. The occupants of the house are the Ambassador and his wife. They too, being in their own house, will probably be unarmed. There will be two house-guests who have arrived today from Moscow and are being given the VIP treatment, plus a diplomat from their Embassy.'

'Whew!' exclaimed Nikki. 'That sounds quite formidable! Presumably the guests are Russians and may be crack shots.I imagine they will have their Tokarev pistols. So there will be three outside and five inside against the two of us. Is there any possibility of us getting out alive?'

John looked earnestly at Nikki. 'Yes,' he replied, 'with a little luck. There are about eight good stone steps leading up to the double front door. The doors open inwards. Immediately inside is a large square entrance hall with a medium-sized oblong table in the centre, three chairs drawn up to the table facing the door and one chair on the opposite side of the table. All other furniture has been removed, which indicates that something particular is going to happen there. We also know that all the staff have been ordered to go to their rooms at five o'clock this evening and to remain there until told they can leave. There will then be a special dinner. As you know, the Russians come to life in the evenings. They work late and they eat late. Is all this clear so far?'

'Absolutely. Now tell me the plan.' Nikki sat there, every muscle taut and his face a study in concentration.

'Right,' said John, 'Now I understand you speak Russian.'

'Yes.'

'In that case,' continued John, 'while we are at Snagov, can you handle the jeep?'

'Certainly, I should enjoy that.'

'So that is settled. You drive the jeep and do exactly as I tell you, instantly. A split second can mean life or death. We shall be wearing Russian Army uniforms. You will be a private soldier and I shall be a captain of the MGB. Edwin has the uniforms, and we'll try them on in a minute. We drive from here to Snagov and straight to the Russian Ambassador's residence. You have to drive straight up to the soldier on the gate, and stop. Keep the headlights full on him. I will wave a large envelope and you say I have a letter to deliver. At the same time I shall get out of the jeep and go up to him. As I deliver the letter to him you must switch off the headlights. I shall then kill him silently with my knife, retrieve the envelope, and climb back into the jeep. You will switch on the headlights and drive down the drive to the house and stop beside the sentry standing in front of the house at the bottom of the flight of steps leading to the front door. I shall jump out waving the letter.

'It will be a repeat performance.

'In the meantime you will back the vehicle a little distance from the house. When soldier number two has been silently killed I will get back into the jeep and you will immediately drive up the flight of stone steps at a good speed so that the impact of the jeep on the double doors will force them to open and you drive straight into the hall. All this will have to be done in one continuous movement at the fastest possible speed. We shall then have to play it by ear, but we do not leave without Lisl.' John's eyes never left Nikki's face. Finally he said, 'Is there anything you want to ask me?'

Nikki leaned forward and said, 'Do you work for British Intelligence?'

John looked at Edwin. 'Yes, he does,' replied Edwin. 'But we don't talk about it. Not now, or at any time in the future. We do not forgive those who betray us,' he added threateningly.

'I can see this plan is both daring and dangerous. If I am caught by the Russians, I shall be tortured and shot. Our Romanian Government are just puppets of the Russians and if the *Securitate* get me they will hand me over to the Russians. I accept the dangers and will come with you. You can rely on me to carry out anything you ask. Believe me, I hate communism with a deep hatred and am prepared to lose my life in the fight against it. At the moment the Communists are holding the country in a tight grip of fear and there is so little I can do about it.'

'Trust John,' said Edwin, getting up from his chair. 'I know the odds are against you. But a daring plan, executed by professionals – coupled with the element of surprise – is usually successful. Unless, of course, you have bad luck or bad intelligence. You are superbly fit, a crack shot, with loads of initiative and a great spirit of adventure. I'm sure you don't panic when things go wrong – you're a survivor. Now John is a professional and a highly skilled operator who has survived many alarming moments. But if you want to change your mind, now is the time. No one will hold it against you. Think before you reply.'

'I've been thinking all the time I've been here. You can count on me. I will go along with you all the way.'

John stood up and grasped his hand. 'Thanks,' he said. 'I appreciate your throwing your lot in with us. I can understand how you feel. I might appear outwardly calm but I always feel tense and a bit churned up inside beforehand. Yet as soon as the job begins, I suddenly feel utterly calm, totally unafraid and mentally in tiptop form. It's all to do with adrenalin,' he added lightly. 'You will probably react in the same way as I do.'

'Here are some Russian uniforms,' said Edwin, going

over to a cupboard and opening it. 'We had better see if any of these fit and make sure you have everything you need.'

John and Nikki were wearing dark shirts, trousers and black shoes with rubber soles. The tenseness dispelled as they tried on the various garments amid bursts of laughter as they looked at each other buttoned to the neck in Russian Army tunics, with the appropriate badges of rank.

There were still two hours to go before they planned to leave so they took off their uniforms, got out the maps and discussed all the pros and cons of what action to take, or not to take, should a particular occasion arise.

'Where do we go when we leave the Russian Ambassador's residence?'

'We must make for Craiova. Do you know the way?' asked John.

'Fairly well. Not all the small roads, but I have driven over there a number of times.'

'Good. That will make it easier.' John looked at Edwin, 'Could you let me have a good length of rope, a ball of string, two or three torches with spare batteries and bulbs, a couple of blankets, a bottle of drinking water and some biscuits.'

'I'll be back as soon as possible,' replied Edwin. 'I'll stow them in the jeep.'

It was an hour and a half later that Edwin returned with a broad smile on his face and carrying a large, rather untidy brown paper parcel.

The other two watched him as he put it on the table and proceeded to open it. 'Just something to keep the inner man happy,' he explained. 'I raided the larder – it's the best I can do.'

'Marvellous,' said John, picking up a thick meat sandwich, 'eat up, Nikki. There's no telling when we shall be able to eat again.'

As they tucked into sandwiches and grapes, Edwin was relieved to see how well Nikki and John got on. They were obviously on the same wavelength and this boded well for the success of this hazardous operation.

'Everything you asked for is in the jeep,' Edwin explained, as he removed all traces of the picnic. 'I've also left you some spare jerry cans of petrol and a container of water in case the engine overheats. Incidentally, is there any chance of recovering the jeep?'

'Yes, Nikki will let you know where you can find it. Thanks for everything, Edwin. You're a real pal.'

23

It was nearly dark when John and Nikki, dressed in Russian army uniforms, climbed into the jeep and drove out of the British Embassy compound towards lake Snagov. Edwin followed closely behind them in his car. He wanted to make sure they were not being followed so he decided to stick behind them until they were in sight of the Russian villa; then he would turn back.

Nikki was at the steering wheel. 'Are you sure you can manage to drive up the front steps and straight through the front doors into the hall? It must be done at speed,' John asked.

'That should be no trouble with this jeep,' Nikki assured him. 'In fact that is a part I am rather looking forward to. I shall have my pistol ready. You never know – you may need some help.'

'Agreed,' said John. 'But once we're in the hall, make sure the jeep is turned facing the door and the steps so that we can make a speedy getaway.'

Nikki nodded. 'Yes,' he said, 'I shall not forget. And you know . . . somehow I can't help thinking about things I don't usually think about.'

'Such as?' asked John.

'I suppose it is because I've never been on this sort of job before – never gone into danger of this kind. Do you think there is another life after this one?'

'I know what you mean,' replied John. 'When I first began this work I felt as you do, always questioning this fact when facing imminent danger and never reaching a satisfactory solution in the limited time available. One day when on holiday I discussed this problem with my mother.

She looked serenely at me and said, "You just have to come to terms with death, that is all you have to do, then you will have no fear whatever happens to you." I was amazed I had not thought of this myself. So I went for a long walk across fields, through woods, up and down hills, and found it was not nearly as easy as my mother had made it sound. I remember sitting on a fallen log forcing myself to deal with this matter, determined not to return home until I had done so. I managed in the end.'

They drove on in silence, each occupied with his own thoughts.

John was studying the map by torchlight. 'We're very near,' he said. 'All set?'

'Yes, I'm ready. Edwin has just stopped and is turning round,' said Nikki, looking in the driving mirror.

John turned round just in time to see the rear lights of Edwin's car disappearing round a bend. They were now on their own.

Nikki drove up to the entrance and stopped. The sentry pointed his rifle and challenged them. Holding the letter in his left hand, with the knife held firmly in his right hand with the blade concealed against his leg in the folds of his baggy trousers, John jumped from the jeep waving the large envelope. The sentry took the letter in his right hand; while letting the butt of the rifle rest on the ground, he held the barrel in his left hand. Like lightning John's left fist landed a devastating uppercut to the sentry's jaw; as his head shot up and he staggered backwards John cut his throat and pulled the body away from the entrance and into the shrubs beside the drive.

Nikki looked away.

John opened the gates and jumped back into the jeep. 'Drive on,' he said curtly.

Nikki drove down the wooded drive, round a bend and

there was the imposing villa before them. A strong light over the door illuminated the flight of stone steps and the large double doors. A sentry was standing to the left of the steps. He pointed his rifle at them and John thought he was going to fire. As the light fell on them the sentry saw that the occupants of the jeep were wearing Russian uniforms. He lowered his rifle and looked towards John as he jumped out waving an envelope as before.

The sentry took the letter and looked at the address. John delivered a left uppercut with tremendous force. The sentry staggered backwards, the blade flashed and with a slight gurgling sound the sentry sank to the ground.

John wiped the knife on the sentry's trouser leg.

Nikki had remembered to position the jeep some way back from the villa facing the steps. He was glad to have something to do; he could not watch another throat being cut; his stomach just wouldn't take it.

John got back into the jeep, took out his Beretta and flicked off the safety catch. 'Be prepared for anything,' he said to Nikki. 'Have your weapon ready. Drive up the steps and into the house!'

Nikki looked at John. Could this be the same man who was eating sandwiches with him only a short time ago? His face was now set and stern, his voice quiet, his speech concise. He moved with speed and lightness and never made an unnecessary movement. He had a natural air of command and expected to be obeyed instantly.

Nikki selected the gear and immediately drove the jeep at the steps as he would have urged a horse to jump a fence. Up they went, the flight seemed steeper than it looked, there was that moment of uncertainty as the front wheels reached the top, wider step. He held the steering wheel in a vicelike grip, he felt his heart thumping, he was holding his breath, he was willing the jeep to go on. He had his foot pressed down on the accelerator; he already had it in the extra gear but it seemed that it needed something more and there was nothing more left.

There was a dull thud and a jolt as the jeep hit the large double doors. Nikki clenched his teeth and pressed on the accelerator with all his force. Suddenly the doors swung inwards, the jeep became horizontal and they drove into a large, square room with bright lights.

Nikki turned the steering wheel as fast as possible to the left but just too late to avoid hitting a large table in the middle of the room. The jeep caught a corner of the table and swung it round, knocking to the floor a man in civilian clothes sitting on the other side of the table. There were two Russian officers in uniform sitting beside him. One of them, a large, elderly man with a florid complexion and grey hair, grasped the table with both hands in order to prevent himself from being thrown backwards on to the floor. His chair was now tilted on to its two rear legs with the Russian's body wedged firmly between the chair and the table. John noticed he was a General.

The other officer, a Major, was about thirty, short, dark and slim. He sprang angrily to his feet drawing his pistol from its holster.

John had taken in the entire scene at a glance. Someone had been knocked to the floor and the table was now pushed half over him. A Russian General was holding on to the table and an alert young officer was about to shoot him. He had also noticed a female sitting on a chair wrapped in a blanket a little apart over on the right.

John sprang from the jeep. 'I have orders from Moscow to remove the prisoner,' he said calmly in Russian.

'Do not believe him!' shouted the General, struggling to his feet and levelling his pistol at John.

Instantly two shots rang out and the General fell, his face covered in blood. The Major was only wounded in his right arm; he transferred his gun to his left hand and fired. John felt the bullet lodge somewhere in his left shoulder as he picked up the woman in the blanket while Nikki shot the Major dead.

'You are Lisl von Althof?' asked John.

'Yes,' came a whispered reply.

At that moment the door to the left of the hall opened and there stood the Russian Ambassador with his wife and servants just behind him. John almost threw Lisl into the jeep, then faced the Ambassador.

'Orders from the Kremlin, Comrade Ambassador,' John spoke in Russian. 'Do not move or I shall shoot.'

Nikki had now driven the jeep round the table and was facing the door.

John climbed into the jeep with his Beretta still trained on the Ambassador's party. It was then that he saw the civilian still sitting on the floor – everything had happened so quickly. Their eyes met and time stood still. It was as if someone had hit him between the eyes. 'Right, get out of here,' he hissed at Nikki between his teeth.

Nikki swung the jeep towards the door and went down the flight of stone steps too fast for safety or comfort. Suddenly they were faced by three Russian soldiers rushing up the steps clutching their rifles. The two on either side of the steps managed to jump out of the way but the jeep hit the soldier in the middle. He fell backwards and the jeep bounced over him.

'Faster!' ordered John. 'Keep your head down and go!'

John fired at the two soldiers who now had their rifles raised. He hit one of them. *Smack, smack, smack* came the sound of rifle bullets as they hit the drive, the jeep and the trees.

Thank God for the woods and the bend in the drive, thought John, and for the darkness.

As they swung out of the gates and turned right, Nikki switched on the headlights. 'Whew!' he exclaimed, letting his whole body slump. He would have given anything to stop and just have a moment's rest.

'Concentrate!' shouted John. 'We shall have the whole force of Russian Intelligence after us. Drive as fast as you can. Stop for nothing. Be ready to shoot our way through if necessary. If there is a road block, drive at it as fast as possible and try to force a way through. If you can't, then it's each man for himself. Dive for cover and try to get away. Leave Lisl to me.'

His thoughts returned to the scene at the Russian villa. He could not have made a mistake! The man was sitting on the floor with the light from the chandeliers shining on his face. He was in no doubt, yet it seemed so unbelievable, just too bizarre. He would not think about it now, it must wait for later.

He checked his Beretta and reloaded it. Then he turned round. 'Lisl, are you all right?' he asked.

'No,' came the whispered reply. 'I can't travel much further.'

John climbed over and knelt beside her. 'Here are some blankets. Let me try to make you more comfortable,' he said encouragingly, while folding a blanket into a pillow. He lifted her head gently and put it on the folded blanket; with the other blankets he did his best to protect her body from the hardness of the jeep with its angular corners. 'My name is John. Ron Fenton was a friend of mine. We will get you to safety,' he said, throwing the remaining blanket lightly over her. He climbed back beside Nikki.

'Everything all right?' he asked.

'So far, OK,' replied Nikki. He was looking straight

ahead, peering into the darkness, concentrating on the road with its numerous potholes. Fortunately he knew this road well and was aware that it was important to be far from Bucharest before the Russians could organise searches and roadblocks.

John checked Nikki's gun, a German Walther PPK, and reloaded it, then sat beside him with his own Beretta in his right hand, alert and ready for whatever lay ahead. His shoulder was painful but he could still move his left arm and hand; it didn't feel as if it was bleeding any more, just painful and uncomfortable. He wanted to prevent it from stiffening up so he kept moving it gently in a circular movement.

'Did you get hit?' asked Nikki.

'In my left shoulder,' John replied. 'But it's all right, I can manage.'

Nikki had turned north and they drove on in silence. This road was in comparatively good condition so long as they kept to the centre. It was very quiet at this hour of the night; two Russian army lorries had rattled past them going in the opposite direction and so had a few civilian cars. They had overtaken a horse and cart, which had only a lantern hanging from the back, and two small old cars.

Suddenly the jeep begun shaking. Nikki put his foot on the brakes and slowed down. 'We are in Ploiesti!' he said. 'I'm always taken unawares by the cobblestones, they certainly shake one up!'

John climbed into the back, 'Are you all right?' he asked Lisl. There was no reply, no movement. He shook her gently. 'Lisl!' he repeated, 'is something wrong?'

He reached for the torch and shone it on her. The pale, thin face was still; her eyes were closed and she looked lifeless.

My God, thought John, if she's dead then all this effort

is in vain; the consequences did not bear thinking about. He felt for her pulse but it was impossible with the jeep bumping about like this.

'How much further with these cobblestones?' shouted John,

'Not much longer,' came the re-assuring reply. 'We'll soon be turning off the main road and taking the road to Tirgoviste.'

John waited. He felt the swing as they left the main road and the ride became instantly smoother. He felt her pulse again. Relief swept over him: she wasn't dead. Not yet, at any rate. There was a faint pulse, but it was very irregular and she was unconscious. He covered her carefully and climbed back beside Nikki.

'How is she?' inquired Nikki.

'Unconscious and, although I'm no doctor, I think she's very ill. But we must get as far as possible tonight before the search for us can spread to the countryside. At first light we must turn off to a remote village and find a bed for Lisl and rest up for the day. What are the people like in this area?'

'All peasants,' explained Nikki. 'All members of Maniu's National Peasant Party. They hate communists and they hate the Russians for occupying their country. Although we were occupied by the Germans, they did not upset our economy as the Russians have done. Now everyone is suffering and our own Communist Party is trying to starve the peasants into submission. Maniu has been arrested and flung into prison for life – in the harshest conditions. He used to move about the country never spending more than one night in any place. They are very pro-British.'

'That's just as well, because the first thing we must do when it's light is to get hold of a reliable car, something inconspicuous if possible. You must let Edwin know where he can find the jeep.'

They passed through Tirgoviste and turned off to Gesti, keeping up a steady average of ninety kilometres an hour, regardless of the condition of these smaller roads with pot-holes, lorries and peasants in carts travelling through the night to reach the market by morning. Soon after leaving Gesti they joined the main Bucharest-to-Pitesti road, where they could travel faster.

'It won't be dark much longer, so we'd better get rid of these uniforms now. We'll bury them in these woods,' John said as he began struggling out of his tunic. His shoulder hurt desperately as he pulled it over his head. Nikki slowed down and pulled off the road into a siding in the woods. John took the spade and began digging but his shoulder was painful and the ground was like a rock, even in the woods. Nikki grabbed the spade and, with tremendous vigour, dug a hole where they buried the uniforms, stamped down the loose earth and covered the area with leaves and branches.

John walked over and looked at Lisl.

'Better or worse?' inquired Nikki.

'No change as far as I can tell. At least she's still alive! I don't want to stop until after Rimnicu Vilcea, by my reckoning from the map, that will be another eighty kilometres.'

'Hold on, and I'll get you there before dawn,' replied Nikki, who loved a challenge.

He pressed his foot down on the accelerator and gripped the steering wheel. John was sitting bolt upright, watching the road ahead and occasionally turning round; he still held his pistol ready to fire instantly if necessary. This was one of the major roads in the country and John was certain that sooner or later someone would be searching it for them. He prayed silently that their luck would hold. Everything depended on it.

Dawn broke as they hurtled through Pitesti. John looked

at the clear light on the horizon with its soft apricot glow that turned into palest lemon which in turn melted into the palest grey of what was left of the night sky. He looked at his watch. He looked at Nikki. The strain of the night was showing. It was six hours since they left Bucharest and Nikki had been at the wheel all this time without a break.

'Just coming into Rimnicu Vilcea,' announced Nikki.

John looked at the map. It wouldn't be safe to drive on much longer in the jeep; by now there would be a country-wide search for them. Nikki looked exhausted. His own shoulder was feeling worse and then there was Lisl. She was his main concern.

He studied the map more closely. 'Take the first road left in the town and drive towards Tirgu Jiu, then take the second turning on the left to the village of Bile Govora. We must chance our luck and rely on the hospitality of the village. It's off the beaten track and, if the map is correct, the road only goes to the village.'

'It should be all right,' Nikki reassured him. 'These people have little connection with the outside world, they are simple and kind and accept strangers at their face value. We should have no trouble.'

The colours on the horizon had faded and the sky was now the palest shade of blue; the sun was just up and the temperature rose with it. Nikki swung the jeep to the left and drove down a mud track littered with stones and holes. On either side was grassland where flocks of sheep were grazing, being looked after by shepherds who were sitting or lying on the ground. When they saw the jeep they jumped up and stared from under their wide-brimmed, floppy black felt hats. They were dressed in a collection of ragged clothes. Their dark skins were weathered and tanned, their hair was long and unkept and their black eyes looked unsurely at the strangers.

175

Nikki stopped the jeep and waved some paper money at them. 'Good morning!' he called in Romanian, 'We are thirsty and thought you would have some milk in your village. Here you are,' he continued to wave the money. 'This is for you. Perhaps we will see you later.'

They all carried rough sticks, some quite long. Very slowly they moved forward, bunched together until they were quite near the jeep. Nikki threw some coins at them. They grabbed these up without taking their eyes off Nikki and John. One of them darted forward and snatched the paper money from Nikki's hand, then they all scampered back to their flocks and stood watching as Nikki drove off in a cloud of dust.

They could see a small cluster of houses a little way off, with bony cows wandering about in search of grass. They drove into the centre of the village and stopped. Some of the houses were wooden and some rendered a sepia colour with decorative friezes around the top of the walls. They had high, sloping roofs with wide, overhanging eaves. They had the neat and clean appearance of the chalets in parts of Austria. The window frames were of wood and so were the fences around each garden; these were also decorated with an intricate pattern. The village looked attractive and tidy.

Although it was early the peasants were astir and smoke was rising straight up into the cloudless blue sky. There was no wind and the air was pleasantly warm.

John turned to Nikki, 'You're the native. We need somewhere to rest. Food, hot water, and a good woman to care for Lisl. See what you can do.'

Nikki climbed stiffly out of the jeep, stretched himself and yawned. He realised for the first time how tired he felt; he had difficulty walking, his shoulders and arms ached, his pelvis was stiff and his eyes felt as if they were out on stalks. He ran his fingers through his hair and looked around. People were standing about outside houses looking at them. There were children clinging to their mother's skirts and peering round the open doors. Thin, hungry-looking mongrels rushed up to him barking noisily.

He walked towards the largest house where a middle-aged woman was standing at the door looking at him. The dogs followed him, yapping and barking. As he walked up the pathway a man came out of the house, pushed his way past the woman and stood in front of her.

Nikki smiled. 'Good morning!' he said cheerfully, 'We need your help. We have been travelling all night and my friend and I are tired and hungry. We also have a lady with us who is ill. Can you please give us food and somewhere to rest. We have money and can pay you.'

A small crowd had surrounded the jeep and were inspecting it with interest.

The man to whom Nikki had spoken turned and whispered to the woman for a moment, he then walked over and talked to the other men. Nikki waited patiently while they spoke with each other.

The man finally turned to Nikki and asked, 'Who are you, and where do you come from?'

'My name is Vascescu and this is my friend,' John jumped out of the jeep and shook hands all round. 'Look! And you will see this lady is ill,' continued Nikki as he walked over to the jeep and drew back the blanket a little way to show the inert form of Lisl with her eyes closed and her face ashen. The peasants pushed each other and peered into the jeep. There were gasps from the women; some put their hands out to touch her; there was instant sympathy.

One of the men turned to Nikki. 'We would like to help you,' he said, 'but will it bring trouble on our village?'

'No,' replied Nikki. 'No one knows where we are and no one will look for us here. If we could rest for today, we will leave tonight. And if the Russians come looking for us, you can say we're not here.'

'Ah! The Russians!' they said and they drew their fingers across their throats and spat on the ground. 'We do not like communists,' they said. 'We will help you.'

John picked up Lisl and carried her into the largest house; the woman went before him and beckoned to him to follow her upstairs to a room with a large bed in the centre. She removed a white lace cover from the bed and turned down the pristine white sheets. John laid Lisl gently on the bed.

She opened her eyes.

John smiled at her. He wondered if she would survive the journey; she looked so fragile; a puff of wind might blow her away. She just lay there where he had put her, only her eyes, drained of colour and light, moved to take in her new surroundings. She had lost much of her hair with the fever and what was left was matted and dark with sweat. He saw the dark circles under her eyes and how thin her face and hands were.

She turned her head and looked at him with hollow eyes.

'You'll be all right here,' he told her gently. 'We're in a remote village where you can rest. You must also eat. We have a long and uncomfortable journey ahead of us, and we must leave tonight.'

'Where are we going?'

'To England.'

She nodded her head in understanding.

John left the room and returned almost immediately with the woman, who had been waiting outside the door. She ran over to Lisl, took both her hands and made soothing sounds as if dealing with a child. John left them together.

He found Nikki in the woods at the back of the houses with the jeep hidden deep in the undergrowth. Some of the men were scuffing their feet in the dust to obliterate

178

the tracks. Nikki beamed at him. They had unloaded the
jeep and everything was being taken into the house where
Lisl lay upstairs.

'Best to keep everything with us,' Nikki explained.
'Something might vanish as a souvenir. This house belongs
to the Headman. He will give us food and a room to
sleep in.'

They were given a bucket of water and took off their
shirts and began washing.   'You have been wounded.' The
Headman's wife looked anxiously at John.

'It's nothing,' muttered John as he began washing away
the blood.

'Let me see it,' continued the woman, who picked up a
piece of cloth and a pointed knife from the table. She passed
the knife through the flame of the fire and poured out a bowl
of hot water.

'Sit down,' she said. 'You are so tall I cannot reach.'

John looked doubtful as he sat down.

'Don't worry,' Nikki reassured him. 'These people never
go to doctors – there are none for miles around. They are
experienced at looking after each other. Just hang on to the
table, and grit your teeth,' he added lightly.

One of her strong hands held his painful shoulder tightly.
It hurt. With the other hand she prodded about with the knife
in the wound.

John gritted his teeth.

'Ah!' she exclaimed, as the bullet fell to the floor. She
stooped down, picked it up and examined it carefully.

John held out his hand. She gave it to him and he put it
in his picket. He didn't want to leave any evidence behind,
and so would dispose of the bullet later.

The woman washed the wound with hot water, put a
home-made white, paste-like ointment on it, tore the white
cloth into strips and bandaged the shoulder. She smiled and

patted him with the satisfaction of a job well done. John thanked her. She picked up his bloodstained shirt and went off to wash it.

Some of the men came in and explained to Nikki that the shepherds they had passed would deny all knowledge of having seen a jeep and would send a warning of anything suspicious. The woman put black bread, thick dark jam and a large bowl of yoghurt on the wooden table. John and Nikki devoured the food ravenously; she then carried in a bowl of milk still warm from the cow and told them that she would be preparing a meal for them to eat later in the day.

But now they must sleep.

Lisl's body sank into the feather bed while kind hands removed the blanket that had been wrapped around her. She felt the roughness of the peasant sheets against her bare arms and legs; she noticed the whiteness of the sheets and the wide band of embroidery along the top.

All was so clean.

She looked up at the kind face of the young woman who had washed her and was now smoothing down the bed. She noticed that her thick black hair was braided, her cheeks were rosy and her dark eyes were full of concern. She went out of the room and soon returned carrying a bowl of hot soup. She was wearing a red blouse and her full black skirt swung from the hips as she walked, showing bare, well-shaped brown legs. She wore no shoes and her feet were covered in dust.

She smiled at Lisl. 'This is rice cooked in the same water with a chicken. There are also some pieces of chicken. This will be good for you. I hope you will like it.' The woman put her arm around Lisl's shoulders and fed her like a small child while saying words of encouragement the whole time. Lisl drank the soup gratefully and tears ran down her face, partly from weakness and exhaustion but also because of all the tenderness and kindness from this simple young woman. It was all too much for her. The woman left her and Lisl fell asleep.

John opened his eyes and looked at his watch; it was three o'clock and the afternoon sun was still scorching outside the house. He again thought over the events of yesterday. He had Lisl and that was the most important thing. But he was still horrified and he felt the blood rush to his head when he remembered that moment of recognition in the Russian Ambassador's house. It didn't bear thinking about; the implications were too far-reaching. The problem was: what should he do about it and how would it affect him? No, there was no quick answer, he couldn't think about it now – it simply had to wait;, there were more pressing things to be seen to.

He looked across the room at Nikki fast asleep on the floor on a bed of home-made cushions and rugs. John stood up and went over to Nikki. He wished his shoulder didn't hurt so much – it had become stiff while he slept and it felt as if the bandages had stuck to the wound.

'Wake up!' he said, shaking Nikki. 'We have things to do before leaving.'

Nikki sat up. 'I can't believe it,' he said. 'It's after three o'clock. I feel as if I had only just fallen asleep!' He yawned.

'Listen,' said John. 'There is something I want you to do. I want you to get sheepskin coats, hats, boots and gloves for Lisl and myself. I also want some spare sheepskins.'

'Whatever for?'

'There is only one way I can think of to get across the frontier. The Russians will have pulled out every stop, so this is the plan. I have a friend who drives a refrigerated truck from Trieste to Bucharest and back once every ten days. That's why we need the sheepskins because it will be cold in the van.'

'Are you mad?' exclaimed Nikki. 'You can't be serious!'

'Can you think of a better idea? He brings a full load of fruit and vegetables to Bucharest – which goes to the Russians and the top members of the Romanian Communist Government – then on his return journey he stops at Craiova to fill up with carcasses of meat from the abattoir. A seal is put on the doors at the abattoir and this remains unbroken until the load is delivered in Trieste – unless the Customs people are suspicious, in which case they have a look inside. But that is unlikely. There are two frontiers to cross, from Romania into Yugoslavia and from Yugoslavia into Trieste. Lisl can rest, hidden in Trieste, until I can safely take her to London.'

'But will she be able to stand the cold? What is the temperature inside one of those trucks?'

'About forty degrees Fahrenheit, but you would probably understand Celsius better. In Celsius it's about five degrees – a mild winter's day, in fact. You have it much colder here every winter – sometimes minus fifteen Celsius. I shall have to take the risk with Lisl. The temperature here now is about forty degress Celsius, so I'll try to prevent her body from losing this warmth for as long as possible by insulating her with sheepskins.'

'And what happens to me?' asked Nikki.

'When we reach Craiova our ways must part. You must go back to Bucharest as fast as possible by any means you can find. Carry on your normal life and make sure everyone believes you have been innocently occupied. If you are missing for too long people will start asking questions. We must ditch the jeep soon and get a car.'

Nikki looked at the map. 'The only possible place will be Tirgu Carbunesti.'

John was anxious for them to be on their way, but also:

'I'm hungry again,' he said. 'Do you think they'll be able to give us another meal?'

'Of course,' replied Nikki. 'These people are most hospitable.'

They went downstairs and found the woman of the house stirring a large black pot over the fire. She turned round, gave them a smile and, pointing to the pot, said, 'For you. It is simple food but good. Eat now. Here are your clothes.' She handed John his shirt she had washed. Then she placed two steaming bowls on the table.

'What is it?' asked John.

'Stewed mutton,' replied Nikki. 'Try it, you will find it excellent. It is cooked with herbs from the fields and mountains with any vegetables they happen to have – and always cabbage.'

She also put bowls of rice, black bread and goat's-milk cheese on the bare table and signalled for them to eat.

When they had finished their meal John and Nikki went upstairs to see how Lisl was and to warn her that they must leave soon. They found her sitting up in bed finishing a similar meal to the one they had just eaten. She still looked pale and drawn but the rest had obviously done her good.

She smiled when she saw them.

'How are you?' they both asked together.

'It is a wonderful bed,' she replied. 'I slept well and ate well and am feeling much better. I still cannot believe all that has happened.'

'Don't think about it,' said John. 'It's best to leave all that behind us for now and to concentrate on the present. I'm afraid it's going to be a tough journey to Trieste. We're leaving here as soon as you are ready.'

'I won't be long,' she said as they went downstairs.

John turned to Nikki. 'We have to leave now, but first you must get the sheepskin clothing we need – get a few extra skins if you can. Here is money for the skins and also for our stay. Pay them well.'

Nikki spoke to the woman, who was standing by the fire cooking the evening meal for when the men would return from the fields. She pointed out a small house where, she explained, a very old man lived alone. His wife had been long dead and he was too old to work in the fields. He spent the days treating the skins of the sheep they killed for their own use and making them into garments. Various women helped with the stitching.

Nikki began by admiring his work, then he explained what he needed. The old man got up from the pile of sheepskins he was sitting on, rubbed his chin, scratched his head and walked over to a heap of clothing in a corner. Nikki looked around. The room was full of skins; they were piled high everywhere. Together they sorted through various heaps and eventually Nikki decided on a selection of hats, gloves, boots and long coats and half a dozen extra skins.

In the meantime John had collected the jeep and parked it outside the house where Lisl was. The old man and Nikki struggled over to the jeep weighed down by the garments, and piled them in. Lisl came slowly out of the house looking pale and uncertain, with the young peasant woman's arm around her. By now women and children were crowding round the jeep, with a sprinkling of men as they came in from the fields.

John looked across at Lisl. Her face was colourless and her eyes looked larger than ever. Her fair hair had been washed and cut short. The young peasant woman had explained that after a fever it is best to cut what hair is left to make it strong. She was wearing a peasant blouse brightly embroidered with red and blue, with the round neck tied loosely in front. She was wearing a black dirndl skirt and had in her hand one of the black headscarves all peasant women wear. These generous peasants had given her their clothes.

How delicate and lovely she looks, he thought. There was a refinement about her that was exaggerated by the simple peasant clothes. John helped her into the front of the jeep, thinking she would be more comfortable there as they drove over the rough tracks.

Nikki got into the driver's seat and John sat on the sheepskins in the back. They shook the many hands hands outstretched to them, shouted their thanks and farewells and waved and drove away slowly, trying not to make too much dust as they drove past the houses. They continued waving until they were out of sight.

They left the dirt track and once on the road drove towards Tirgu Jiu. 'We must drive as fast as possible,' John urged. 'By morning the Russians will be organised and nowhere will be safe.'

'Rely on me,' replied Nikki, 'and we will be in Craiova before dawn.'

As they drove along John threw the bullet that had been taken from his shoulder into the bushes at the side of the road; it would be unwise to have a Russian bullet if they were searched; it might be connected with the shooting in the Ambassador's Residence.

They had not been driving far when Lisl complained she felt tired.

'I'll make a bed of these skins in the back here,' said John as he stood up. Nikki stopped the jeep and John jumped out. He helped her climb from the front into the back. 'Make yourself snug on these,' he said as he put them around her like a nest. Lisl lay down on the skins and shut her eyes.

After they had been driving for some time John, who had been studying the map, told Nikki to take the next turning on the left.' This is a minor road leading to Craiova,' he explained. 'We are unlikely to meet many vehicles at this hour but be ready to stop the moment you see the lights of Tirgu Carbunesti.'

It was not long before they saw lights just ahead of them.

'Swing the jeep off the road and drive deep into those bushes so that we can't be seen,' said John pointing to a copse on the right.

Nikki swung the jeep sharply to the right, off the road, and steered it through some trees round the back of the copse. He then turned it and drove into the depth of the copse so that the jeep was facing the road. The tyres made only the slightest impression on the earth baked hard by the summer sun.

John turned to Nikki. 'I don't care how you do it,' he said, 'but please find us a car – we can't drive into Craiova in this. It's only a short walk to Tirgu Carbunesti, and here's a wad of money. I'm sure you can think up an irresistible story, such as your car has broken down and your friends must get home to feed the cat!'

'What make would you prefer? Rolls Royce?' Nikkie teased, as he set off towards the lights.

John got out of the jeep and found a large branch that had fallen from a tree; he dragged it in a zig-zag pattern over the tracks the jeep had made, so that no search party would see that a vehicle had left the road. He lay down on the dry leaves beside the jeep. 'This is where we have a rest,' he said to Lisl, who was still lying on the nest of skins in the back of the jeep. 'If you can sleep, it would help you get through the difficult journey ahead.'

'Tell me about the journey,' Lisl asked. 'Which route are we taking, and how do we cross the frontier?'

'An Italian friend of mine will be collecting a load of carcasses in Craiova and will deliver them to Trieste. We'll travel with him in the back of the truck.'

'Amongst all the meat? Is that possible? How cold will it be?'

'Yes,' replied John in a quiet but firm voice. 'It *has* to be possible – there is no other way. You know how difficult it is to get out of this country. And once the truck is sealed, it is not searched at the frontier unless there is a good reason.'

'How cold will it be?'

'About five degrees Celsius.'

'My God!' exclaimed Lisl. 'Is that what these skins are for?'

'Yes, and by the time you have on one of those coats, plus hat, boots and gloves, you'll feel well prepared to face the cold. I've also got spare skins to sit on and put over us.'

The idea of being locked in a van, with no air or light surrounded by carcasses, appalled Lisl. She couldn't bear to think about it. If only she felt fit. Feeling so ill made something like this seem impossible.

'Is there no other way?' she asked.

'No, I can think of none. Think of it as sitting in the garden in mid winter, then it won't seem so bad. We'll be together and I'll try to think of amusing stories to tell you all the way.'

'I'll do my best,' she replied. 'You've done so much for me, I don't know how to repay you. I know you are risking your life for me.'

'We should get some rest while we can. You should try to sleep.' With that John stretched out and shut his eyes. He could sleep at a moment's notice anywhere; he had trained himself to do that. He knew that someone approaching would awaken him instinctively; this was

187

something else he had taught himself. He never understood how these things happened but they were invaluable in his job, just like being able to awaken at any set moment; all he had to do was to tell himself the time he wanted to wake up and he would do so at that precise moment; it never failed.

John had no idea how long he had been asleep, but when he opened his eyes he saw headlights turning off the road towards the copse. He jumped up, flicked the safety catch off his Beretta and walked towards the headlights, keeping himself covered by the undergrowth. The vehicle stopped, someone started walking towards him. He waited, then recognised the large form:

'Nikki?'

The figure stood still. 'Yes, it's me. Put that gun away – you make me nervous.'

'Did you have any trouble?' John asked anxiously.

'None at all. I explained that my car had broken down and I couldn't wait to have it repaired because my wife was having a baby and we must reach the hospital tonight. I paid quite a lot to hire it,' Nikki continued, 'but it is a Cadillac and in good shape. I checked it over and filled up with petrol.'

'Excellent!' said John. 'Now . . . '

Nikki buried the grenades and transferred the sheepskins to the car. He saw John dragging a large branch. 'Leave that to me,' he said, 'don't aggravate your shoulder. Anyway, what do you want this for?'

'We must camouflage the jeep, it's important that no one finds it. It would be best, later, if you could drive Edwin here. He'll never find it otherwise.'

John helped Lisl to the car, while Nikki covered the jeep with leafy branches.

They drove off towards Craiova.

'This is luxury!' exclaimed Lisl, stretching herself out on the back seat.

John turned towards her. 'Make the most of it while you can,' he said smiling, pleased to see her looking better.

24

Boris Molohovski had received a message which he deciphered himself. It was marked for his eyes only, top secret and immediate. It read:

Harcourt last seen in Romania with Austrian woman Elizabeth von Althof. Watch all crossing points from Austria and Yugoslavia. Interrogate and dispose leaving no trace.

The message had come from Moscow.

A long drawn out *Ahhh!* came from Molohovski. So that is what Harcourt has been up to, he thought, and wondered how he had slipped through the net and got out of Trieste without his knowledge.

He summoned his aides and the intelligence staff and gave them their orders. Finally he said, 'I do not want a border incident. No one must be able to trace their deaths back to us. If anyone makes a mistake in any way there will be serious consequences. They must be caught and killed at all costs. This office will be manned day and night, so keep me informed.'

They went silently away to carry out the Colonel's orders.

Next, Molohovski called his Deputy in to take charge of the office while he himself visited contacts in Trieste to discover if Harcourt had already returned. He immediately called on his opposite number in the Yugoslav Embassy.

Stanko Logar greeted Molohovski with his accustomed civility. After a friendly greeting he asked, 'And what can I do for you this morning?'

'My dear Stanko,' said Molohovski with studied informality, 'I was just passing and realised it is a long time since I have seen you, so decided to visit you on the spur of the moment. I hope you don't mind.'

'Of course not. Delighted to see you at any time. Let me pour you some tuica, or perhaps you would prefer vodka?'

'Tuica would do splendidly.'

Logar selected two small glassed and filled them to the rim. With a steady hand he put them on a small table and sat down on the sofa beside his guest. They each took a sip and swallowed slowly, savouring the first drink of the day.

'Have you seen any of our friends recently?' inquired Molohovski.

'I was at a party given by the British Consulate last night. All the usual people were there. The food was good.'

'Was Harcourt there?' asked Molohovski, with careful casualness.

'I do not remember seeing him,' replied Logar. 'But the room was full and I could have missed him.'

'It is of no importance,' replied Molohovski. 'It was just that I have not seen him around these last few days and if there is something happening we communists must stick together – you agree?'

'Of course,' agreed Stanko. 'Have no fear on that score.'

'I have reason to believe that Mr Harcourt is trying to bring someone into your country illegally and then to come on here. He would be coming from Romania. I would be personally grateful for your co-operation.' Molohovski put his glass on the table and looked Logar straight in the eye.

'Can you tell me more about who will be coming with Mr Harcourt?'

'I can only tell you that she is a young woman. It is of the greatest importance that we are informed immediately where and when they arrive. It could make it very awkward for Marshall Tito when he goes to Moscow next week if they travelled through your country and we were not informed. You understand?'

'I understand completely, but I hope you intend no incident in our country.'

'Of course not. You have my word on it. No harm will come to either of them in any way. We just want to ask the lady one or two questions in connection with a former Russian lover she had. I like what little I know of Mr Harcourt and would wish him no harm. After all, he is one of us. We are all engaged in the same sort of work,' he added smiling.

'You can rely completely on our full co-operation. I will take action immediately to have our borders watched for them. Rest assured they will not slip through.'

Molohovski stood up. 'I am most grateful,' he said, 'and if there is anything we can ever do to help you, you only have to ask. I will detain you no longer.'

They shook hands warmly, and Logar escorted Molohovski to the door.

When Stanko was alone he sat quite still, deep in thought. A few pieces of the jigsaw puzzle were falling into place, but there were still some important pieces missing. He realised that something unusual was afoot for Molohovski to have become personally involved and for Harcourt to be escorting this unknown woman from Romania. Who could the woman be? He was quite certain the Russians had poisoned Harcourt's predecessor, and he hoped Harcourt himself would survive. He had always liked him and they had helped each other in the past.

He signalled the Ministry of the Interior in Belgrade, asking to be informed personally if John Harcourt, accompanied by a woman, arrived in Yugoslavia, probably from Romania. He informed them of the Russian interest. He then ordered his people to keep a vigilant watch on the frontier and throughout the Free Territories, both Zones *A* and *B*.

25

Sir Gerald Downey walked briskly into Section *B*.

Hugh jumped to his feet. 'Good morning, sir,' he said. 'We didn't expect you back for another two days.'

'I wasn't needed any longer,' replied Sir Gerald, walking over to the window. 'My sister has her family to support her and, as you know, I'm concerned about our chaps on the Continent. What's the latest news?'

'I've contacted every intelligence network and agency and our own agents personally. No one has seen or heard anything of Harcourt – with just one exception: Edwin Hobbs said he couldn't speak at the moment and would come back to me, but he has not done so. Romania is a long shot but I thought it worth trying. I was planning to go to Trieste myself to see what I could find out on the spot.'

'No,' replied Sir Gerald, walking back across the room. He stood with his hand on the door handle. 'It's better for you to stay here and keep tabs on everyone and be ready to rescue Harcourt – so long as it doesn't compromise us or any of our people. This includes friendly Governments.'

'Understood, sir. We've also been unable to find out what's happened to Elizabeth von Althof.'

'Well, if we don't hear soon we can presume her dead. She was still suffering from typhoid when she was kidnapped and could not survive too much rough treatment.'

'That would be a disaster, sir, since it is she who probably has the vital information for which Fenton and Wilson have already been killed – and now perhaps Harcourt as well.'

'I know all that,' said Sir Gerald tersely, 'but never cry over spilt milk. One thing is certain, we cannot go on losing agents of this calibre at this rate, or there will be an investigation and if the press gets hold of it then all hell will break loose. Keep me informed of events, no matter what time of the day or night. By the way, you'd better earmark a replacement for Harcourt.'

'Yes, sir. I'll see to that.'

That evening Hugh talked the whole episode over with Julia. 'Gerald must be exhausted,' she said, 'travelling to the south of France and back and attending a funeral all within these few days. How did he look?'

'Terrible! And so was his temper, but he held a tight rein on himself. I breathed more easily when he'd left the room – he might have exploded at any moment.'

Julia got up from the armchair and went over to the sofa. She sat beside Hugh and took his hand. 'You know John and I worked together for quite a time, and I simply refuse to believe that anything awful has happened to him. He has a sixth sense. He used to say how he felt the bristles go up on the back of his neck and a tingling go down his spine when there was danger threatening and this had always given him just enough time. Don't be depressed, darling, it never helps.' She kicked off her shoes, tucked her feet up on the sofa and gave Hugh a reassuring smile.

'I know,' he replied wearily. 'And Gerald fears an Inquiry. Every Member of Parliament believes he knows better than anyone else how to run the security services. They make me see red. They stand up in the House, spouting away about something they don't begin to understand. They're just a bloody nuisance!'

'Don't get too het up darling. What you need is food!' and she wriggled her feet into her shoes and led the way to the dining room.

'Dick even suggested that John could have defected,' continued Hugh.

'Never!' exclaimed Julia, leaning across the table towards him. 'That is out of the question. It's not part of his character. So forget it. Anyway, what made Dick suggest it?'

'Something Gerald said to him, but he didn't tell me what it was. But in one thing Dick is right – and that is, when someone is missing and security is involved, one mustn't let personal relationships blur one's judgment. Every possibility must be considered.'

'Perhaps John had no time to let you know what he's up to. Or he may have sent a message that never arrived, and is unaware that you don't know.'

'You're very loyal.'

'It was you who said we must consider every possibility!' Julia replied archly, smiling at him.

He walked round the table and, standing behind her chair, placed his hands on her shoulders. She leaned back, placed her hands over his and raised her face. She felt his waistcoat buttons dig into the top of her head as he leaned over and kissed her lightly on her forehead.

'Thank you for a delicious meal,' he said affectionately. Julia always made him feel better; more relaxed. He smelt the fragrance that was always about her in the evening. A mixture of make-up, hair shampoo and the scent he always gave her, Jean Patou's 'Moment Supreme'.

Next morning Hugh walked into Dick Reynold's office and found the Chief there discussing the effects on the Intelligence set-up should Harcourt have defected to the Russians, or been a double agent all along. Sir Gerald said the possibility must be considered, but warned against getting jumpy and seeing spies under the bed. He stressed the importance of keeping him informed immediately about anything and everything in this connection, no matter how trivial.

26

Nikki drove into the outskirts of Craiova as dawn was breaking. The town was already beginning to stir and John suggested they stop at the first café that was open. The area was dirty and run-down, but Nikki saw a café owner putting tables on the pavement outside his café. He stopped the car and John got out.

'Beggars can't be choosers!' he said as he opened the back door to help Lisl out.

They found a table at the back of the café where Nikki ordered coffee and bread. They were soon given three steaming cups of strong black coffee and some slices of heavy black bread. The coffee was foul but they were grateful for the hot liquid and, as they finished, John and Nikki felt the tiredness leave them; they were revived.

Nikki paid and asked if the abattoir was in the area.

'No,' replied the owner, 'you will have to drive nearly to the centre of the town.' He appeared to be running the café on his own. He was short and dark with small brown eyes that looked quickly from face to face. He moved quickly, clearing the table and wiping over the wooden surface with a grubby cloth as he spoke.

'Could you tell us exactly how to get there?' Nikki asked.

'Follow this road for about two kilometres. You will then come to a junction of five roads. Do not take the first three roads, but take the fourth one. Drive along the road a short way and take the second turning on the left. Go round a corner then take the first on the right. It is the building on the right. You will see the area for cattle beside it.'

They got back in the car and drove off following the

directions they had been given. The abattoir was not difficult to find. There were a few soldiers about and some policemen, but no one took any notice of them. All was activity and noise. The iron pens were mostly full of pigs, while the cows and sheep were on the spare ground being tended by their owners with the help of shepherds, cowherds and dogs.

John and Lisl remained in the car while Nikki went in search of someone who could tell him when Valentino was expected. He asked in the office. They knew Valentino; he was a regular customer. They could not say when he would be arriving; perhaps today, perhaps tomorrow or even the next day. They would just have to wait.

Nikki parked the car under a tree in order to get some shade during the hottest part of the day. They made Lisl as comfortable as possible on the back seat; so long as the car remained in the shade with the doors open, it was bearable. John sometimes sat in the car and at other times wandered about, but he never went far from Lisl.

Nikki had disappeared a little while ago. He now returned with his arms full of bottles of lemonade, a large water melon, bunches of black grapes and, in his hands, thick slices of dark bread with slices of beef between them. A broad smile of satisfaction had spread across his face.

'Look what I've managed to find!' he said, dropping it all on the front seat of the car.

'You are wonderful!' said Lisl, sitting upright and looking much brighter. 'How could you have guessed that the one thing I wanted in life was a water melon?'

'I just knew,' grinned Nikki. Meanwhile John had used his knife to cut the melon into portions. There was silence as they first ate the water melon and then devoured the bread and meat.

'I was in need of that,' said John, carefully wiping his

knife and concealing it again in his clothing. He opened a bottle of lemonade and passed it to Lisl. She had trouble drinking direct from the bottle. They all laughed as the lemonade ran down her chin. She handed the bottle back to John. 'By the end of today I shall be as good as you two,' she joked. There was an easy camaraderie between the three of them, as if they were old friends.

John and Nikki decided to take it in turns to sleep while the other kept watch; from the car they could see the office where the truck drivers had to report before loading. This helped to relieve the tedium of waiting.

As night came on, the abattoir closed and the place cleared of people. Those who had driven their cattle in, now drove them back to spend the night in the fields on the edge of the town, where the cattle could graze and be given water. They would return at dawn and be the first to be slaughtered in the morning. Any trucks still full of cattle unloaded their cargo into the now empty pens and these would also be slaughtered the following morning.

In order not to be too conspicuous, they left the abattoir and drove down a nearby road out of the town until they found woods where they could park the car, hidden from the road by the trees. They felt tired with the boredom of hanging about, so they set about getting some rest, but one of the men was always awake on guard throughout the night.

Next morning, when they reckoned the abattoir would be busy and they would not be noticed, they drove back and parked under the same tree and settled down to another day of waiting.

John walked amongst the cattle and lorries looking for Valentino. His great fear was that he might miss him; there was so little organisation. Trucks were left wherever the driver felt inclined and cattle wandered about among them.

It was amazing how the owners knew their own cattle. The man at the gates of the slaughterhouse decided whose turn it would be by whistling and shouting to the herdsmen and drivers. Then amid much shouting, running, barking and waving of sticks, the cattle would be driven through the gates, which were then shut until the next batch were required.

Suddenly John saw Valentino. He came out of the office carrying a large piece of paper in his hand and disappeared among the trucks. John almost ran, fearful of losing him and, at the same time, afraid of drawing attention to himself. As fast as he dared he wove in and out of the trucks, looking to right and to left and often turning round. He stumbled and almost fell as a pig rushed through his legs pursued by a ragged urchin. Valentino was his only hope; if he drove away without them . . . No, he would not think about that; he must find him.

As he rushed round a truck, he came face to face with him.

'Valentino!' he cried, clasping Valentino's arms with both his hands, 'thank God I've found you,' he said in Italian.

'*Mamma mia!*' shouted Valentino, looking shocked. 'Carlo, what are you doing here? Are you in trouble? Where are you rushing to?' Valentino held up both hands in bewilderment and looked uncomprehendingly at John.

'I need your help,' said John desperately. 'You'll remember when I left you in Bucharest, I told you I was visiting a friend while her husband was away?'

Valentino nodded.

'Well, he has been so cruel to her that she can stay with him no longer and is coming to live with me. You know how impossible it is for anyone to leave this country – she would be imprisoned, tortured and probably killed if she were caught. You must help me, Valentino.' John pleaded.

Valentino shook his head. 'No, that is impossible. I can take you, but no one else. You have a passport. It is too dangerous to smuggle someone out. You realise the consequences if we were caught? No, I am not yet ready to leave this life!' He was shouting and gesticulating.

'Come and meet her,' John took Valentino by the arm and led him to the car. 'She's in a friend's car. He's a good friend and has risked a lot for both of us.'

They walked in silence to the car.

'This is my friend Nikki, who drove us here,' said John. Then he introduced Valentino, and added:

'He says he cannot help us.'

'Impossible! Impossible!' Valentino emphasized vehemently.

Nikki walked off and left them.

John turned to Lisl. 'You must meet my friend Valentino too,' he said. 'He has disappointing news for us, in that he's afraid to help us.'

Lisl smiled at Valentino and held out her hand. He took her hand, kissed it, and suddenly realised how thin and delicate it was. He then noticed how frail and fragile she looked.

'You are so thin and pale – you look as if you need some good meat!' Valentino said jokingly, pointing to the abattoir. They laughed and John hurried to say:

'I told you her husband ill-treated her. This is how I found her. I couldn't leave her in this condition. I *had* to bring her with me. I bet you would have done the same,' he added.

At that moment Nikki returned with a bottle of wine in each hand. 'One must never miss an occasion for a drink,' he said, beaming at Valentino. 'Let us drink to you and your journey and to friendship!' He handed one bottle to Valentino and put the other to his lips. He then passed his bottle to John.

Lisl refused wine.

The three men sat on the grass beside the car talking and drinking. John and Nikki shared one bottle; Valentino drank the other easily by himself. Their conversation was light and easy, with Valentino doing most of the talking. Lisl was sitting in the car, half listening to them and at times lost in her own private thoughts.

Valentino stood up. 'I can stay no longer,' he announced. 'I must load the truck and be on my way.'

The other two men rose too. 'Just a minute, my friend,' said Nikki, putting an arm round Valentino's shoulder. 'I have never heard of an Italian who refused to help a lady in danger. As you can see, her husband has nearly killed her already. Do you want the *Securitate* to finish off the job? They would not be very nice to her, as you know.' (Lisl winced.) 'It is not really so dangerous,' continued Nikki. 'Just put Lisl in the back of your truck behind the meat and put Carlo there to keep her warm,' and he laughed at his own suggestion.

'It's true, Valentino,' urged John. 'And once the doors have been locked and the seal put on, they will not be opened until you unload in Trieste.'

'But first the meat has to be loaded,' said Valentino, obviously agitated. 'How to load the meat with the official watching all the time and to hide Carlo and Lisl without anyone seeing? It is impossible!'

'Look at this beautiful sick lady. You *have* to help her.' Nikki put his arm around Valentino's shoulders. They were both of Latin races and understood each other. 'Our friend Carlo has something for you – he knows you will want to help him,' continued Nikki persuasively, looking meaningfully at John, who took some paper money from his pocket and handed it discreetly to Valentino.

'Perhaps you could use some of these notes to persuade the official to go for a little walk,' John suggested. He went to the car and rummaged under the front seat and brought out a round tin of Player's cigarettes and gave it to Valentino. 'I believe a few cigarettes work miracles in this country,' he said. 'There are fifty in this tin.'

'Ah!' said Valentino taking the tin. 'With this I can do business.' The wine had done its work and Valentino was wavering. He looked at Lisl. 'She will never survive the cold,' he said.

'As it happens, we have sheepskin coats, hats, boots and gloves with us,' John explained.

'At this time of the year!' exclaimed Valentino.

They looked at each other and then they began laughing.

'You had the whole thing worked out,' said Valentino, grinning. He slapped John on the back. 'All right, I will do this for you Carlo and' – he turned to Lisl – 'for this beautiful lady. But I must make one thing clear. If it goes wrong and you are discovered, I shall deny knowing you or even having seen you before.'

'That's understood,' said John.

'Where are all these sheepskins?' Valentino asked.

John and Nikki staggered with them from the car. They had been made with the hide on the inside and the untrimmed, unwashed wool on the outside. In the winter, the Romanian soldiers on sentry duty always wore similar sheepskin coats in order to survive the very low winter temperatures. This is what had given John the idea.

'When do we get into the truck?' Lisl asked anxiously.

'As soon as I am loaded and ready to go,' Valentino explained. 'Get over near the meat store,' he continued, 'but try to look as if you are part of the scene. Once I am

202

loaded and have lured the official away, you two get in and put those clothes on. Remember, don't make a sound while the doors are open.'

'While we're waiting for you to load, could Lisl sit in the cab while Nikki and I stand about?' John suggested, knowing that Lisl would be unable to stand for long.

Valentino readily agreed.

They locked the car and walked over to the truck which was parked a little way off beside the meat store.

'Perhaps we could share a bottle of wine in Bucharest on my next run,' Valentino suggested to Nikki as he climbed into the truck. Nikki was delighted at the suggestion. 'That is a date I shall look forward to,' he replied as he handed the sheepskin clothing to Valentino, who put them in a corner at the back of the truck with the hats and boots at the bottom, making it look like a pile of old skins.

While Valentino went off to the meat store, John helped Lisl up the high step into the cab and shut the door, leaving the window open. He and Nikki walked a little way off. They watched as Valentino returned with the official followed by a string of loaders bent over by the weight of huge sides of beef and carcasses of lamb and pork. This was the moment of parting between John and Nikki. They both felt how a bond had grown between them in this short time, born of danger and excitement. John was drawing patterns in the dust with his shoe. Nikki could not stand still; he walked up and down as if waiting for a train. Then he said quietly, 'I don't want to quit now. Couldn't I come as far as Trieste? Then I would feel the job done.'

'No, Nikki,' John replied firmly. 'Your job is done here and I'm more grateful than words can say for your help and comradeship. It's been most successful so far – gone like clockwork – and much of it was your doing. I couldn't have managed without you. Of one thing I'm certain, that

203

it was you and your vino that made Valentino change his mind and risk taking us to Trieste. Don't forget to let Edwin know where his jeep is hidden and, most important, not a murmur to anyone about this little operation.'

'I promise,' said Nikki sadly.

They shook hands and Nikki walked over to Lisl to bid her farewell and a good journey. He then went over to the car determined not to leave until they were safely on their way.

John wandered over to the truck and stood by the cab door.

Valentino stood beside the truck checking his list as the loaders toiled from the meat store with their loads. They were experienced at this work and while two stood in the truck hanging the vast sides of beef on large hooks and stacking the smaller carcasses of lamb and pork on either side of the vehicle in order to make a balanced load, the loaders worked nonstop until the official told them to halt. The official and Valentino checked their papers and nodded to the loaders that all was in order and they could go.

As the loaders went into the meat store Valentino turned to the official, whom he knew from previous visits and asked:

'Would you like a nice piece of meat for your family?' Without waiting for a reply he took a long butcher's knife from a piece of cloth that had been lying on the floor at the side of the truck and, jumping into the truck, cut off a generous chunk of rump steak.

'Take this,' said Valentino, wrapping the meat in the cloth that had been round the knife. I know it is impossible to buy beef here because of the price. Put it directly in your car, no one will know.'

The official looked quickly around and saw that there was no one nearby and no one looking in their direction.

He grabbed the meat and went quickly to his car which was parked on the far side of the meat store. Valentino looked round the truck.

'Quick!' he hissed to John. In a flash John had lifted Lisl out of the cab and run round the back of the truck with her. He jumped into the truck and turned round to help her, but Valentino was already there. He picked her up and put her inside.

'Get to the back and put on the sheepskins while the doors are open, but remain hidden and silent,' he whispered urgently as John helped Lisl past the carcasses.

The truck was a six-wheeler with doors only at the back. The cab was separate. There were four rails running the length of the truck on which were hanging carcasses of beef reaching down to the floor, almost touching it. On either side of the truck and on the floor between the hanging carcasses were the carcasses of sheep and pigs, lying everywhere. John had helped Lisl to get to the back of the truck, stumbling over carcasses and pushing aside the hanging beef. They quickly put on the sheepskin clothing. The coats were very long and came to the ground; the fleece on the outside was long and thick and sticky from the lanolin in the wool. As they were putting on their hats they heard the doors bang shut and, whereas it had been dim before, the inside of the truck was now pitch-black.

They could see nothing.

After the official returned, he put a seal on the doors. 'Have a good journey,' he said as Valentino switched on the refrigeration before climbing into the cab and starting up the engine. As he passed Nikki he gave him a discreet thumbs-up sign; Nikki winked and drove off.

27

'We must look like a couple of sheep,' said John, determined to keep their spirits up.

Lisl laughed. 'My coat is so long I can't move,' she said,
'but thank God we're on our way.' The truck lurched and
bumped over the pot-holes; she clutched John and the
carcasses all around them prevented her from falling.

'Hold on a moment,' said John as he went on his hands
and knees searching for the spare skins. He felt around and
gathered them into a corner. He needed more room and
it was difficult being in such total blackness. He pushed
some carcasses, but they were so heavy they only moved
a little way. He stretched a sheepskin on the floor and then
stood up.

'I've put a sheepskin on the floor beside you – let me
guide you.'

As she moved she stumbled over her coat, which was
trailing on the floor. John grabbed her and picked her up
to put her on the sheepskin.

'Oh!' she cried. 'Oh! I can't bear it!'

'What is it?'

'I hit something, it scratched my face, it was hard and
cold. I can't go through with it. The smell is terrible! So is
the blackness! I can't bear to touch all these things around.
I had no idea it would be like this!'

John sat her on the sheepskin. He placed another one at
her back, draped it around her as best he could, then leant
against the wall and slid down on to the floor beside her. She
was silent and John hoped that she would eventually sleep.

But then she began sobbing.

'Cheer up,' he said gently. 'Look on the bright side.' He

put an arm round her shoulders. 'You have already escaped the Russians and the *Securitate*, and we're on our way to freedom,' he spoke positively and cheerfully.

He gave her an encouraging squeeze. 'You're still ill,' he said. 'That's why you feel like this. I warned you it would be uncomfortable – tell yourself you *can* do it. *Will* yourself to survive. Remember I will look after you.' With that he pulled a spare sheepskin over them.

Her sobbing abated and she sniffed.

'I've never yet met a girl who wept and had a handker-chief! Borrow mine,' John said. He held it in front of what he believed to be her face. She took it and blew her nose noisily then gave it back to him. She was recovering.

It was strange sitting there in pitch darkness. They sat close together, fearful that if the truck lurched too violently they might be hit by a swinging carcass. They sat in silence; learning to accept the discomfort, the bumps, the sudden lurches, the idea of all that meat around them and so near, but above all the darkness and the cold air getting gradually colder. The cold was made worse by the fact that their bodies had become acclimatized to the very hot summer. John pulled the sheepskin up over their heads and faces in order to keep the cold air out.

Lisl had her head on his shoulder and seemed composed and silent.

And so the time passed.

The last few days had been so full of action and danger. Now John could only rely on Valentino to deliver them into Trieste. He knew that the net would be closing in on them and he wanted to use this enforced inactivity to think over the last few hectic days.

He was certain he had not been mistaken about who he had seen at the Russian Ambassador's Residence when he rescued Lisl that night. There could be no reasonable explanation for his presence there. And if it was as John feared? It was too awful to contemplate. The question really worrying him was: had he himself been recognised despite his disguise? Although he had spoken only one or two sentences, and those in Russian, his voice might have given him away. Also, their eyes had met. And in that moment, when time stood still, he felt he had been recognised.

What could he do?

Where could he turn?

He knew he was in mortal danger and would not be safe even in Trieste. Worse still, not even in England. He must contact Hugh, but not on the telephone. He would have to risk it and go to London. The trouble was that everything would be denied and he would be accused of losing his mind. Or a case of mistaken identity. Just one person's word against another's. His mind raced on and he had no idea how long he had been sitting there. He now knew what it was like to be a fugitive.

'I am so very cold. I can't stop shivering,' complained Lisl.

John came back to the present with a jolt. He took off his gloves and felt her hands. They were frozen. He felt her body shivering. Her face was like ice.

'My coat is huge,' he said. 'There's room for both of us. Put your arms out of your coat but keep it on your back and come inside my coat. I'll make you warm.'

He put his arms around her cold, shivering body and pulled her to him. He pulled the sheepskin round them and put one over their heads. Lisl snuggled up to him, putting her face against his neck and her hands on his chest. Slowly the heat of his body stopped her shivering and the warmth went through her.

The closeness of her body disturbed him. He thought of

past loves and of Anna and wondered if he would ever see her again. No matter how he felt now about Lisl, he knew he could never take advantage of the situation they were in. Yet he did not deny to himself that he found her very desirable.

'Are you feeling better?' he asked.

'Yes, much better. I feel myself again.'

'Good. Now tell me something. Did you know that James had been killed?'

'Oh, no!' she exclaimed. 'He was going to London to explain that I have some very important information for the British Government. What happened?'

'He was murdered and thrown out of the Simplon Orient on his way to London. He was to have stopped off in Trieste to see me.'

'Who killed him?'

'I don't know, but I can make a shrewd guess it was our friends the Russians. After Radu Negulescu visited you, he was found in his bed shot through the head. Then, after you were kidnapped, Doctor Ionnitiu and his wife were arrested and have not been heard of since.'

She gasped. 'This is terrible, and the doctor was so kind to me. I'm so afraid. How can we hope to escape them?' It was more a statement than a question.

'We can,' replied John. 'But we must be constantly on our guard – both the Russians and the *Securitate* will be looking for us.'

Just then the truck stopped.

'The frontier. This must be Turnu Severin,' John whispered. They held their breath, trying to hear. They could hear Valentino: he seemed to be shouting. Then there were other voices; these now moved round to the back of the truck, near the doors. John pushed Lisl gently away from him and took out his Beretta. Very carefully he stood up, pressing his back against the wall of the truck, trying not to touch the carcasses. He stood there ready. He wasn't going to be caught unarmed, and neither would he give in easily.

Then there was laughter. Some more loud voices, but they were moving away from the truck. A door slammed and the truck jolted forward.

'Well done Valentino!' said John, flicking back the safety catch. 'Now we have no-man's-land, then the Yugoslav border.'

'What do you think Valentino did?'

'I expect he bribed them. The frontier guards will sell their souls for a few cigarettes.'

'We need luck,' Lisl murmured, almost to herself.

No-man's-land seemed wider than John had remembered it to be. He remained standing, being careful to keep his balance as the truck bumped along. It was no good deciding what to do beforehand, he would have to wait and see what happened and then make a split-second decision.

The truck slowed down, finally stopping with a jerk. John nearly fell over. This time there were voices immediately at the back of the truck and they could hear Valentino shouting.

Then the heavy doors were swung open.

'There is the meat,' Valentino was saying; he sounded angry. 'I bring the same load every time; and this is my usual load. You never wanted to see it before. Why today?'

'Strict orders from Belgrade to search everything, even refrigerated trucks. A soldier jumped into the truck. 'Bring a torch, Maric,' he called to a comrade. He had turned with his back to John and was facing outwards with his hand outstretched waiting for someone to bring the torch.

John had caught hold of Lisl and pulled her face down on to the floor of the truck. She was completely covered in sheepskin. He squatted down beside her putting an arm protectively over her. His coat was right up over his face and his eyes looked out through the long, shaggy fleece that hung down from his conical sheepskin hat. He had his pistol ready beneath his coat for fear the light might shine on the metal.

They hardly dared breathe.

The soldier took the torch and began flashing the light around the truck. He prodded at the hanging sides of beef with the end of his rifle and kicked at the carcasses lying on the floor. He took a few steps into the truck and, flashing his torch around, peered into the back. 'You've got some good sheepskins there,' he said. 'You won't miss one.' He lunged forward, caught hold of the fleece of the skin covering Lisl, and at the same time turned, dragging the skin behind him, stumbling over the carcasses and knocking into the hanging beef.

John had frozen and was absolutely still, tense and ready. As the soldier caught hold of the fleece and turned, he lifted the arm that was over Lisl so that the soldier could drag the skin easily away. He feared she might move or cry out.

The soldier jumped out of the truck and immediately there were noisy arguments over the sheepskin.

The doors banged shut. There was much talking as the Yugoslav Customs sealed the load. With no show of haste, Valentino climbed into the cab and, with his usual cheerful farewell, drove off.

As the truck moved away John relaxed. 'Are you all right?' he asked. 'That was a near thing. I thought for a moment we'd had it.'

'I thought I should die,' she replied, sitting up. 'I felt my heart stop beating.'

'You did well. You remained silent and you didn't move. That's what saved us. We're now in Yugoslavia, but they have obviously been alerted and are co-operating.' Then he asked:

'We have one sheepskin less, are you very cold?'

'Yes. It seems to get colder and colder in here,' she replied.

'The fan makes it worse,' John replied. 'They have to keep the air moving or the meat would go bad. But I have been colder and more uncomfortable, and somehow that helps. It's much harder for you because you are ill. By rights you should be in a nice warm bed with people fussing over you and pandering to your slightest whim. Instead all I can offer you is an arm to go round you, a body to keep you warm and a shoulder on which to rest your head.'

'I'm not complaining,' she said weakly, 'but I feel so tired and ill and weak and unhappy that I just want to . . . ' She began to sob.

'Don't cry,' he pleaded. 'It will make you feel worse. You're still alive and you will recover from this fever and from the ordeal you've been through. Just hang on a little longer, and I'll find you food and comfort in Trieste. Come,' he said drawing her close to him. He wrapped the sheepskins around them, pulling one right over their faces. When you're warmer you'll feel more cheerful.'

'I'll be all right,' she replied with more composure, 'people have lived through much worse. I'll try to sleep.'

'Good,' he replied, holding her tightly. 'I shall probably doze off myself.

She put her head on his shoulder and he rested his head on hers.

But neither was able to sleep. Besides the cold, there was the movement of air and the noise of the fan, combined with the hardness of the floor. There was also so very little room to move. Lisl was just grateful for the warmth of his body. They remained still and silent, absorbed in their own thoughts until they felt the truck stopping and starting and the noise of traffic. Then the truck stopped altogether and the cab door slammed shut.

'This must be Belgrade,' John said quietly. 'Valentino is probably having something to eat in one of the little cafés.'

'Lucky Valentino!' said Lisl.

'How I could do with a good steak!'

'Don't mention meat!' protested Lisl. 'I don't think I shall ever eat meat again after this journey!'

'Lisl, I don't want to distress you, but did you realise that everyone who has had contact with you has been killed?'

There was a long pause, then she said in a strained voice, 'You are telling me that Aleksandr Petrovich is dead?'

'Yes.'

'I knew it! I knew it! I have known it for a long time,' but the hurt was still so great; she had buried it away and now it had been resurrected. Because of what John had just told her, there was no longer any doubt or hope; just a vast blankness stretching to eternity. She felt numbed, mentally and physically.

The cab door slammed and the truck jolted forward, stopping and starting, obviously still in Belgrade. After a time the driving became less irregular and John guessed they had left Belgrade behind and were on their way to Zagreb and Trieste.

The silence continued until John could bear it no longer. 'Lisl, are you all right?' he asked gently.

She didn't speak. He wished he could see her face. It was so difficult talking into the darkness. Although the road from Belgrade to Zagreb was straight and it was possible to drive really fast, it was a long way, especially when there was nothing to see. Just blackness. He felt Lisl shudder. He held her tightly and kissed her very gently on the top of her head. 'We must accept that we have a long, cold, tedious ride ahead of us,' he said.

'I know,' she whispered, and put her head on his shoulder again.

At long last they reached the Yugoslav–Trieste border at Sezana. The truck stopped and there was the usual shouting around the truck that John now associated with border crossings. Nothing happened and the truck moved on.

They were now driving through no-man's-land. They had left Yugoslavia behind and were on their way to the Free Territory of Trieste.

'Just hold on a little longer,' John urged. 'We're nearly there.'

'I feel faint,' she said.

'Just a little longer,' he pleaded. 'I know you can do it. You'll feel better once we're out of this truck. If I could have my arm back for a little while? It's felt dead for some time.' As he pulled his arm away his fingers had pins and needles. He stood up and swung his arm, which hit a carcass – it was hard and painful. So he just stood still and let time do its job.

It was only a short journey to the Trieste side of the border. The truck stopped and there was immediately a great deal of shouting. There always was, thought John, when a group of Triestinis got together. He could hear Valentino's voice, louder than the others.

'Ah! Luigi, you are coming with me? Good.' Valentino shouted. 'Jump in and we go. I'm ready for my bed.'

'Not so fast,' replied the Custom's officer in charge. 'I see from your papers that you have a load of meat from Romania. Correct, or not?'

'Correct. My usual load from Craiova.'

'Then why is there a Yugoslav seal on the door?'

'The Yugoslavs did it!' shouted Valentino, waving his arms in a gesture of helplessness. 'I loaded up as usual in Craiova, but when I reached the Yugoslav border at Turnu

Severin, the Customs officials broke the seal and made no trouble, so why do you? If Luigi comes with me he can inspect the load when we reach the warehouse.'

'Sorry, Valentino, but we must open the truck. It is irregular to have papers of loading from one country and a seal from another,' replied the Customs official, firmly. 'I trust you, my friend, but I do not trust the Yugoslavs! You know how they are!'

'*Mamma mia!*' shouted Valentino angrily, 'how many times must this truck be opened? The meat will be bad before I unload!'

'I will be quick.' The official went close to Valentino and whispered, 'Do you see that car over there?' indicating a small, black saloon parked a little distance from the border crossing. 'Those men are Russian agents, they arrived last night and have been there ever since. We can take no chances, because they may be trying to smuggle someone or something into our country.'

John and Lisl heard the seal snap. The doors were undone and swung open. Bright sunlight streamed into the truck, filtering through the carcasses. The warmth swept in. They were hidden under the sheepskins lying among the sheep and pig carcasses.

The officer was in uniform and armed; he was slight and neat. He sprang lightly into the truck and looked around. 'You must ask me to dinner,' he quipped.

'Any time. You're most welcome,' replied Valentino, affably. 'Which do you prefer, beef or lamb?'

'Always beef,' came the definite reply.

'I'll remember,' said Valentino, as he watched the official walking further into the truck. It took time because the officer did not like touching the meat with his hands, neither did he like the carcasses to come into contact with his uniform. He was a smart and fastidious man.

He was doing a thorough job working his way towards the back.

'The sun is hot on the meat, all the cool air will have escaped by now.' Valentino was becoming anxious.

The official peered around and began clearing a way to go in a little further when he heard his colleague calling him. He turned his head and saw the men from the saloon car standing by the truck, peering in.

He quickly retraced his steps and jumped down from the truck. 'Clear the area!' he ordered. 'Your load is in order,' he shouted to Valentino, who hurriedly shut the large doors. 'I'm in charge. What do you want?' he asked the Russians, pulling himself up to his full height. 'This is the inspection area and I will have no strangers or unauthorised people here.'

He stood glaring at them, full of importance, but within himself worried and uncertain about what he should do about these uninvited observers. He watched Valentino drive away.

The Russians did not answer. They studied their feet and with downcast eyes and hands in their pockets, they walked over to their car and resumed their vigil.

The Customs official went into the Customs' shed, picked up the telephone, rang his Headquarters in Trieste and told them of his problem. They promised to send out a Russian-speaking liaison officer.

As Valentino drove away, John clutched Lisl. 'We've made it! Do you realise we've made it?' he cried, kissing her on both cheeks.

Tears ran down her face.

28

John knew they were in Trieste by the familiar noises. The hooting of cars with their impatient drivers, the ringing of church bells, the shouting and the clanging and clatter of trams.

'We mustn't be seen getting out,' he said. 'How do you feel?'

'Horrible,' she replied. 'I don't think I can stand and I certainly can't walk. I feel dizzy. I think it's my heart.'

'Don't worry. Leave it to me – I'll carry you.' John felt elated, although he knew they were still in danger which could strike at any moment. But at least this part had been accomplished.

The truck came slowly to a halt and Valentino backed it right up to the doors of the meat warehouse. He climbed out of the cab and walked round to the back of the truck where he was greeted by the foreman.

'You're late, Valentino,' he complained. 'I've been waiting for you, as you know there is no one about during the siesta time. No one to unload. Where have you been? What have you been doing?'

Valentino thew up his hands. 'I've been driving, driving, *driving!* he shouted angrily. 'And I'm hot and tired. Where do you think I've been? What do you think I've been doing?' he demanded loudly, 'I've had the load searched twice. Once by the Yugoslavs, and then again here. Something is going on. There were some Russians sitting in a car on the border as if they were waiting for someone.'

'You'd better come back at five o'clock when the others are here. I'm going off now. I was only waiting for you.'

Valentino climbed wearily back into the cab and drove

through Trieste as fast as the traffic would allow, swearing and hooting at anyone who got in his way. The town was fairly clear at this hour in the afternoon and he soon reached his home. The truck stopped with a jerk and Valentino slumped and gave a sigh of relief. The strain had been greater than he realised. He felt all in. What a fool he was to have agreed to do this. He always told himself he would never do this sort of thing again; but when John asked him he found it difficult to refuse. Somehow he could never say No.

He climbed slowly out of the cab and walked wearily to the back of the truck. He glanced up and noted that the shutters were down on the windows as the people rested from the afternoon sun.

He opened one of the heavy truck doors. 'Come out quickly!' he called to Lisl and John. He was agitated and kept looking around.

John had been preparing for this moment. He had removed his sheepskin clothing and was standing in his socks; he had been unable to find his shoes in the dark. Lisl was still in her sheepskins; she was lying back on the carcasses with her eyes shut.

John was desperately thirsty; the refrigeration had affected his throat. He also felt so stiff he had to force his legs to obey him. He picked Lisl up and felt the pain in his shoulder; he gritted his teeth and, pushing aside the carcasses of meat with his head and shoulders, staggered over carcasses on the floor to the open door of the truck where the sudden heat and brilliant sunlight was like receiving a blow to his head. He stood still for a moment and shut his eyes.

'Help me!' he said to Valentino who reached up and took Lisl from him. John jumped down. 'My shoes are in the truck,' he said.

'Not now!' Valentino was agitated. 'Shut and fasten the doors, and follow me.' he cried. 'Hurry!'

Minutes later they entered Valentino's house.

'Mamma! Mamma! We're back!' he shouted. 'Carlo is here with a friend. Where are you?' he called.

Next, Valentino laid Lisl on the sofa. They removed her sheepskin clothing. She had fainted.

'Valentino! Carlo! What a time to arrive! You must be hungry.' The voice came from the floor above as Valentino's mother pulled on a bright pink, loose dressing gown that went to the ground; she slipped her feet into sandals and flip-flopped noisily downstairs.

She looked around in amazement. There was no Valentino and no Carlo but, collapsed on the sofa, was a young woman who was so white and still she might have been dead. She stood still, looked around and listened.

'Valentino! Carlo!' she called in a frightened voice.

'Mamma!' cried Valentino, emerging from the lavatory, followed by John, who had just returned from the garden. He flung his arms around her and kissed her. She pushed him away exclaiming, 'Who is this?'

'She is Carlo's friend, and she is very ill. She needs looking after, Mamma, and good food. I knew you wouldn't mind,' Valentino explained, pleadingly.

'She should be in hospital. You must take her there at once.' She looked at Carlo. 'What is wrong with your friend?' she asked.

'She's been ill-treated and has had a fever. I apologise for bringing her here like this, without warning, but I had no choice.'

Valentino interrupted, 'It is impossible for her to go to hospital, Mamma. Please believe me. She has no passport and no visa. We smuggled her in. We must help Carlo and his friend. Please, Mamma.' Valentino kissed her and repeated, '*Please*, Mamma.'

She looked from Valentino to Carlo and then at Lisl.

'Bring her upstairs. Pedro is away, so she can have his room. But I do not like this, Valentino. You will bring trouble on us all,' and she went upstairs as fast as her ample proportions would allow.

Valentino picked Lisl off the sofa and, carrying her, followed his mother upstairs. The bed was quickly made with fresh, white sheets and he laid her gently on it.

'Leave her to me. Look after Carlo. You both need a bath and clean clothes.'

Valentino went downstairs and his mother closed the door.

'We need beer,' announced Valentino, going straight to the refrigerator. He handed John two cans of beer. They sank into easy chairs and drank the beer straight off.

'Whew! That's better!' exclaimed John. 'A journey like that makes you really appreciate home comforts. Valentino, you are a good friend. How can I thank you? You were marvellous, the way you dealt with those frontier guards and got us safely here. Perhaps one day I shall be able to do something to repay you.'

Before Valentino could reply his mother entered the room.

'Who is this poor bambino upstairs, and what have you two been up to?' she demanded, standing over them.

'Mamma, we can explain everything.' Valentino spread his hands in an explanatory gesture. 'But first we must eat. Carlo is famished and I must go back to the warehouse and unload.'

'You have not eaten? No wonder you look so tired.' She looked at Carlo and shook her head. To her food came second to religion; she considered it unpardonable that anyone should be hungry in her house.

'I cook immediately. Wait a moment,' and she busied herself in the kitchen. 'I make a special soup for your friend. What is her name?'

'Lisl,' replied Valentino. He then told her how he had met Carlo and Lisl at the abattoir and smuggled them in.

'I do not want the police here!' she said sternly.

'They won't come unless you talk. Please don't tell anyone about Lisl. No one knows she is here, and once she is fit Carlo will take her away. Please help, Mamma. Carlo loves her very much.'

'All right. So long as there is no trouble. If you aren't careful you will lose your job. Promise me never to do this sort of thing again.'

Valentino promised, and once the meal was over he took his truck back to the warehouse to unload.

It was sixteen hours later that John awakened. He felt remarkably better but was ravenously hungry and his throat was dry. He went into the kitchen where he found the remains of a meal still warm on the top of the stove.

He knew that for the present Lisl would be safe in this house and well cared for. When she was fit enough he must find a way of getting her to London. His original plan had been to get to Trieste and go to his flat; having put Lisl in a safe flat, he would have resumed his normal way of life. He would have contacted London and found a way of getting her there; Hugh and Julia would have looked after her.

But now everything had changed. Ever since that night at Snagov in the Russian Ambassador's residence. The upturned chair. The figure on the floor. Had he been recognised? Surely there was recognition in those eyes. He would never forget that moment . . .

And now Russian agents and the *Securitate* would be in

Austria and Trieste, making inquiries, ready to kill. They would never let them reach London, they had too much to lose if their source were blown.

He dared not go anywhere near his flat, yet he could not stay too long with Valentino. They had many friends and visitors and he did not want to compromise them. He decided to get a room nearby, and when Lisl was better, to ring Hugh at his home and tell him what had happened. It was a risk using the telephone but he could think of no other way. He needed help.

This was a poor district and he easily found a room with a family for a few lire. He had just the bare necessities for sleeping and washing. He told them he would eat out. He bought himself a pair of large dark sun-glasses. With these, his darkened hair, his bronzed skin and his casual, old clothes, he felt he could pass easily for an Italian workman.

The food in these cafés was awful – even the coffee was bad – so John decided to risk going a little way into town to have one good meal. He found himself walking down the via Carducci; he walked into the first café and ordered a meal. When he had finished eating he ordered coffee. It was a warm evening and he took off his dark glasses and polished them. He looked up straight into the eyes of Anna Marieva who was sitting by herself at a small table drinking coffee.

She looked startled as if she recognised him and half rose as if to speak. It was also a shock to John but he relied on his changed appearance. He continued to look through and past her without a change of expression. He then replaced his dark glasses and sipped his coffee in total composure.

Having received no response, Anna sat down and blushed with embarrassment. She finished her coffee and left, looking straight ahead.

John realised he had made a grave mistake coming into this area of the town and he had a sinking feeling in the pit of his stomach that no good would come of this. He paid the waiter and returned to his room with a foreboding that would not be dispelled.

The next evening Anna and her uncle were sitting at the bar of the Rouge et Noir, where Alberto was mixing their usual drinks, when she decided to tell her uncle of the incident in the café the previous day.

'You must have been mistaken,' her uncle assured her. 'No one has seen Mr Harcourt for some time. That is correct, isn't it, Alberto?'

'Si, signor. Everyone is asking for Signor Harcourt. Has the Signorina seen him?'

'Well,' replied Anna, 'I feel sure it was Mr Harcourt because I recognised his voice when he spoke to the waiter. But he looked different; his hair was black and his clothes were awful, like a workman's. He looked right through me; there was not a glimmer of recognition. I was so embarrassed!'

'Never mind,' said her uncle, consolingly. 'It was just a case of mistaken identity. I have made that mistake myself.'

'Was it here in Trieste that you thought you saw Signor Harcourt?' Alberto asked the question casually.

Anna told him about the café and how she would never be able to go there again: she would be too embarrassed in case she should see the same man again. Alberto listened attentively and then moved away to serve other people who had just come in.

29

Edwin Hobbs was just finishing a late Sunday-morning breakfast, when the telephone rang – it was Radka.

''allo darleeng! Come and 'ave some lunch. I 'ave a friend 'ere ooh wants to see you. Come soon, then we can 'ave a drink.'

'I can think of nothing I should like better,' replied Edwin. 'Who is your friend?'

'That is to be a surprise. Come as soon as you like. We are waiting for you.'

'Thank you. I shall be along in half an hour.'

When Edwin arrived, Radka greeted him with her usual flamboyance.

''allo, you naughty boy, what 'ave you been doing since I last saw you?' and she flung her arms around him, not expecting an answer.

Looking past Radka, Edwin saw Nikki. He was not altogether surprised because it was well known that they were lovers. Edwin grinned at Nikki. 'How are you?' he asked, shaking him formally by the hand. 'I haven't seen you lately – have you been away?'

'It is so stuffy now in Bucharest, I went into the country for a few days.'

'Did you enjoy it?' Edwin asked, looking hard at Nikki.

'Yes,' he replied smiling. 'It made a great change and I feel much better for it. Much fitter.'

Just then Radka decided to find out why the drinks were so long in arriving and to tell the cook that they would have lunch just as soon as it was ready.

Nikki took this opportunity to tell Edwin briefly how things had gone and where he would find the jeep. Edwin was delighted and reminded him of his promise of secrecy.

They had a happy lunch, full of laughter. Edwin soon took his leave because he had another appointment.

Radka's husband, Todor, had left that morning for a conference in Sofia, so she had immediately rung Nikki and asked him over for lunch. Ever since arriving in Bucharest Radka had formed a liaison with Nikki; there had never been anyone else. Nikki was sophisticated, he knew the rules and would never overstep them. He was a playboy and fun.

They had learned to understand each other over the years, neither being jealous or possessive. They came together briefly whenever they felt the need for each other and the opportunity was there. They were always happy times which they looked back on with pleasure. And now they looked forward to some happy times before Todor returned at the end of the week.

The Bulgarian Ambassador's wife was giving a tea party the next afternoon and Radka had been invited, along with most of the other Diplomat's wives. She looked forward to going because this was a chance for the wives to let their hair down. There was little intellectual conversation, it was mostly gossip. Somehow the women found out even the most secret events long before their husbands heard of them officially, if at all.

Radka selected a pale blue classic-style dress that had come from a Paris fashion house. She threw three gold chains round her neck; they came almost to her waist. She put on a matching gold bracelet and delicate white sandals. She sprayed herself generously with 'Je Reviens' and told Nikki she would return as soon as she could politely do so.

The Bulgarian Ambassador's residence was in the Strada Paris. It was a large, beautiful house of classic elegance. The butler was standing in the open doorway and he showed

Radka into the drawing room. It was about six o'clock when she arrived and most of the other wives were there.

The maid, dressed in black with a small white apron trimmed with lace and a white cap on her head, offered Radka weak tea with lemon; there was also sweet white wine. Servants moved around with large silver trays of tiny cakes and bon-bons.

Between the armchairs, which were filled with large, soft cushions, were scattered beautifully carved fragile gilt chairs with delicate gilt cane seats. Radka sat on one of these chairs, sipping wine and enjoying the sweet cakes. The evening was still very hot and she kept pushing her hair off her forehead.

Around her were the wives of the Russian, French and Italian ambassadors. Her hostess flitted from group to group, staying just long enough to have a little conversation and then going on to the next group. The language being spoken was English, for the benefit of the Russian and American wives who did not speak French.

''ave you 'eard about Princess Doina and 'er butler?' asked Madame le Journot. ''ow 'er 'usband found out about them sleeping together because she talked in 'er sleep and kept calling out, "Stefan, my darling"? Now the Princess is 'eartbroken because the butler 'as been sent away. 'ow can she manage without a butler, I ask you?'

'Eet must be impossible. And eet is difficult to find a good butler. I would rather do without my 'usband than my butler,' said Radka light-heartedly. 'I also know someone 'oo talks in their sleep,' she added, wanting to contribute to the gossip.

The eyes of all three women fastened on her. 'Tell us, yes, tell us,' they said impatiently, laughing in expectation.

Radka was enjoyin this. 'Eet ees not my 'usband,' she teased, then paused. 'Eet ees Nikki Vascescu.'

'Ah, ha!' exclaimed Signora Grimaldi, who had a tender spot for a romance. 'I heard he is now your lover. Is that so?'

Radka pouted and said, 'My 'usband is away a lot and I 'ave known Nikki for a long time. I love my 'usband as I love my dog. You understand?'

'Tell us what your Nikki says in his sleep,' asked Mrs Larkin in her South American drawl.

''e 'as often talked in 'is sleep before but never as interesting as last night.' Radka was now in her element, her audience eager to hear what she was going to say.

''e spoke in Eenglish all the time,' she continued. ''e shouted, "'old on, John. 'ere are some bad pot'oles. I will drive as fast as I can." 'e was very excited, waving 'is arms about. Then 'e said, "You look and see 'ow Lisl ees. I 'ope she will live until you get to Trieste."'

'What were they going to do in Trieste?' asked Signora Grimaldi.

'I leaned over Nikki and said, "darleeng, 'oo ees this John?" and 'e said, "British Secret Service, good with a gun, better with a knife." "And this Lisl?" I said. "'oo ees she?" But 'e did not speak any more, 'e just went on sleeping. 'e 'ad been asleep all the time.'

The Russian Ambassador's wife leaned forward and murmured:

'Did you ask him about it in the morning?'

'Are any of you going to the British Embassy garden party?' asked Mrs Larkin, changing the subject.

They were all going and eagerly joined in discussing clothes and the difficulty of finding any suitable hat. At that moment their hostess rejoined them and Mrs Larkin went in search of the British Ambassador's wife.

Natalia Chebrukova would not be put off so easily. 'Did you talk to Nicolai about his dream in the morning?' she persisted.

Radka was bored and she stood up, preparing to leave, 'No, I forgot all about eet. Eet was only when Madame le Journot told 'er story about Princess Doina that I remembered. I will talk to Nikki when I get back and find out if 'e remembers anything.' They shook hands and Radka went to find her hostess and make her farewells.

In the meantime Mrs Larkin had found Lady Neville. She took her to one side and said:

'I have just heard Radka Antonov tell how Nicolai Vascescu – you know he is her lover – talked in his sleep last night about a British Secret Service agent called John. It seemed that Nicolai was driving fast along some road with pot-holes, taking this John and some woman called Lisl to Trieste. They wondered if this Lisl would live. Just thought your old man might like to know.'

'Thank you. I'll tell him. It never ceases to amaze me what one hears here.'

'That's why I come. Harry always says to me, "You go to all the hen parties you can. It's the darnedest thing, but that's where all the information comes from. You can't beat the girls for gathering news." That's what he always says and so I trot along like an obedient wife to do my bit of gathering.'

'I know,' murmured Lady Neville understandingly. 'It's a blessing that our tour here is only for three years.'

'That's a sure thing,' and Norma Larkin wandered off.

When she reached home, the first thing Radka did was to find Nikki. He had bathed and shaved and was in his white linen dinner jacket, sitting in the drawing room, relaxed on the sofa, drinking chilled white wine. He stood up as she entered the room. 'How was your tea-party? Let me pour you a drink,' he handed her a glass of chilled wine.

'Everyone was there,' she replied, sinking on to the sofa

close beside him and linking her arm through his, 'I deed my best to make the party go. Unless everyone contributes a story the 'ole theeng becomes so boreeng, so I told them about you talkeeng in your sleep last night. They were all very interested, especially Natalia Chebrukova.'

Nikki became instantly alert. He pulled his arm away and turned towards her. 'I talk in my sleep?' he said incredulously. '*Do* I talk in my sleep? What did I say?'

'Darleeng, eet was very amusing, you 'ave a great imagination. You should write a book.' Radka was kittenish and teasing.

'Tell me,' he implored, a trifle too urgently. 'I must know.'

She pouted. 'Don't be so serious. Eet was all good fun. You talked about some journey you 'ad made with a British Secret Service agent called John and a sick woman called Lisl. You were dreameeng – eet wasn't real.'

'What else did I say? Can you remember anything else?'

'No, notheeng else.' She thought for a moment. 'Ah, yes. The road 'ad pot'oles and this John and Lisl were goeeng to Trieste.'

He jumped up from the sofa, his face ashen white and agonized. With quick paces he walked up and down the room, clasping and unclasping his hands.

Radka sank further into the cushions. 'What ees the matter?' she asked. 'Why do you look like that? You frighten me.' She picked up a cushion and clutched it to her. 'You deedn't really go on that journey with a British agent, deed you?' she asked in a frightened whisper.

With an effort Nikki pulled himself together. It would be fatal if Radka found out; the whole of Bucharest would know in a few hours. He must take control of the situation before it was too late.

He smiled at her. 'Of course I never went on any journey with any secret agent!' he assured her. 'What an absurd idea!'

'But you acted in such a strange way.' Her eyes were large and round. 'You frightened me. I 'ave never seen you like this before.' Her face was screwed up and she buried it in the cushion to hide the tears, and added miserably, 'I was 'aving such a 'appy time and now eet ees all spoiled.'

He sank down beside her on the sofa and took her in his arms. 'Forgive me if I frightened you,' he said as he kissed the wet tears on her face. 'Radka, my sweetest, don't cry. Try to understand how I felt. I was quite taken aback that you should have disclosed such an intimate detail of our association to people who are only acquaintances. But now that I have had time to reflect I realise it is not important and they will all have forgotten about it already. It was just a silly dream and gave you a good story for your tea-party. Did they all enjoy it?'

'Yes. All of them. Especially Natalia Chebrukova – she wanted the story to go on and on. She never joins in very much, though. She is very boreeng.'

'Perhaps they don't have gossip in Russia,' Nikki suggested as he got up to refill their glasses. He decided to return to his own house just as soon as he was able to allay Radka's fears and to regain the carefree, happy atmosphere that had always been the essence of their relationship.

Edwin showed no surprise when Nikki, looking utterly dejected, arrived at his house just as he was sitting down to lunch. That morning Sir Rupert had sent for him and told him about some story circulating among the Diplomat's wives. He had looked Edwin straight in the eye and asked him what he knew about it.

Hesitantly, Edwin admitted he had been on the fringes

of this operation and that he had not wished to involve the Ambassador in such a clandestine affair.

Having reached the height of his career, Sir Rupert was, generally speaking, kindly and easy-going towards his staff, but behind this facade was an alert and shrewd brain. As Edwin stood on the pale blue carpet looking at the immaculate figure seated before a French period writing table, he felt just as he had felt at school when sent for by his headmaster. He felt the blood rush to his face and his body went stiff.

'Who are these people?' H.E. looked stern and spoke shortly.

'John Harcourt, my opposite number in Trieste, to whom I report on the MI6 side. And an agent from Austria – Baroness Elizabeth von Althof, sir.'

'What were they doing and why did you get involved?'

Edwin thought rapidly. It was difficult serving two masters and he had found in the past that it always worked better to keep the diplomats in the dark in all matters where murder was likely. So with the best interests of MI6 at heart, he looked for a moment at the official portrait, hanging directly behind Sir Rupert, of King George VI, wearing the crown of state and ermine robes, and decided to circumvent the truth:

'As I said, sir, I was just in on the fringes. The whole event was shrouded in secrecy. Should there be a leak, the lives of these two people would be at stake.'

'But now there *is* a leak,' H.E. interrupted.

'That could be a disaster, sir.'

'How did this Romanian, Vascescu, get involved?'

'I will find out, sir, and let you know.'

The Ambassador nodded a dismissal.

Edwin turned and left the room, closing the heavy door silently behind him.

Sir Rupert leaned back in his chair and shook his head. He knew it was useless trying to get anything out of these Intelligence boys; they always knew more than they would admit.

Now Edwin faced Nikki and without any preliminary said, 'I advise you to leave the country immediately before you get a Russian bullet in the back.'

'I don't know what to say.' Nikki was abject. 'I gave you my word. Wild horses wouldn't have dragged this from me. I have let you all down. I had no idea I talked in my sleep. Do you think it will harm John?'

'It will hardly help him!' Edwin replied tartly. 'Here's a British passport and exit visa with a false name and occupation. Get out of the country today before you cause more harm; go anywhere you choose, but lie low for a while, I implore you. Take this money, it will help you with expenses. Go now.' He stood up and held out his hand.

Nikki grasped it, turned and walked from the room. Emotion welled up in him and his eyes filled with tears. He could not remember when he had felt so awful, so full of remorse. He vowed that somehow, some day, he would make up for this betrayal. Unless he did so he knew he would never recover his self-respect.

30

Boris Molohovski walked up and down his office impatiently.

A message was coming through in code from Moscow, to be decoded personally by himself. He had received a similar message only the other day; what could this one be? He always felt nervous on these occasions because it might be a recall. His mind raced back over recent events as he tried to remember every little incident. Any comrade could have reported him for some breach either real or unreal. He could think of no lapses, but in Josef Stalin's Russia there were many false accusations and people were often never heard of again. He endured agonies while he waited.

The cypher clerk brought the message in and left the room immediately. Molohovski locked the door, then took out his handkerchief and wiped the perspiration off his forehead and hands before sitting at his desk and opening the code book. As he progressed he felt his heart beating faster, his breathing become shorter and the colour rush to his cheeks. This was what he had always wanted but hardly dared to hope for. It would be a just reward for years of hard work.

He strode to the door, unlocked and opened it. 'Ivan Alexandrov, I want you here!' he shouted. 'Listen to this!' he said, unable to hide the excitement in his voice. Ivan stood in front of the desk, aware that something important was about to be revealed. 'I have just received this coded message from Moscow.' Molohovski read it out:

John Harcourt and Elizabeth von Althof travelling by road from Snagov, Romania to Trieste. Should arrive Trieste now. Imperative they are dealt with immediately. Seal all exits and carry out thorough search. Yugoslavia has promised full co-operation. You must ensure local Trieste co-operation by any means. On successful completion you will be promoted to London.

'We *must not* let them slip through our hands,' he continued. 'We must increase our efforts, employ more agents.'

'Congratulations, Comrade Colonel. I hear that for our work London has more possibilities than anywhere else.'

'I think they say in England, "not to count the chickens". First we must catch these two. We will work day and night, checking and rechecking hospitals, hotels and pensions. All restaurants and cafés. Travel in trams and buses, walk the streets, talk to people. Scour the town. Remember, this is a clandestine operation. No one must realise what we are doing. We have our contacts in the police prisons – use them. We have money – be generous with it, and we will get results.'

'Leave it to me, Comrade Colonel. Nothing will be left to chance. I will see to everything immediately.' Ivan had some good agents in the town, he could rely on them and they were not squeamish. He returned to his office to step up the scope and pace of the search.

Left alone, Boris Molohovski leaned back in his chair and put his feet on the desk. He lit a long, black, Russian cigarette and smiled to himself as he drew on it, inhaling deeply, and allowed himself a few moments of indulgence as he thought of life in London. He had never been to England; he knew it would be a whole new world.

Having spun the web, he sat in his office like a great spider waiting impatiently for the fly. He continued smoking throughout the night. He drank innumerable cups of strong black coffee to keep himself awake. Sometimes he got up and walked around the room and poured himself a glass of vodka. Time passed slowly, but to curb his impatience, he counted the number of paces he took in each direction.

In the early hours of the morning there was a knock at the door. The guard entered. 'Someone to see you, Comrade Colonel, his name is "Uno".'

'Show him in.'

In came Alberto, the bar attendant from the Rouge et Noir.

'Yes, Uno? What brings you here at this hour?'

'Comrade Colonel, while working at the bar I heard something that might be of interest to you.'

'Go on. What is it?'

'I heard Signorina Marieva telling her uncle, Signor Papadopolous, that she had seen a man in a café in the via Caducci who she felt sure was Mr. Harcourt. She recognised his voice when he spoke to the waiter, but his hair and eyebrows were very dark, almost black. She jumped up to speak with him but he looked right through her as if he had never seen her before. The Signorina was so embarrassed that she hurriedly left the café.'

'When was this?'

'Yesterday evening, Comrade Colonel.'

'You have done well, Uno!' Molohovski unlocked a drawer in his desk with a tiny key, took out a wad of lire and handed it to Alberto. 'Come directly to me if you hear anything more in connection with Mr Harcourt. This is very good information.' He stood up and patted Alberto affably on the back. Alberto backed away towards the door, bowing slightly, as if to royalty.

The moment Alberto had left the room, Molohovski was on the telephone summoning his staff. He described Harcourt's changed appearance and ordered them to find and arrest him, if possible without anyone noticing, and not to hurt him too much because they must first discover where von Althof was. They should disarm him, handcuff him, bring him here and lock him up. It might be necessary to render him unconscious. They must try not to alert the Allied Military Staff or the Trieste police.

Boris Molohovski now felt confident that he would get results very soon.

31

Sir Gerald burst into Hugh's office. 'Look at this!' he said, flinging a Foreign Office telegram on to the desk. 'We're in a bloody mess! The Ambassador is embarrassed, the Minister wants an immediate explanation and I shall have to see the P.M.'

Hugh stood up, picked up the telegram and read it. 'So that's where he is!' he exclaimed. 'Why ever didn't he let us know what he was planning to do?'

The Chief was fuming. Hugh had never seen him so angry. 'Get Harcourt back here!' he ordered. 'This is crass irresponsibility! With this coming out at a wives' tea-party, we shall become a laughing stock. What answer am I to give the Minister and what am I to tell the P.M.?'

'We had better tell them the truth, sir, hand't we? That we knew nothing about these exploits and this has come as a complete surprise to us.'

'That sounds pretty feeble,' sneered Sir Gerald. 'Draft me a reply for the Minister and I'll see him in half an hour, then I'll see when the P.M. can see me.' He stalked from the room.

As soon as Hugh had taken the reply, all neatly typed, to Sir Gerald, he contacted Interpol. He outlined to them what had been revealed at an Embassy wives' tea-party and asked for help in tracing the whereabouts of John Harcourt and Elizabeth von Althof and to assist and protect them if necessary. He knew he could count on their help.

The Minister had not been pleased with the explanation and the P.M. made it quite clear that it was Sir Gerald Downey who was left holding the baby and that it was he who must take responsibility for the actions of his operators and, whatever happened, to keep it out of the press.

Sir Gerald and the whole Secret Intelligence Service were in disgrace. Hugh was glad when it was time to go home.

Thank God for Julia, he thought, as he put his latchkey in the door. She was so even-tempered. He put his bowler hat on the hall table and stuck his black, rolled umbrella in the stand and walked into the kitchen.

'Hello, darling!' she said, greeting him with her usual smile. 'Had a good day?'

'Disastrous!' he replied, kissing her. 'Leave the cooking and come and have a drink.'

'I can't! This is the *moment critique*. Sit here and we can talk while I finish cooking. We could have our drinks here,' she suggested.

He poured himself a large whisky-and-soda and a gin-and-tonic for Julia, then returned to the kitchen. While sitting on the kitchen stool, he told Julia all that had happened during the day.

She listened intently. 'At least John is alive,' she said, prodding the potatoes with a long, kitchen fork. 'He must have had a very good reason for doing all this on his own.'

'You still have faith in him, I see. I'm not so sure myself, but you may be right. He always had an independent streak. If only he had carried out this operation of his with someone who didn't talk in his sleep!'

Julia laughed. 'That's not something one usually checks. But probably why you married me, come to think of it. In case you gave something away in your sleep, you knew I had security clearance!'

Hugh went over to his wife and kissed her gently on the back of her neck as she bent over the stove. 'Gerald goes about looking like thunder,' he said, 'and the whole place is doom and gloom. I think this is the right moment for me to go to Trieste and be on the spot. I'll suggest it to the Chief tomorrow. He might agree this time.'

'Yes,' she nodded, taking the sauce off the stove, 'John may need help, especially if Elizabeth von Althof is still ill. I shall miss you, darling, so don't be away too long. Everything's ready, so let's go into the dining room. I hope this trouble hasn't taken away your appetite?'

'No fear of that!' he replied. They always tried not to let the events of the day spoil their evenings together.

The next morning Hugh arrived early at the office and found Sir Gerald already there.

'Good morning, sir.'

The Chief looked up, unsmiling. He was looking haggard, as if he had not slept all night. Hugh cleared his throat. 'If it's all right with you, sir, I'll go to Trieste to be on the spot.'

'No. I've decided to go myself,' came Sir Gerald's terse reply. 'I shall need tickets and my usual hotel reservation. Everything must seem as normal as possible. I shall go tomorrow, so give me a last-minute report first thing tomorrow morning. I shall also want a list of all our agents in the Balkans.'

'Yes, sir, but you know the list cannot leave this section.'

'I am perfectly aware of the regulations,' was the frigid reply.

Hugh returned to his office to find a message had been received that a man resembling John Harcourt, except that his hair was dark and his clothes rough, had been seen in Trieste. In fact the informant was certain it was Harcourt. This was from an Italian Intelligence A1 source.

Hugh immediately informed Sir Gerald, who was now all the more anxious to get to Trieste. Out there he would not have the Minister breathing down his neck, asking questions it was preferable not to answer; best to keep these politicians out of it as much as possible. Anyway they wouldn't understand and the less they knew how the Service operated, the better. The Minister was becoming nervous in case Harcourt's escapade should leak out and questions be asked in the House.

32

John was angry with himself for having gone into the café in the via Caducci; it had been a mistake. He knew that a mistake like this could be disastrous. He feared that Anna had seen through his disguise and he could only hope that she would be doubtful and keep the encounter to herself.

He bought some rolls and a salami sausage from a small shop in the dingy area where he was living. He ate his way through the sausage and knew that he must get out of Trieste with Lisl without delay.

She had no passport – the Russians had taken it – so he would have to get her a false one by visiting the contact who had always done this work for Ron. It was a risk going there but he would have to take it. First he must have photographs of Lisl; he would get these now. On reaching Valentino's house he found Mamma watering the flowers near the front door. She looked up. 'Carlo!' she exclaimed, 'Where have you been? I thought you had forgotten us!'

'Mamma, I could never do that,' he replied, embracing her. 'How is Lisl?'

'Come and see for yourself,' she said proudly and led the way into the house, down the passage and into the sitting room. 'See? I have looked after her well for you. Just look at her!' and she flung out an arm towards Lisl.

Lisl stood up. 'I'm much better,' she said smiling and walking towards them.

John went to her and took both her hands. 'So I see,' he said, turning towards Valentino's mother. 'She looks wonderful! In two days time I shall be coming to take her with me. You have been marvellous, Mamma, how can I thank you for all you have done?'

'No need for thanks. You are Valentino's friend, and that is enough for me. Valentino is a very good son to me – but must you go away so soon? Where will you go?'

'In two days time I can tell you more.'

'All right! All right!' she said looking hard at John. 'You look thin. I shall give you a large dish of Mamma's special spaghetti Trieste – the recipe is my own. How is your shoulder?'

'Healed completely, thank you. I can now do everything without feeling it.'

'It is good to be young and healthy. Now I make the spaghetti.'

'Mamma, there is just one thing. I want to take photos of you and Lisl; have you a camera?'

'Of course, but first we eat,' and she disappeared into the kitchen.

John turned Lisl's hands over, they were very white and thin; he looked into her face; it was so pale and her grey eyes looked larger than ever. There was a spiritual quality about her that made her unlike any other girl he knew. He was greatly attracted to her.

He kissed her fingers. 'You're so beautiful,' he murmured.

'I feel a fraud,' she replied, smiling at him. 'I'm so much better but Mamma will still not allow me to do anything, and she waits on me hand and foot. I have kept my promise to you and have not left this house.'

He released her hands. 'Good,' he said. 'Continue to remain inside until I come for you. When Mamma gets the camera, we'll take photographs of each other and I'll get passports for us. We'll travel to England by easy stages, but it's urgent that we get out of Trieste. I can get the passports quite quickly, then we can take a local train to Udine and decide from there how to go on.'

242

'All right, I'll be waiting. Now that Sascha is dead, I shall have no peace until I reach England and pass on his secret. It is what he would have wished.'

'You could tell me – it's better that two should know.'

'No,' she replied with finality. 'I promised Sascha to tell no one outside England. Please don't ask me again.'

John realised that Lisl had made up her mind and there was no point in pursuing the matter further.

'I have to be careful,' he told her, 'because I am being followed – although I managed to shake them off on my way here today. I should really like to come here every day, but it would be far too dangerous. I enjoy being with you.' He took her hand.

Lisl lowered her eyes and gently withdrew her hand. 'Be careful, John,' she said. They are so clever. Remember those who have been killed in the last few months.' She looked at him anxiously.

Then they heard Mamma calling from the kitchen, 'Come, children. The meal is waiting.'

After the meal they took the photographs, including some together with Mamma. John put the reel in his pocket and slipped quietly out of the house. As he walked into the street he looked up and saw the face of a man watching him from a window across the road. They are too near, he thought. I must move her from here tomorrow.

The next day he rented a two-room flat in a run-down district and went off to collect Lisl; she was so defenceless where she was, he would rather have her with him. He had handed the film to his passport contact; the forged passports with false names would be ready in two days time.

Mamma came into the bedroom carrying a jug of steaming coffee. Lisl sat up in bed rubbing her eyes. 'I shall miss this moment when I leave here. It's one of the best moments of the day.'

'I hope Carlo has somewhere comfortable for you to stay,' said Mamma as she poured the coffee into a large cup, 'and that it's not too far from here. Then we can visit each other.'

'We shall know in two days time,' Lisl said. 'I'll dress quickly, then we can spend all day together.' She put her cup on the bedside table and got out of bed.

She dressed with her usual care and went downstairs to the bright little sitting room where the sun streamed in until midday. She had just settled herself on the sofa in her usual corner, when there was a ring at the front door. She heard a male voice saying in Anglicised Italian, 'Signora, I have come to visit your guest.'

Mamma led a tall, elegant, middle-aged gentleman into the room and went out, shutting the door behind her. Lisl could see by the cut of his suit that he was English.

He took a step towards her holding out his hand, 'Baroness von Althof,' he said, shaking her hand, 'I am delighted to meet you at last.'

She gazed at him. She had seen the face before, somewhere, but it was only a hazy recollection. She had certainly not heard the voice before.

'I am John Harcourt's senior officer and I have come from London to take you back with me,' his voice was cultured, his English educated. 'You are in great danger and must leave here at once. Please collect your belongings and come with me immediately. I have a car outside.' He spoke with authority.

'But I promised John to wait for him, and he will fetch me tomorrow.'

'Plans have been changed and Harcourt is meeting up with us later. There is not a moment to be lost and the sooner we meet up with him, the sooner we can leave Trieste.'

Lisl's mind was in a whirl. This man was used to being obeyed instantly. If John was in danger she must be quick. She ran upstairs, collected her few possessions and asked Mamma if she could have a small basket to put them in.

'To leave so suddenly!' exclaimed Mamma, flinging her hands in the air. 'What will Mamma do without her bambino? What shall I tell Carlo when he comes?' She put her arms around Lisl and drew her to her ample bosom, while large tears rolled down her cheeks.

'Where are you taking her, Signor?' she asked.

'Have no fear, I shall look after her well,' he reassured her, taking Lisl by the arm and propelling her to the door, down the path and to the waiting car. Mamma followed and when they stopped at the car both women wept, locked in a warm embrace. He opened the car door, helped Lisl gently but firmly into the back and turned to Mamma.

'Goodbye and thank you for all you have done,' he said, climbing into the back and sitting beside Lisl.

As the car sped away she waved until Mamma was out of sight, then she wiped the tears away and glanced at the face of the man beside her. She noticed the greying hair and the brown, bloodshot eyes and the autocratic expression. She saw how tightly the skin was stretched across his cheek bones.

'What's your name?' she asked.

'They call me GOD,' he replied, looking straight ahead.

'You must be very powerful,' she ventured, watching his face.

'I wish I were,' he turned towards her and gave a one-sided smile.

They lapsed into silence and Lisl tried to remember where

she had seen him before; it was quite recently, she thought; but perhaps she had been mistaken.

The car drew up outside the entrance to the Excelsior Palace Hotel. Lisl's companion told the driver to wait, helped her out of the car, propelled her through the hotel door, across the marble hall to the gilded lift. They went up to the first floor.

The suite was spacious and luxuriously furnished. Off the little entrance hall, an open door revealed a large bathroom with two wash-hand basins and a large bath, all made of white marble mottled with light brown. The walls and floor were of dark green marble mottled with black. The taps were gold.

He opened a door and they went in to a large, light room. 'Do sit down,' he said. 'Will you have some sherry?'

'Thank you,' she murmered and sank into a large arm-chair. She noticed the offwhite sofas and chairs, the off-white carpet, the crystal light fittings and the long, wild-silk French blue curtains.

He handed her the sherry, walked across the room and opened the long casement windows that led on to the balcony which curved round the room they were in and also the two smaller rooms. Looking across the balcony, through the supporting stone pillars, Lisl could see the blue Adriatic Sea from where she was sitting. She sipped her sherry and felt herself relaxing. It seemed a long time since she had been in surroundings like these.

He sat on a chair opposite her. 'We should drink to the fact that at last we have met,' he said, raising his glass.

She raised her glass in reply. 'I thought we were in a hurry, that there is danger and we must leave Trieste immediately. When do we meet John? I don't understand . . . why are we here?'

'I'm waiting for a friend. He should be here any time now.

246

While we are waiting you could unburden yourself to me. Tell me the secret you have kept so well,' he smiled at her.

'How do you know I have a secret? What do you know about me?' Lisl asked in a low voice, putting her glass on the table.

'Have no fear,' he smiled and leant towards her. 'I know of your relationship with Colonel Ivanov and that he passed on to you some vital information, which you were only to disclose once in England. But I have come to take you back to England. So you can safely tell me everything, I am Harcourt's boss, I was Fenton's boss, in fact I am the Head of British Intelligence. Believe me, you can trust me. I have come especially to help get you and Harcourt to safety.'

Lisl sat there stunned – she had not been ready for this. Her contacts had been Ron Fenton and more recently James Wilson and John Harcourt. She knew there were people above them, but they were all faceless and nameless; always referred to as 'London'. Now sitting before her was the Great White Chief himself. No wonder they called him GOD, she thought.

'What do you know about Aleksandr Ivanov?' she asked.

'I have read all the interrogation reports.'

'Colonel Ivanov wanted to disclose to British Intelligence the precise workings of the MGB in Moscow, also where Russian agents are working in England, with details of their networks.'

'Have you that information with you?'

'Yes,' she replied. 'Here,' tapping her forehead. 'Colonel Ivanov made me memorise everything.'

'Please accept my condolences on the death of your friend. It was a most sad and unpleasant business. But if you will tell me the names of the Russian agents in England, then you will be doing what he intended to do.'

'I will begin by telling you what Aleksandr Petrovich

247

considered the most important information and that is the real name of the best British agent working for the Russians. His code name is "Apex" but his real name is Gerald Oxborough Downey. Aleksandr wanted a new life in England for himself and for me in exchange for this information.'

He looked at her as if she had not spoken and asked, 'Who else knows about this? Have you told Harcourt?'

'No! No! No one.'

The atmosphere had changed; his eyes and voice were as cold as steel.

Lisl felt afraid.

There was a knock on the door and in walked a thickset man with dark hair and dark penetrating eyes set far apart in a Mongolian face. The two men shook hands.

'My name is Molohovski. I received instructions to assist you in any way you need. Can I be of any help?'

'Yes, I was expecting you. This is Baroness von Althof. I will leave her with you. I believe you have received instructions regarding her.'

A gleam spread over Molohovski's face. 'Yes, I will take care of her', he said meaningfully. 'And by this evening we should have Harcourt.'

'I'm going to England and nowhere else!' Lisl said defiantly.

Molohovski caught hold of her wrists. 'Sit down and shut up,' he snarled at her, pushing her roughly into a chair and standing over her.

33

The door was opened by Valentino's mother. John gave her a kiss and went inside.

'I've come to collect Lisl,' he said. 'I know I said I would come tomorrow, but I have found somewhere for her to stay, so I decided to come for her this morning.'

'Ah, ha! You are too late. A tall English gentleman came here just a short time ago. You have only just missed him. They went away together in a car. I heard him tell the driver to go to a hotel, but I did not hear which one.'

'What did he look like?'

'He did not smile, he was very English and correct. Although he was not young he had no wrinkles, not even tiny ones. His eyes were brown and the whites were red.'

'My God!' came an agonised cry from John. He rushed from the house and ran into the road where he jumped on to a passing tram, which went swaying and clanging through the town. He felt absolutely calm and his mind was working in top gear. His worst fears had been realised; he only hoped he would be in time.

He jumped off the tram while it was still moving, sped down the road to the Excelsior Hotel, up the three steps and across the foyer to the reception desk. GOD had always stayed here in the past, he hated inferior hotels and this was the best one in town, so it was worth trying first. There were three new arrivals booking in. He looked around for someone to help him and spotted a waiter he knew.

'Antonio! Can you help me?' he called out. The waiter came towards him. 'I'm looking for a tall, distinguished, English signor, who will only have arrived a few days ago.' John tried to look unhurried.

'Yes, that will be Signor Williams. He always stays here. Very elegant gentleman. He has just come in.' Antonio went round the desk to look in the register for the room number.

A large young man, who had been sitting in the lounge just off the foyer reading a newspaper, jumped up. He looked towards John. Their eyes met.

'Nikki! exclaimed John. 'What the hell are you doing here?'

'I had to find you. I talked in my sleep and it was repeated at a Diplomatic tea-party. The Russians know about you and Lisl. I am mortified.' Nikki blurted it out breathlessly. 'I betrayed you. I would have cut my tongue out first. How can you ever forgive me?' He looked desperately unhappy. 'I recognised your voice just now.'

'Room number one hundred and four, signor,' said Antonio, bowing slightly.

'Grazie,' John gave him a tip and turned to Nikki. 'Have you a gun?' he asked in a low voice.

'Of course.'

'Then come with me. We have to rescue Lisl again. It may be a rough-house.' John bounded up the wide carpeted staircase, two steps at a time, closely followed by Nikki. He knew the layout of the hotel and found the number without difficulty. It was exactly one floor below the rooms he had occupied when he first came to Trieste. The lower the floor, the larger and more expensive the suite.

The chambermaid was sitting on a chair watching over her floor. John gave her a generous tip and explained that he was staying with his friend Signor Williams and had forgotten his key and could she please unlock the door to suite one hundred and four. She smiled, unlocked the door and opened it for them.

They entered silently, closing the door behind them. They could hear voices coming from the room in front of them, so they opened the door leading to the left off the little entrance hall and went in. This was a bedroom with a balcony running along outside the casement window. Silently they opened the window and stepped on to the balcony; John knew that the balcony ran past the windows of the next room, which would be the sitting room of the suite. Cautiously they stole along the balcony to the next open casement window and listened to the conversation. John peeped in and beckoned to Nikki.

They both took in the contents of the room and its occupants at a glance. They heard Lisl speaking and John heard her saying that the British agent working for the Russians was none other than his Chief. He pulled back and froze, pulling Nikki with him. He heard his name mentioned. He listened as he heard someone else join in the conversation and, being curious, peered in again and saw Colonel Molohovski push Lisl into a chair.

John turned to Nikki and whispered, 'You deal with the shorter man with the black hair and I'll take care of the tall one.'

Nikki nodded.

John hissed, 'Now!' and they rushed into the room through the open casement window.

John went straight for Sir Gerald, who jumped up from his chair, but never stood a chance. John had his arms pinned painfully behind his back. The pain showed on Sir Gerald's face, but John had no pity. He looked across the room and saw that the blow Nikki had delivered to Molohovski had sent him reeling across the floor. Molohovski reached for his gun, Nikki grabbed his wrist and they wrestled on the floor, knocking over tables, with Molohovski still clutching his pistol.

Lisl had jumped up and was standing pressing her back against the wall with a look of utter horror on her face. She was shocked and terrified at the violence around her and looked wildly from one to the other.

John jerked Sir Gerald's arm painfully and said, between clenched teeth, 'When I saw you sitting on the floor in the Russian Ambassador's house in Romania, I vowed that I'd get you, although I knew you would deny it and it would be only my word against yours. But you won't get away with this. You are responsible for the deaths of all our best operators, and many of my friends.'

'I can explain,' replied Sir Gerald with difficulty, his face contorted with pain. 'I don't believe in their ideology and I never received money. When I was working in Moscow I fell in love and had an affair with a Russian woman . . . '

A shot rang out from Molohovski's pistol. It hit the wall above Lisl and small fragments of plaster rained down on her. She gave a little scream and put her hand on her head as if to protect it. Nikki and Molohovski continued to struggle on the floor, overturning chairs and damaging the walls where they kicked them. Molohovski was obviously trained in this sort of contest and Nikki had to rely on his greater weight and size as well as his youth. He was determined to get the gun away from the Russian.

'Go on,' commanded John, continuing to hold Sir Gerald's arm painfully locked behind him.

Between clenched teeth he said, 'We had a child seven years ago, a girl – she's very delicate. I love her and her mother more than anything in the world. More than my life.' He winced. 'They can't leave Russia, and my wife knows nothing about them. The MGB made a deal with me – that my Russian family would be kept secret so long as I kept sending them the information they wanted.' He paused, struggling to remain in control of himself.

'Go on,' said John roughly.

Sir Gerald swallowed and blurted out, 'As a reward, the MGB would fly them to a secret place – for us to be together for a few days.' His voice was coming in gasps as John increased the pain.

'Why were you in Romania?'

'The MGB had arranged for me to meet Tatyana and her mother in Romania if I would help with the interrogation of von Alt—'

A shot rang out and Sir Gerald slumped to the floor, blood spurting from his head.

John sprang across to where the two men were still wrestling on the floor and wrenched the gun from Molohovski's fingers. The chambermaid peered round the door, screamed and rushed away.

The two men stood up, eyeing each other suspiciously. Lisl was still standing transfixed, watching the red stain grow larger as the blood flowed from Sir Gerald's head over the offwhite carpet. He made no movement. With the pistol pointing towards Molohovski, John put an arm round Lisl and drew her gently into a chair. He then stooped down and felt Sir Gerald's pulse.

There was none.

He straightened up, slipped Molohovski's gun into his pocket and turned to the disarmed Russian. 'It's all over,' he said. 'You have just killed your own most important agent. We now know why your people went to such lengths to prevent Colonel Ivanov and the Baroness from giving us the name of the man who has been betraying his country and his colleagues for the past seven years. Fenton, Wilson, Sokolov, Ivanov, to mention just a few. And who can tell how many more?' John looked grim.

Into the room strode a small Italian Triestini in a light suit followed by two members of the local Venizia Guilia police force in uniform. The policemen were small, dark and fierce; they carried their pistols menacingly. John swung round, his hand on the gun in his pocket.

The Italian bowed slightly and introduced himself:

'Benito Cavalli, Head of Security for Trieste, at your service. I heard what was being said as I entered the room. I imagine this man is dead or you would be doing something to assist him,' he waved an arm towards Sir Gerald. 'How did it happen?' he asked sternly.

My gun went off by mistake,' Boris admitted frankly. 'I am Boris Molohovski, a Russian diplomat.'

'I know,' replied Benito Cavalli. 'I know all about you foreign intelligence agents using Trieste as your playground. I have been watching you for some time. This is the fourth murder during the last few months connected with you people. I will have no further murders in this town. They must stop.'

He turned to Molohovski. 'Because of your diplomatic status I cannot detain you, but I shall be reporting this incident to my superior in the Allied Military Government, recommending that you are *persona non grata*. So I suggest you return to your house and start packing at once. Goodbye, Colonel Molohovski!' He bowed slightly, the two policemen moved aside and Molohovski, still puce in the face from the recent struggle, strode from the room.

Signor Cavalli bent down and studied the inert figure of Sir Gerald lying in a pool of blood. He looked at Nikki who was sitting in a chair mopping his brow and was still a little breathless. He then turned his head and looked at John. 'This is an unfortunate accident, Mr Harcourt,' he said, as he deftly removed the contents of Sir Gerald's pockets, not forgetting to examine the lining of his jacket and the soles of his shoes. 'I wonder what the press will make of it,' he said.

'I have no idea,' replied John in an expressionless voice.

'What are you going to do about him?' he asked, jerking his head in the direction of the body.

'I am sure you understand that we have certain procedures to follow, and of course I shall be informing the Allied Military Government, who will give me instructions regarding the body. It would be of assistance if you would write down his name, address, where he works and any other personal particulars you know.'

'The quieter you can keep this, the more grateful everyone will be,' said John as he wrote down the details.

'I understand,' said Signor Cavalli. As he walked over to Lisl, he bowed slightly and kissed her hand. 'Now if my information is correct, you are Baroness von Althof. This must have been most upsetting for you, signorina. How do you fit into all this?'

'She was on her way to England with me,' John answered for her.

'In that case I suggest you continue your journey together.' Signor Cavalli looked out of the window and continued, 'You see that ship moored across from the hotel?'

Lisl and John looked out of the window.

'That is a British frigate which has just finished paying a courtesy call here and will be sailing in one hour's time. I shall speak to the captain. You must both embark now, I shall come with you and see you sail safely away and, Signor Harcourt, since you have now discovered who was responsible for the murder of Signor Fenton and why, I presume you will resume your work in London.'

John grinned at these remarks. 'I just obey orders,' he said. He turned to Nikki. 'Thanks for your help – I couldn't have survived alone. You turned up in the nick of time, so now we are even. What are your plans?'

Nikki looked at Benito Cavalli. 'I am a Romanian and

have left illegally. I cannot go back and would like to join friends in Paris. I also entered here illegally, I have no visa.'

'You will have to come with me. There are certain formalities,' explained Signor Cavalli. 'But I am sure it can be arranged.'

'If there are difficulties, get in touch with me,' John said reassuringly to Nikki. 'Perhaps I could arrange for you to come to England. The Foreign Office, London, will always reach me.'

'Thanks, I will remember.'

Leaving one policeman with the body, Signor Cavalli escorted John and Lisl across the road to the quayside where the frigate was anchored. Nikki and the other policeman came also. They all went on board where they found the Chief British Naval Officer to the Allied Military Government bidding farewell to the Captain. John asked him to get a message to Hugh Compton to meet them when they berthed in England.

All was finally agreed.

Signor Cavalli bowed stiffly to the Captain. 'Thank you,' he said. 'I hope your journey is calm. Goodbye.' He turned on his heel, followed by the policeman.

Nikki kissed Lisl and grasped John's hand. 'Goodbye,' he said. 'I have never had so much excitement, and we have all survived somehow, and I have escaped to freedom! We must all meet again and have a reunion in Paris.'

'My favourite city,' murmured Lisl, smiling at the two men.

'Goodbye, Nikki. You're a good friend,' replied John, shaking his hand. 'Paris it will be.'

Nikki paused a brief moment, grinning, then he turned and walked down the gangway. A moment later there was just the sound of waves lapping the quayside in the warm night.